Disney
PRINCESS

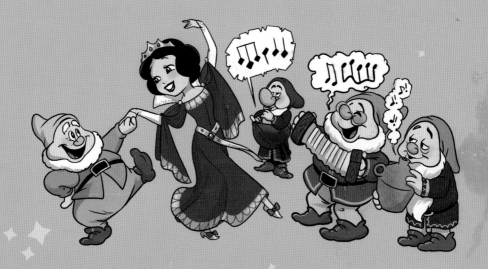

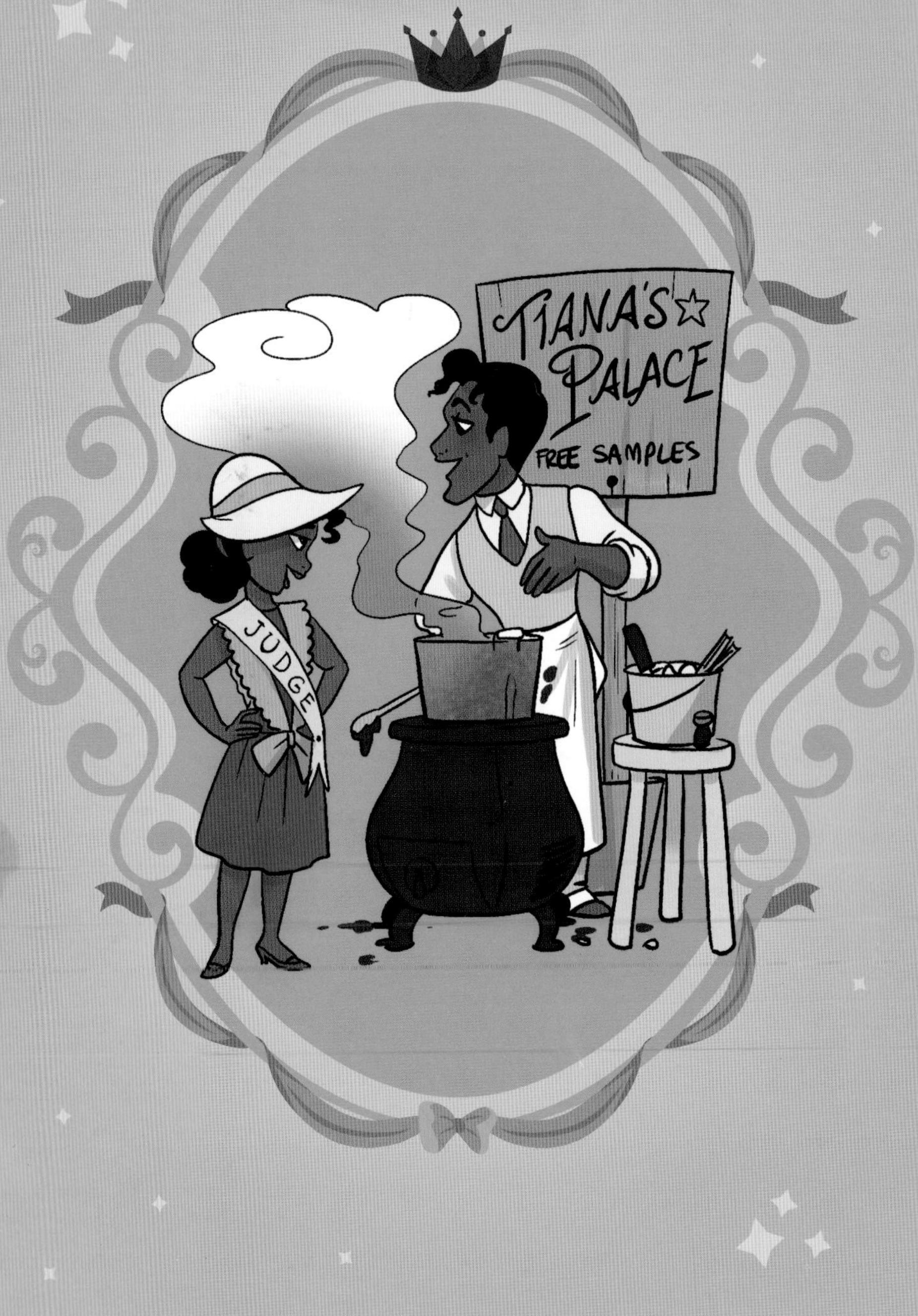
TIANA'S PALACE
FREE SAMPLES
JUDGE

Disney

PRINCESS

Gleam, Glow, and Laugh

Script by
Amy Mebberson
Georgia Ball
Paul Benjamin
Geoffrey Golden
Patrick Storck

Illustration by
Amy Mebberson

Lettering by
AndWorld Design

Cover Art by
Amy Mebberson

Dark Horse Books

Before we jump
into stories with the
Disney Princesses, let's
take a moment to learn
some *quick key details* about
a few of them with these
very informative
infographics!

**Presenting, Rapunzel,
Snow White, and Tiana . . .**

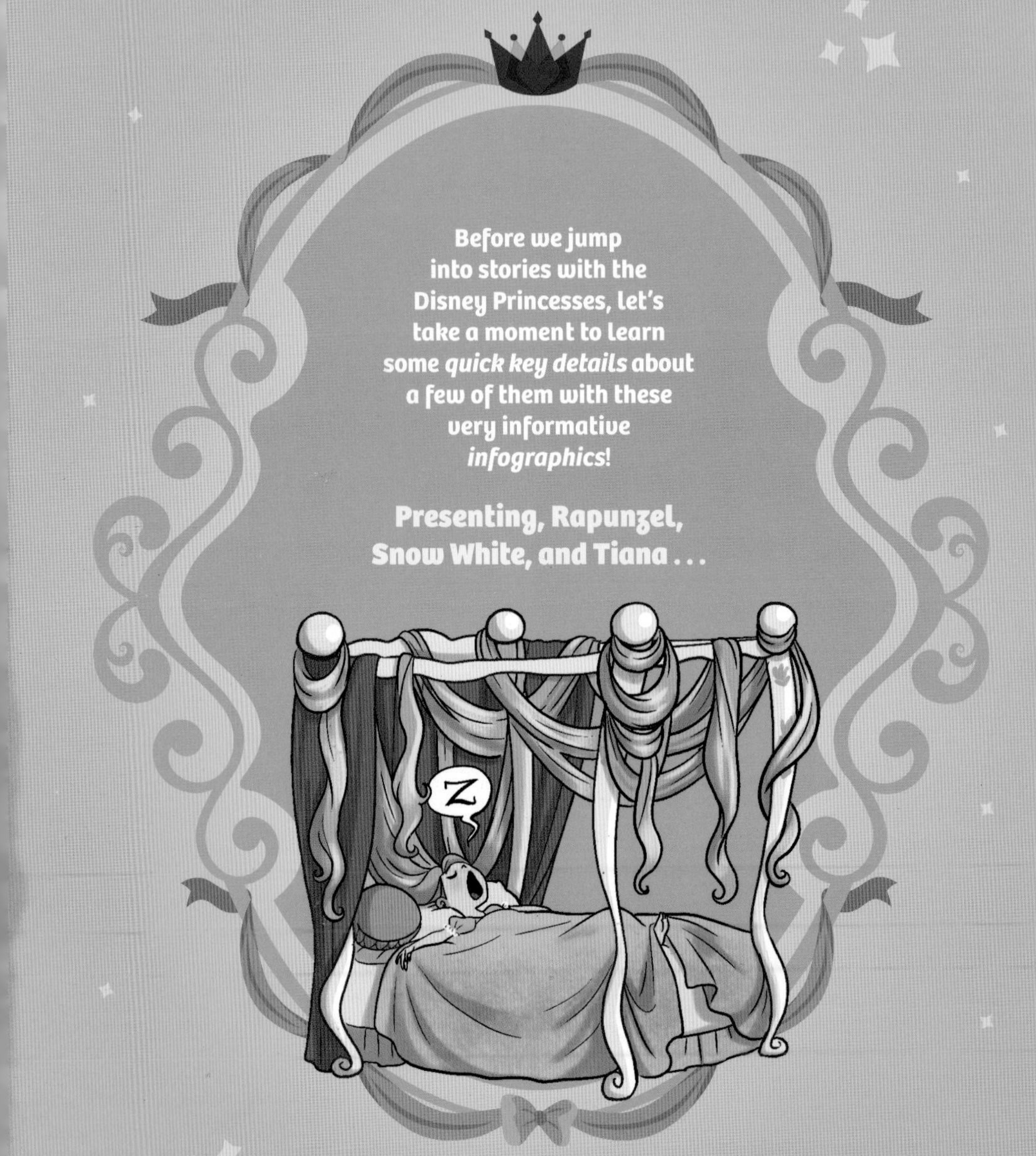

Z

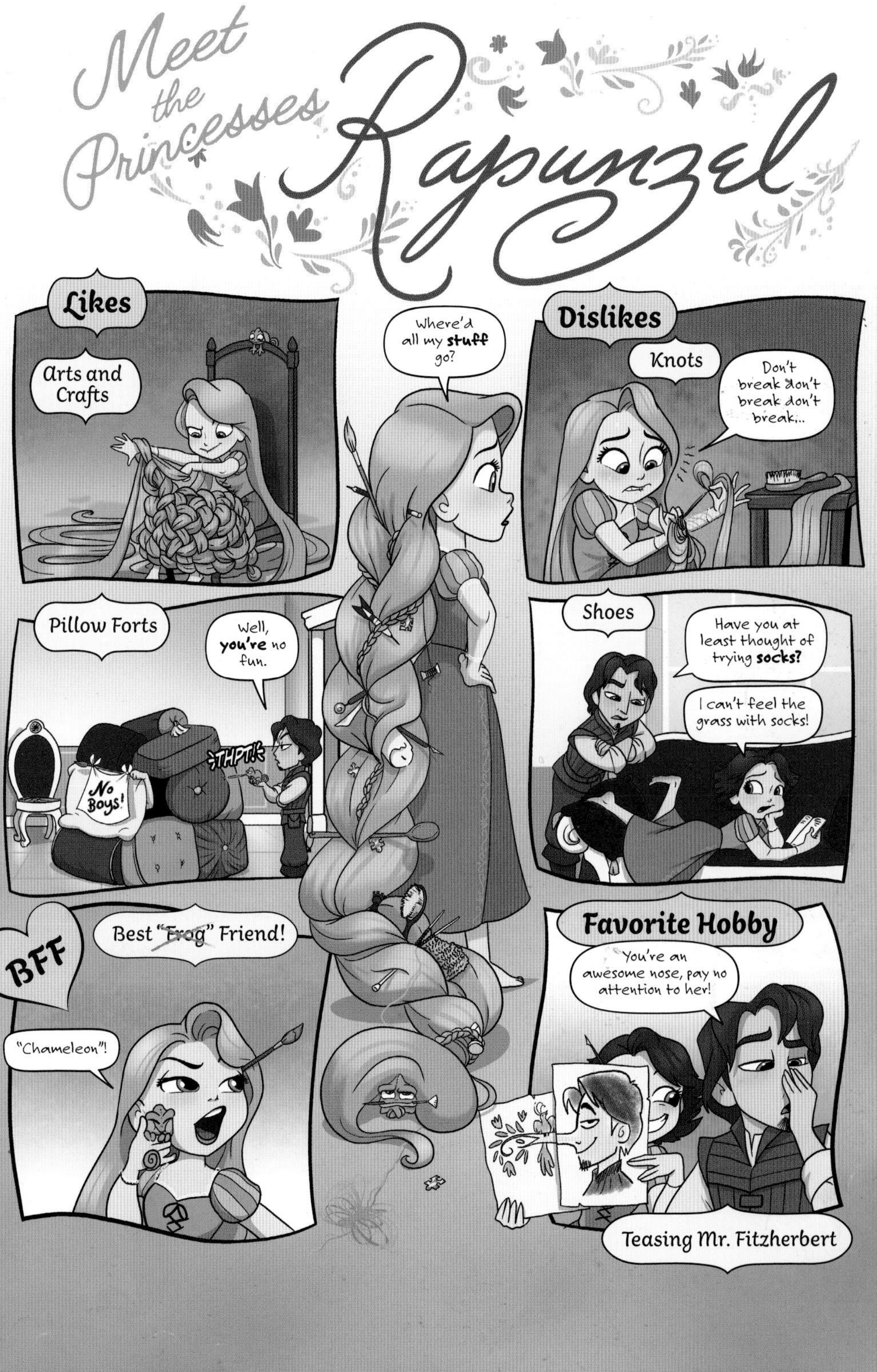
Meet the Princesses
Rapunzel
Likes
Arts and Crafts
Where'd all my stuff go?
Dislikes
Knots
Don't break don't break don't break...
Pillow Forts
Well, you're no fun.
THPT!
No Boys!
Shoes
Have you at least thought of trying socks?
I can't feel the grass with socks!
BFF
Best "Frog" Friend!
"Chameleon"!
Favorite Hobby
You're an awesome nose, pay no attention to her!
Teasing Mr. Fitzherbert

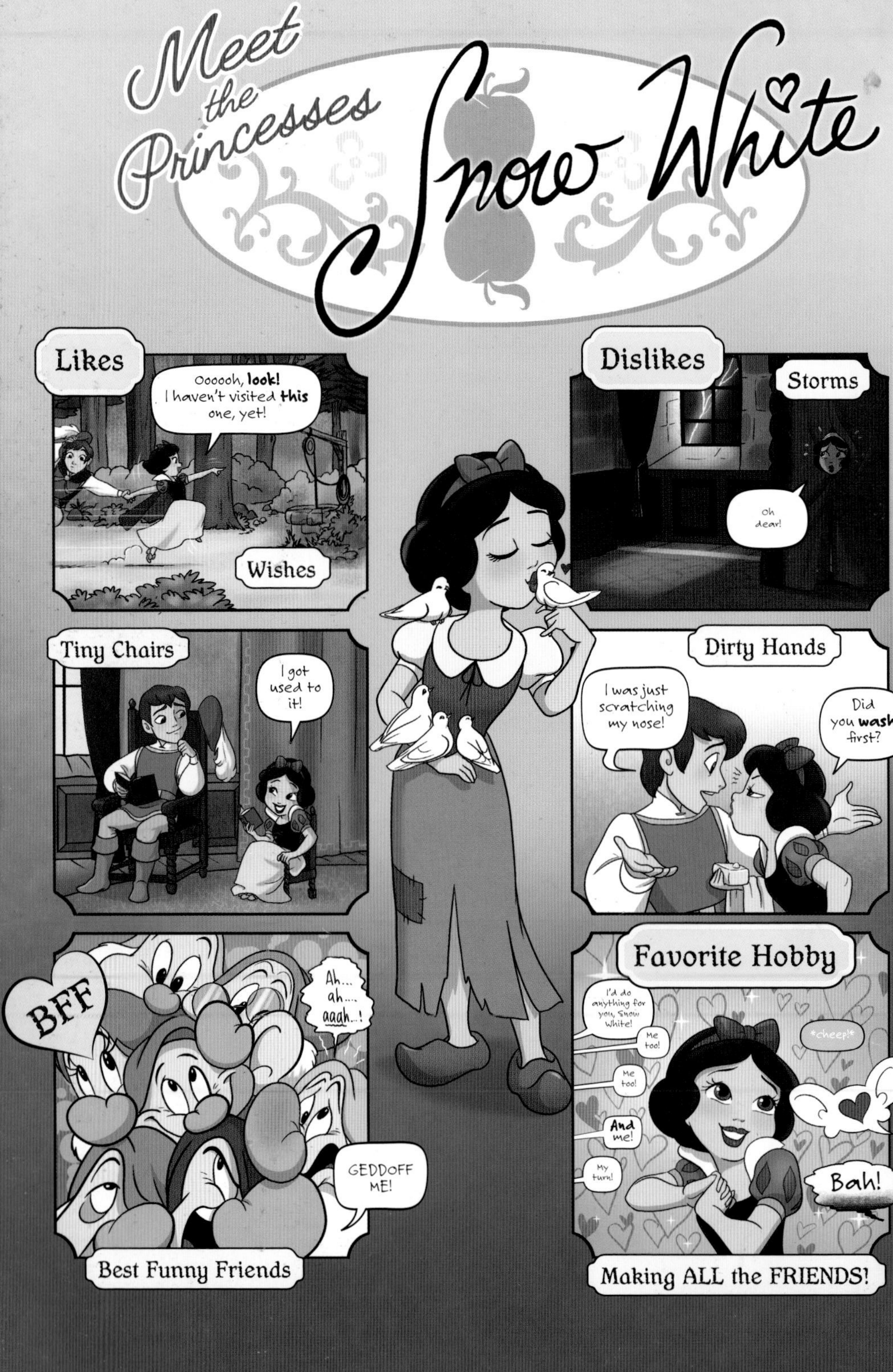

Meet the Princesses
Snow White
Likes
Ooooh, look! I haven't visited this one, yet!
Wishes
Dislikes
Storms
Oh dear!
Tiny Chairs
I got used to it!
Dirty Hands
I was just scratching my nose!
Did you wash first?
BFF
Ah... ah.... aaah..!
GEDDOFF ME!
Best Funny Friends
Favorite Hobby
I'd do anything for you, Snow White!
Me too!
Me too!
And me!
My turn!
cheep!
Bah!
Making ALL the FRIENDS!

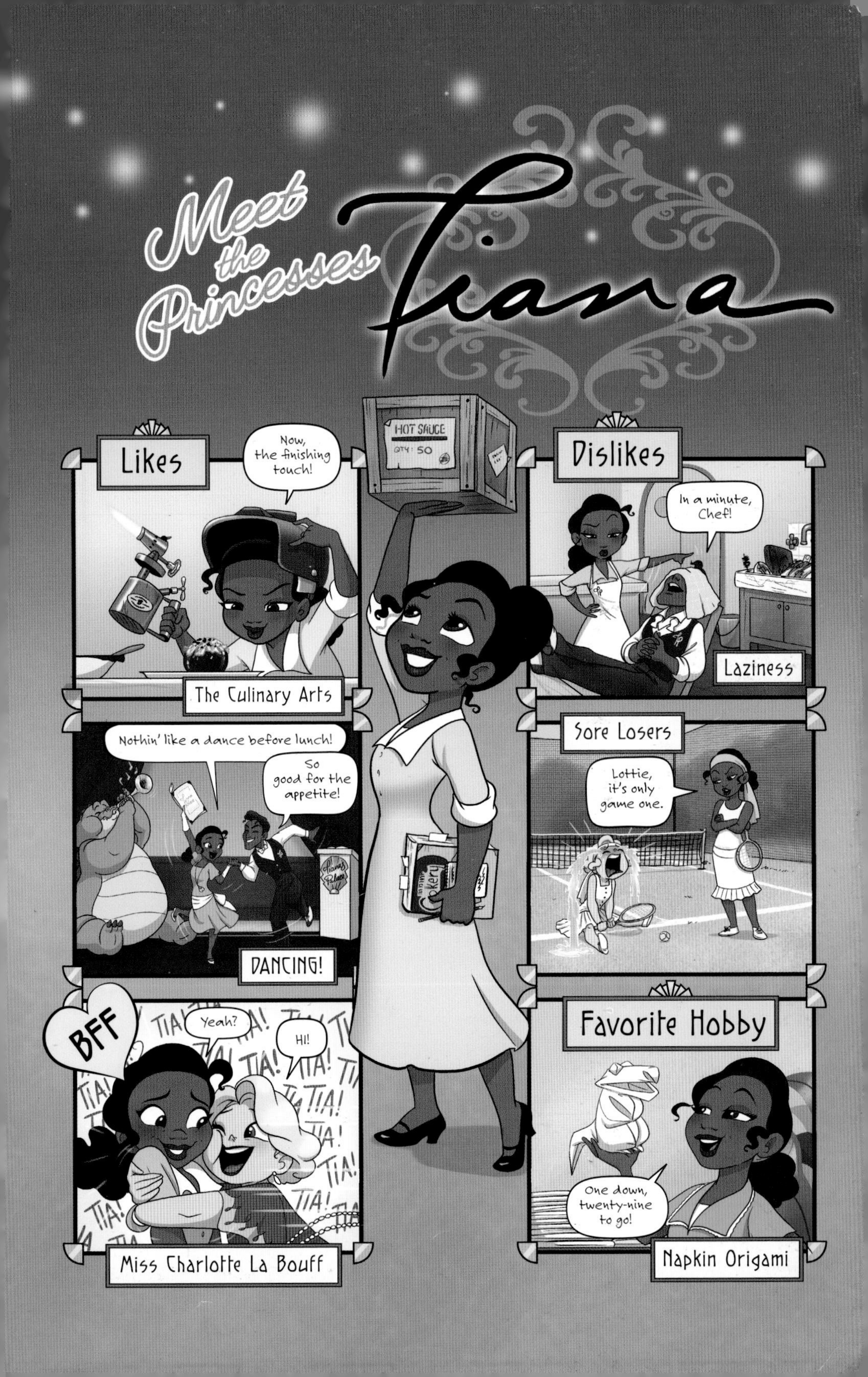
Meet the Princesses
Tiana
HOT SAUCE
QTY: 50
Likes
Now, the finishing touch!
The Culinary Arts
Dislikes
In a minute, Chef!
Laziness
Nothin' like a dance before lunch!
So good for the appetite!
DANCING!
Sore Losers
Lottie, it's only game one.
BFF
Yeah?
Hi!
TIA! TIA! TIA! TIA! TIA!
Miss Charlotte La Bouff
Favorite Hobby
One down, twenty-nine to go!
Napkin Origami

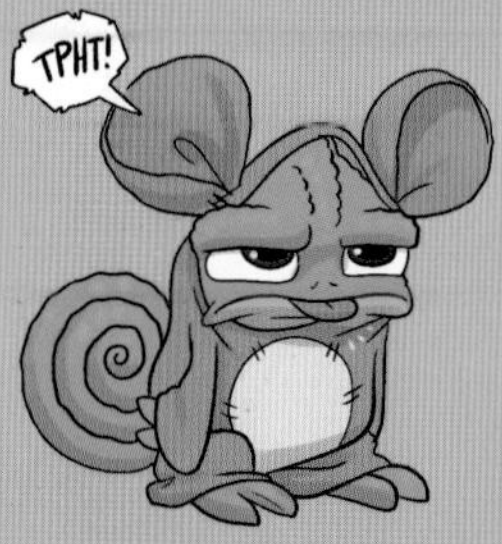
TPHT!

"RAPUNZEL'S ONE WOMAN (AND PET) SHOW"

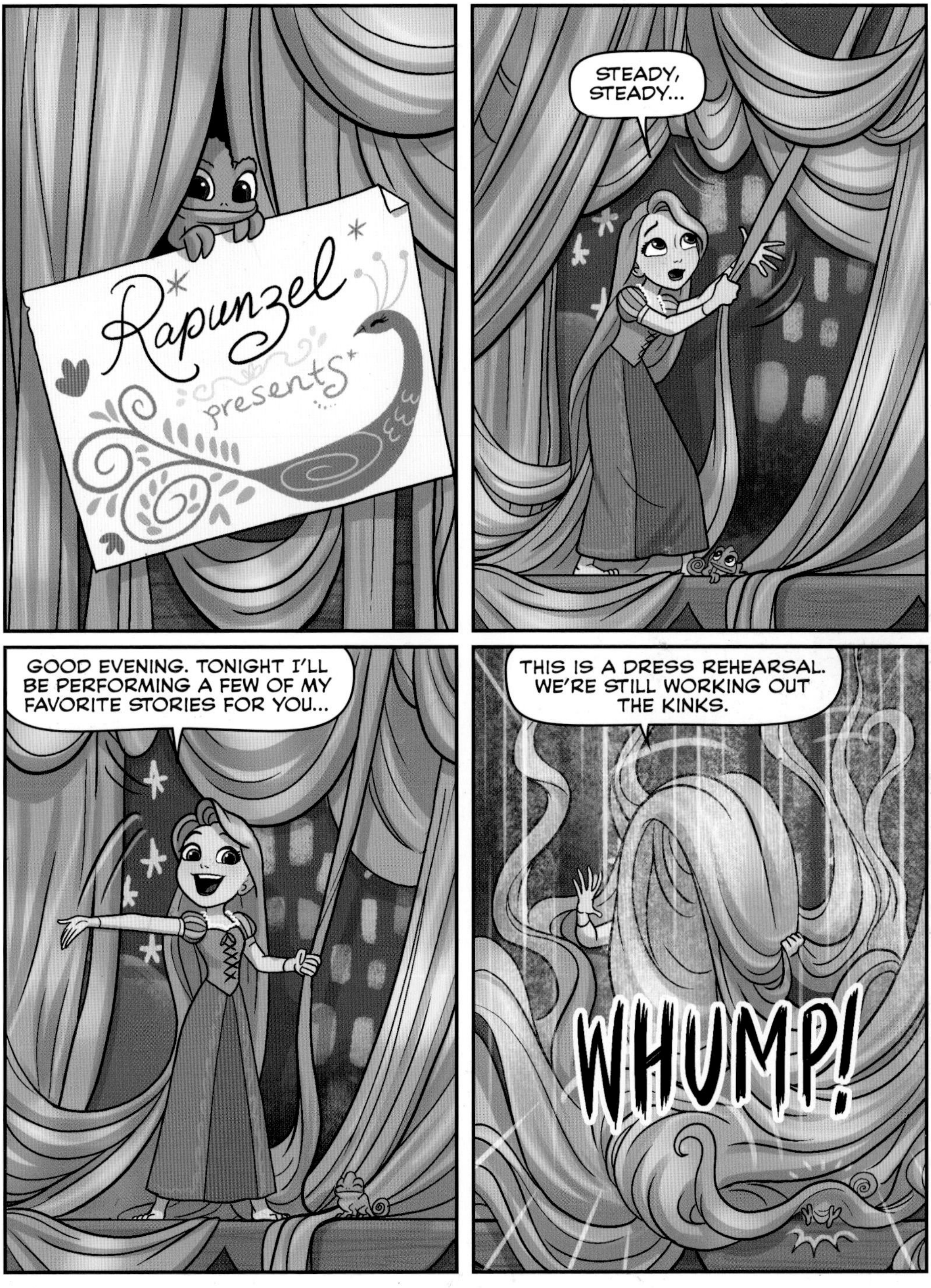

Rapunzel presents
STEADY, STEADY...
GOOD EVENING. TONIGHT I'LL BE PERFORMING A FEW OF MY FAVORITE STORIES FOR YOU...
THIS IS A DRESS REHEARSAL. WE'RE STILL WORKING OUT THE KINKS.
WHUMP!

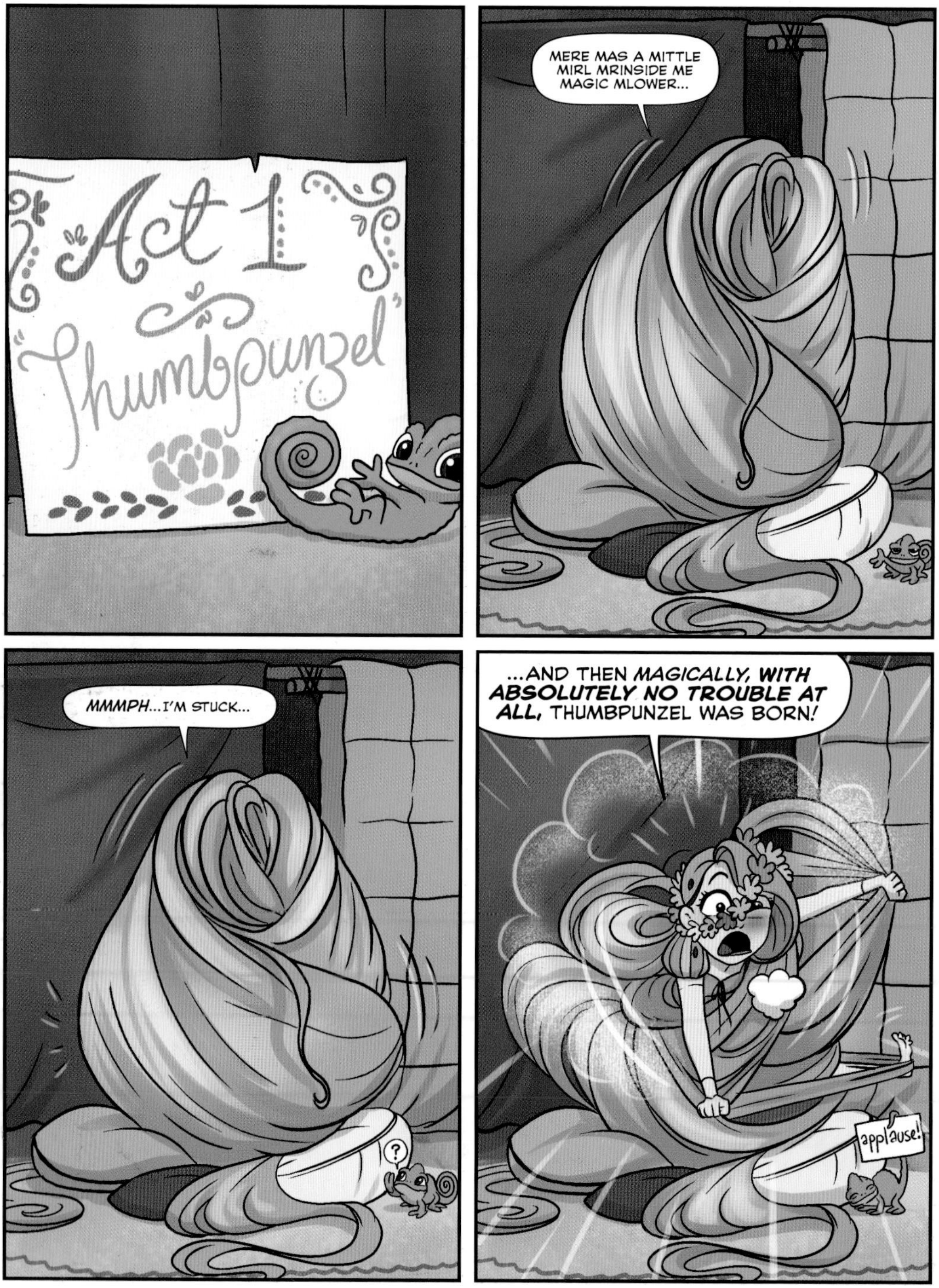
Act 1
"Thumbpunzel"
MERE MAS A MITTLE MIRL MRINSIDE ME MAGIC MLOWER...
MMMPH...I'M STUCK...
?
...AND THEN MAGICALLY, WITH ABSOLUTELY NO TROUBLE AT ALL, THUMBPUNZEL WAS BORN!
applause!

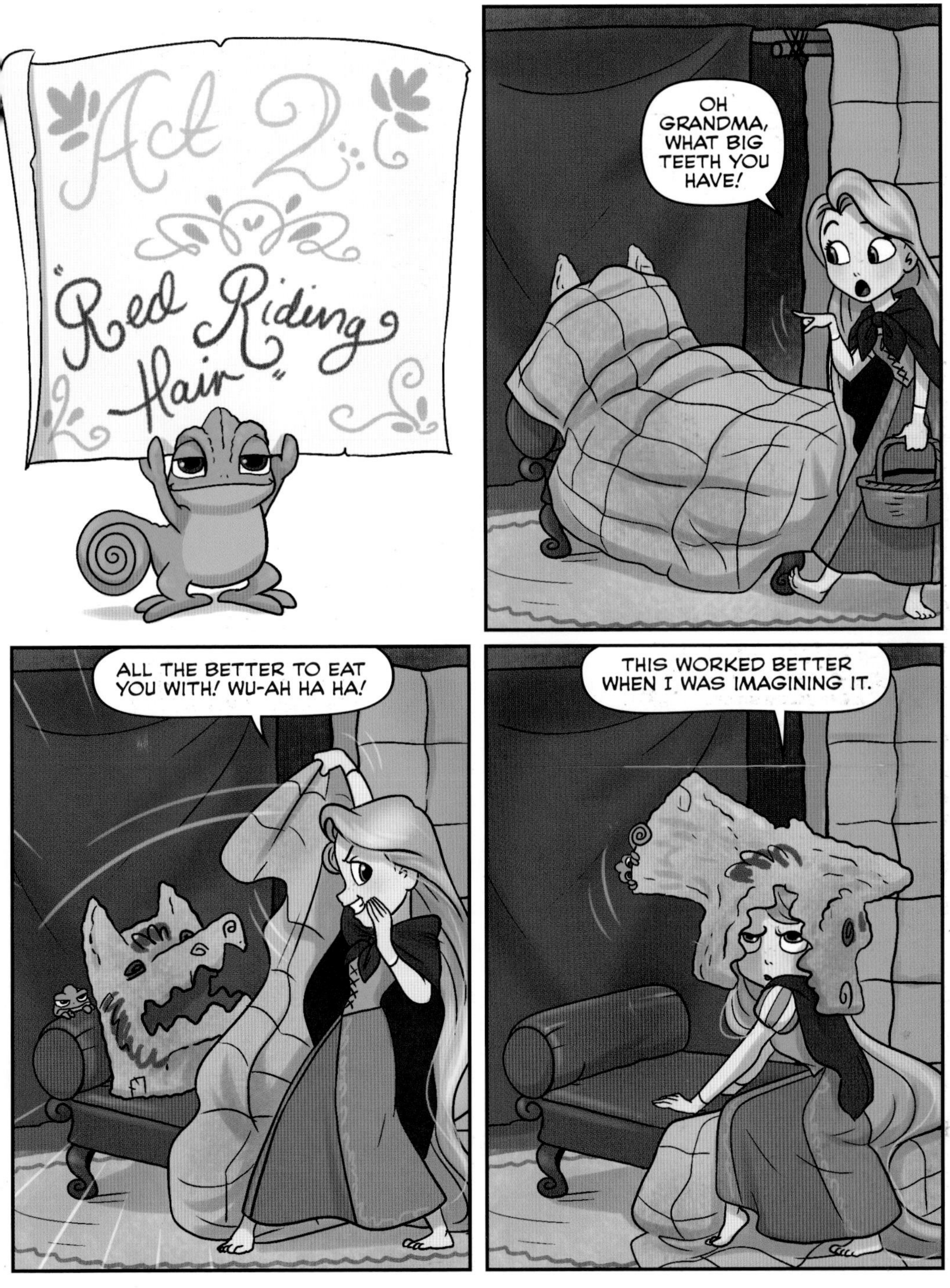
Act 2
"Red Riding Hair"
OH GRANDMA, WHAT BIG TEETH YOU HAVE!
ALL THE BETTER TO EAT YOU WITH! WU-AH HA HA!
THIS WORKED BETTER WHEN I WAS IMAGINING IT.

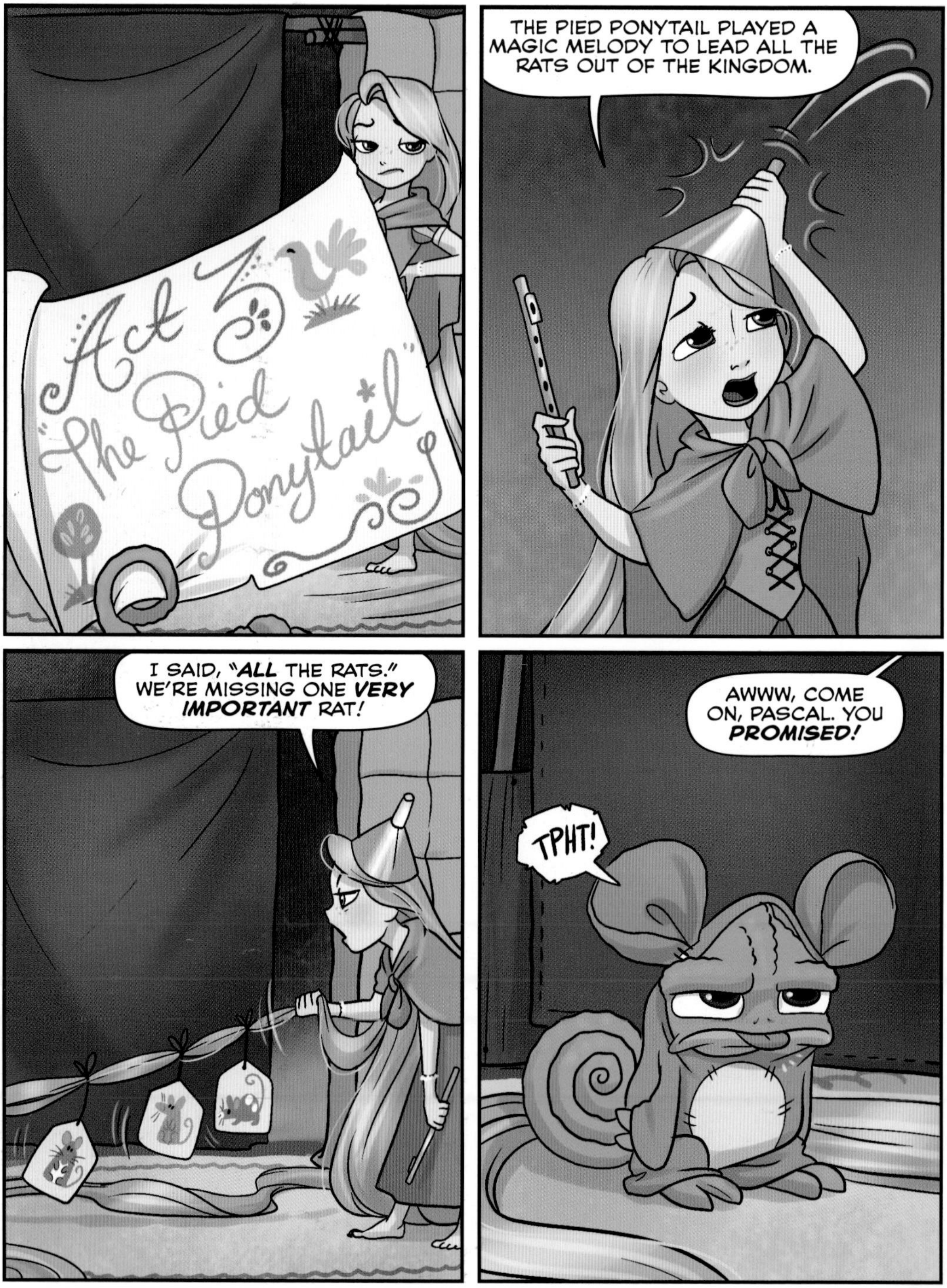
Act 3
"The Pied Ponytail"
THE PIED PONYTAIL PLAYED A MAGIC MELODY TO LEAD ALL THE RATS OUT OF THE KINGDOM.
I SAID, "**ALL** THE RATS." WE'RE MISSING ONE **VERY IMPORTANT** RAT!
AWWW, COME ON, PASCAL. YOU **PROMISED!**
TPHT!

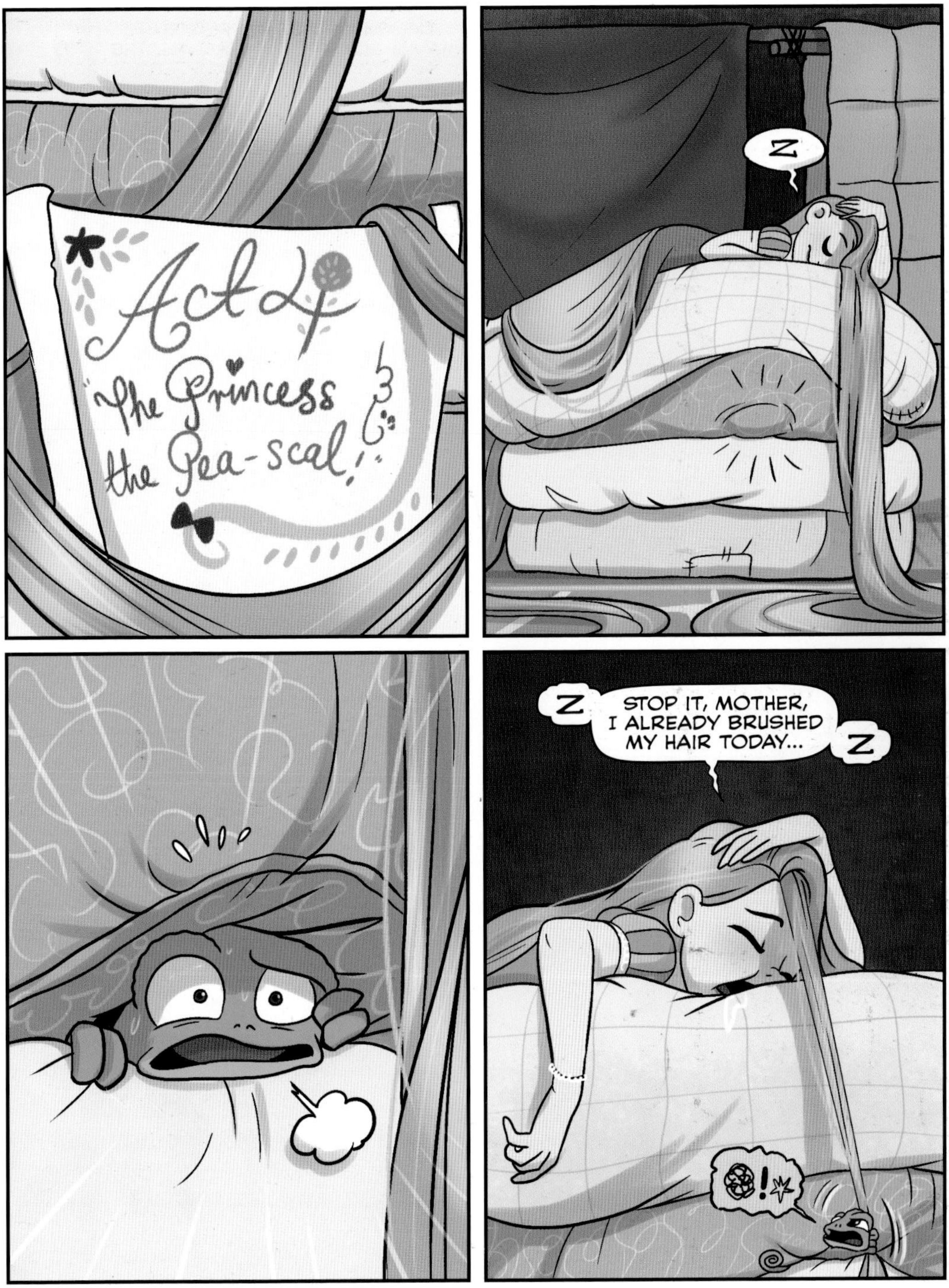

Act 4
"The Princess & the Pea-scal!"
Z
Z
STOP IT, MOTHER, I ALREADY BRUSHED MY HAIR TODAY...
Z
!

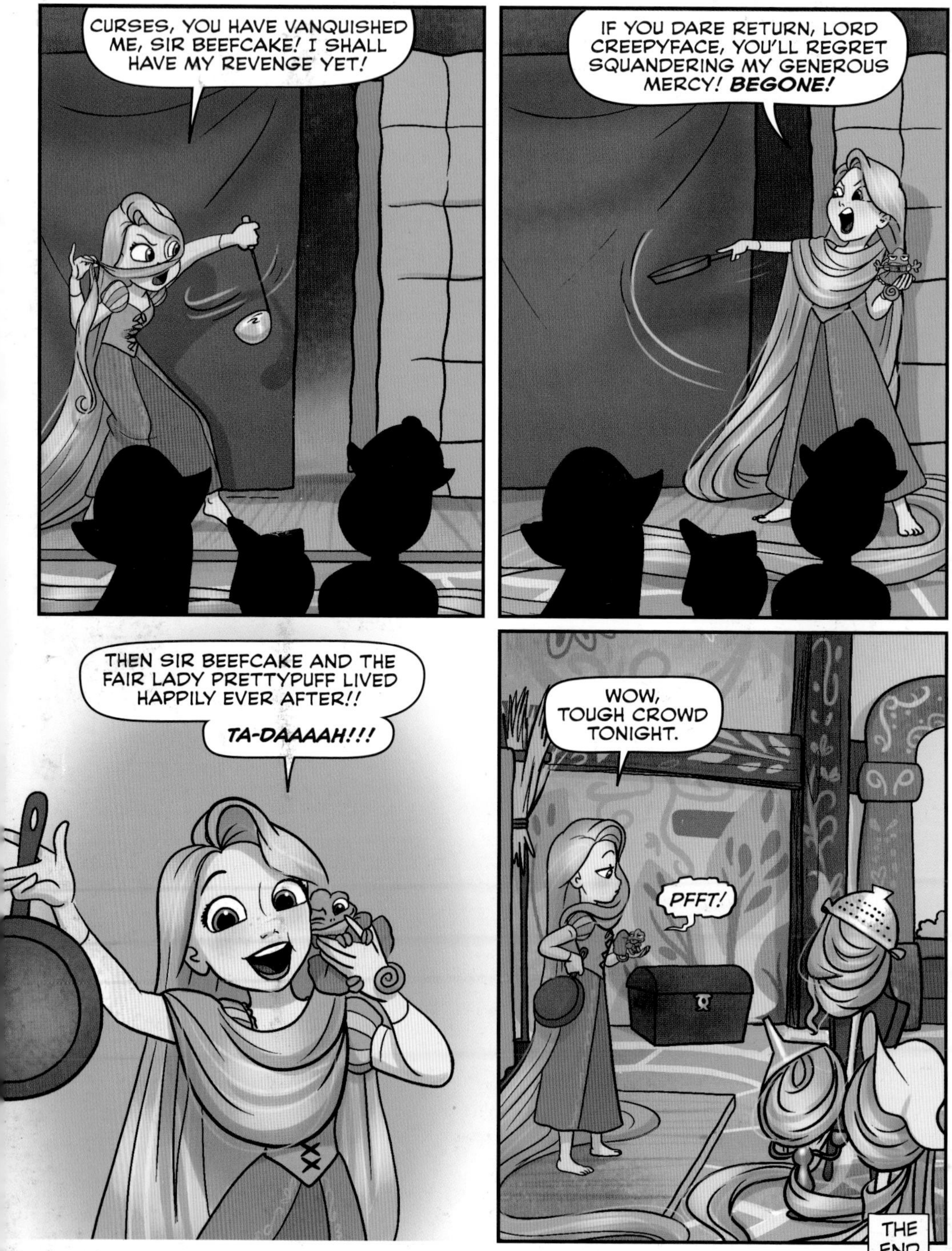
CURSES, YOU HAVE VANQUISHED ME, SIR BEEFCAKE! I SHALL HAVE MY REVENGE YET!
IF YOU DARE RETURN, LORD CREEPYFACE, YOU'LL REGRET SQUANDERING MY GENEROUS MERCY! BEGONE!
THEN SIR BEEFCAKE AND THE FAIR LADY PRETTYPUFF LIVED HAPPILY EVER AFTER!!
TA-DAAAAH!!!
WOW, TOUGH CROWD TONIGHT.
PFFT!
THE END

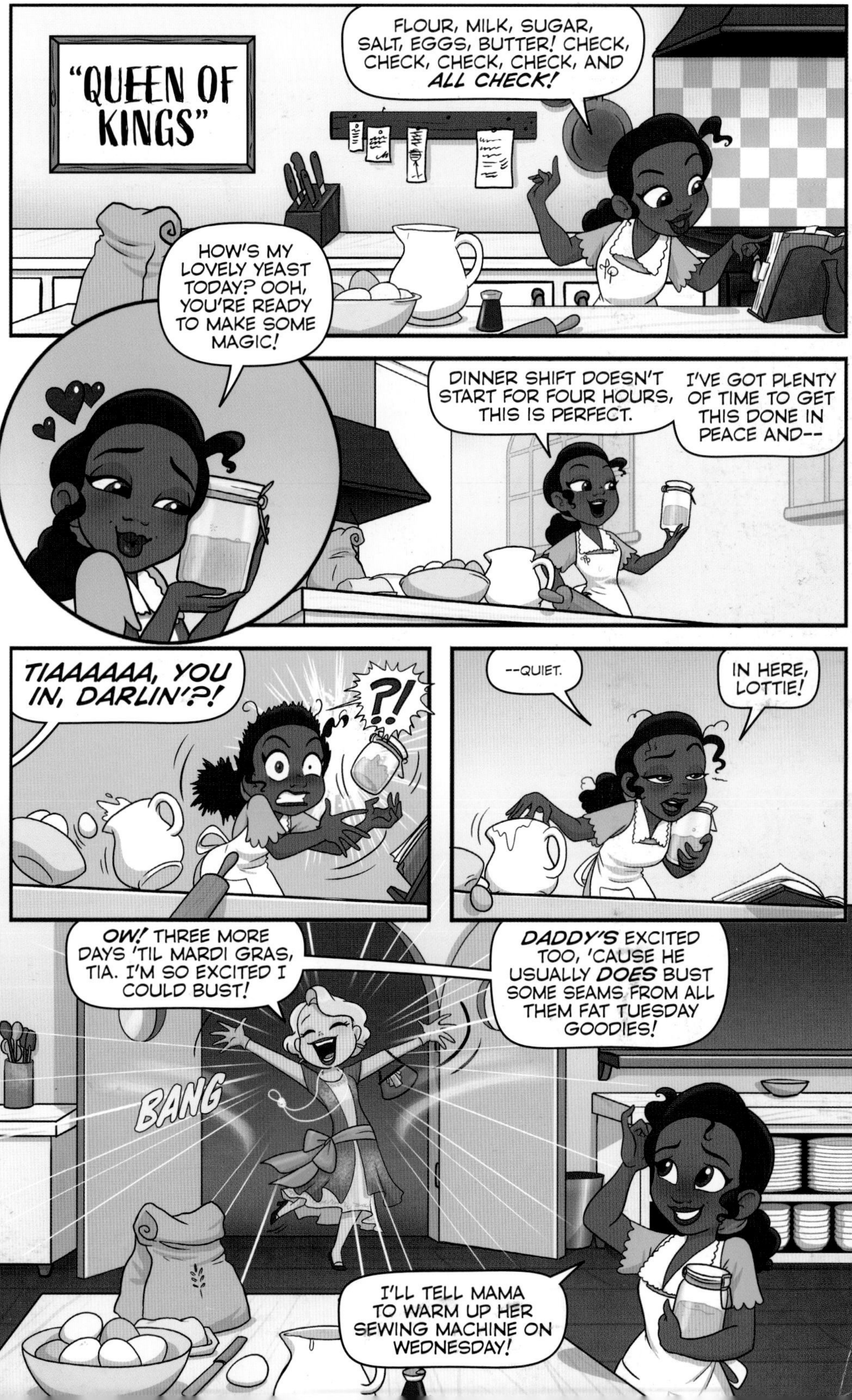

"QUEEN OF KINGS"
FLOUR, MILK, SUGAR, SALT, EGGS, BUTTER! CHECK, CHECK, CHECK, CHECK, AND ALL CHECK!
HOW'S MY LOVELY YEAST TODAY? OOH, YOU'RE READY TO MAKE SOME MAGIC!
DINNER SHIFT DOESN'T START FOR FOUR HOURS, THIS IS PERFECT.
I'VE GOT PLENTY OF TIME TO GET THIS DONE IN PEACE AND--
TIAAAAAA, YOU IN, DARLIN'?!
?!
--QUIET.
IN HERE, LOTTIE!
OW! THREE MORE DAYS 'TIL MARDI GRAS, TIA. I'M SO EXCITED I COULD BUST!
DADDY'S EXCITED TOO, 'CAUSE HE USUALLY DOES BUST SOME SEAMS FROM ALL THEM FAT TUESDAY GOODIES!
BANG
I'LL TELL MAMA TO WARM UP HER SEWING MACHINE ON WEDNESDAY!

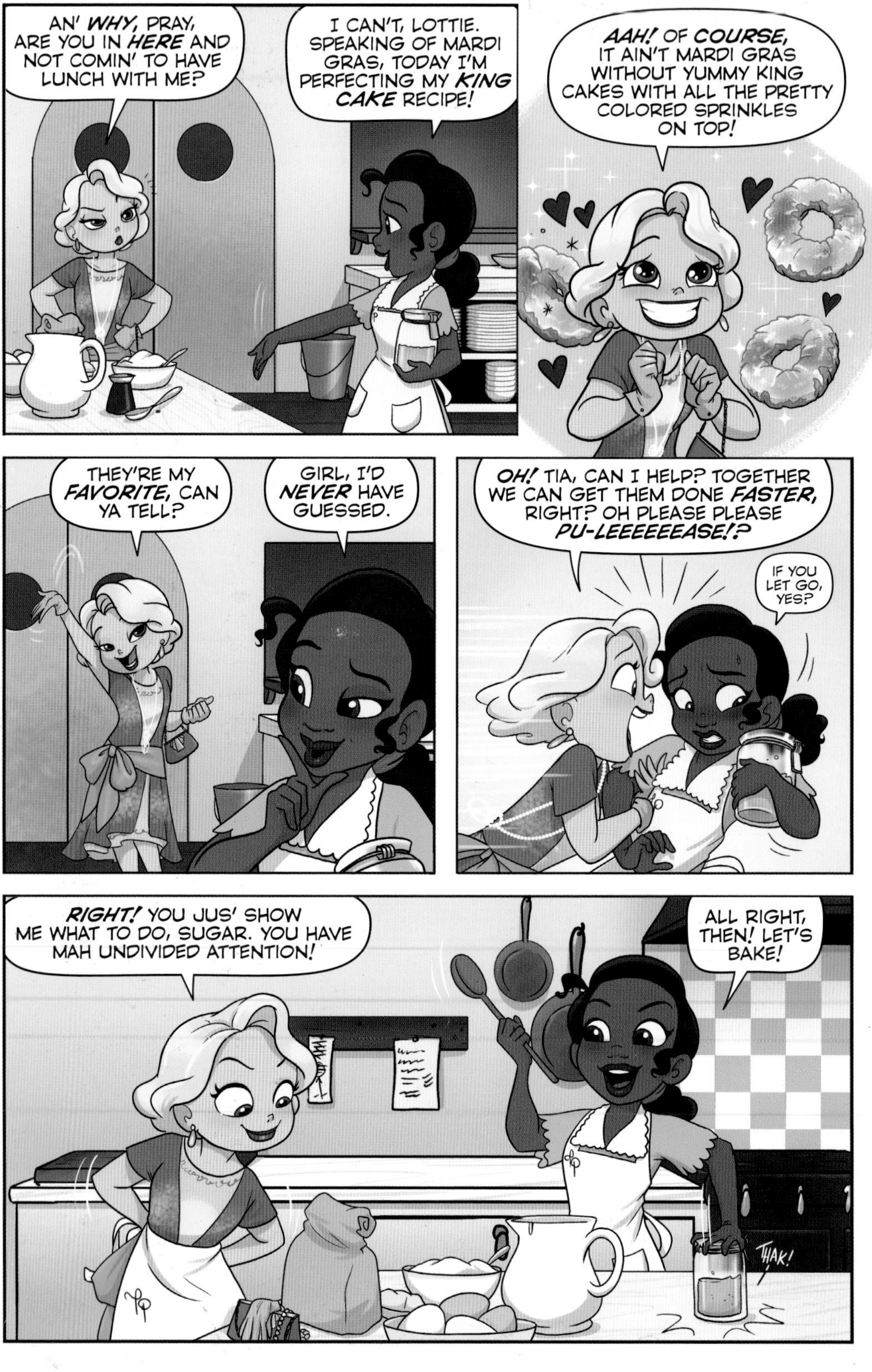
AN' WHY, PRAY, ARE YOU IN HERE AND NOT COMIN' TO HAVE LUNCH WITH ME?
I CAN'T, LOTTIE. SPEAKING OF MARDI GRAS, TODAY I'M PERFECTING MY KING CAKE RECIPE!
AAH! OF COURSE, IT AIN'T MARDI GRAS WITHOUT YUMMY KING CAKES WITH ALL THE PRETTY COLORED SPRINKLES ON TOP!
THEY'RE MY FAVORITE, CAN YA TELL?
GIRL, I'D NEVER HAVE GUESSED.
OH! TIA, CAN I HELP? TOGETHER WE CAN GET THEM DONE FASTER, RIGHT? OH PLEASE PLEASE PU-LEEEEEEASE!?
IF YOU LET GO, YES?
RIGHT! YOU JUS' SHOW ME WHAT TO DO, SUGAR. YOU HAVE MAH UNDIVIDED ATTENTION!
ALL RIGHT, THEN! LET'S BAKE!
THAK!

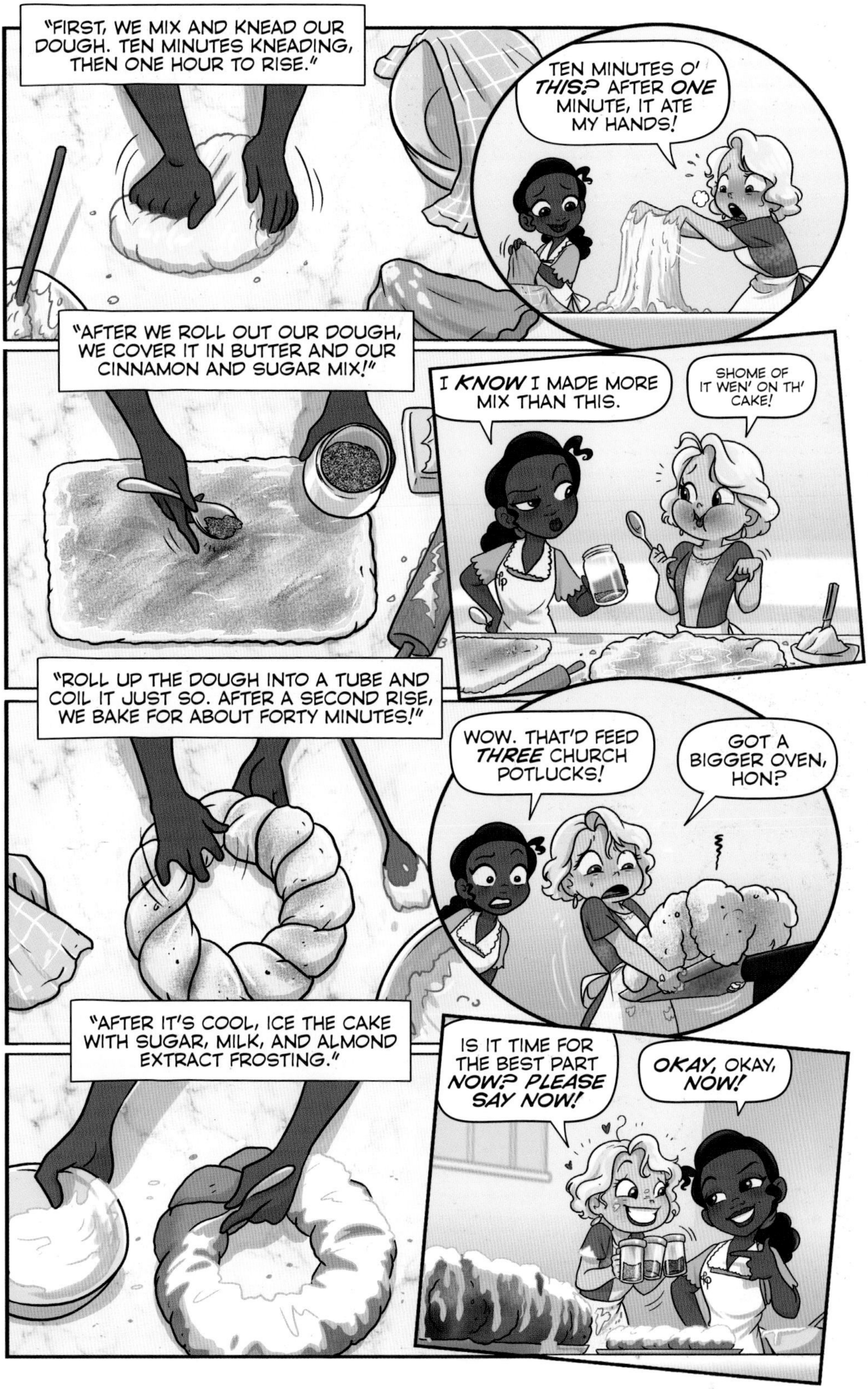
"FIRST, WE MIX AND KNEAD OUR DOUGH. TEN MINUTES KNEADING, THEN ONE HOUR TO RISE."
TEN MINUTES O' THIS? AFTER ONE MINUTE, IT ATE MY HANDS!
"AFTER WE ROLL OUT OUR DOUGH, WE COVER IT IN BUTTER AND OUR CINNAMON AND SUGAR MIX!"
I KNOW I MADE MORE MIX THAN THIS.
SHOME OF IT WEN' ON TH' CAKE!
"ROLL UP THE DOUGH INTO A TUBE AND COIL IT JUST SO. AFTER A SECOND RISE, WE BAKE FOR ABOUT FORTY MINUTES!"
WOW. THAT'D FEED THREE CHURCH POTLUCKS!
GOT A BIGGER OVEN, HON?
"AFTER IT'S COOL, ICE THE CAKE WITH SUGAR, MILK, AND ALMOND EXTRACT FROSTING."
IS IT TIME FOR THE BEST PART NOW? PLEASE SAY NOW!
OKAY, OKAY, NOW!

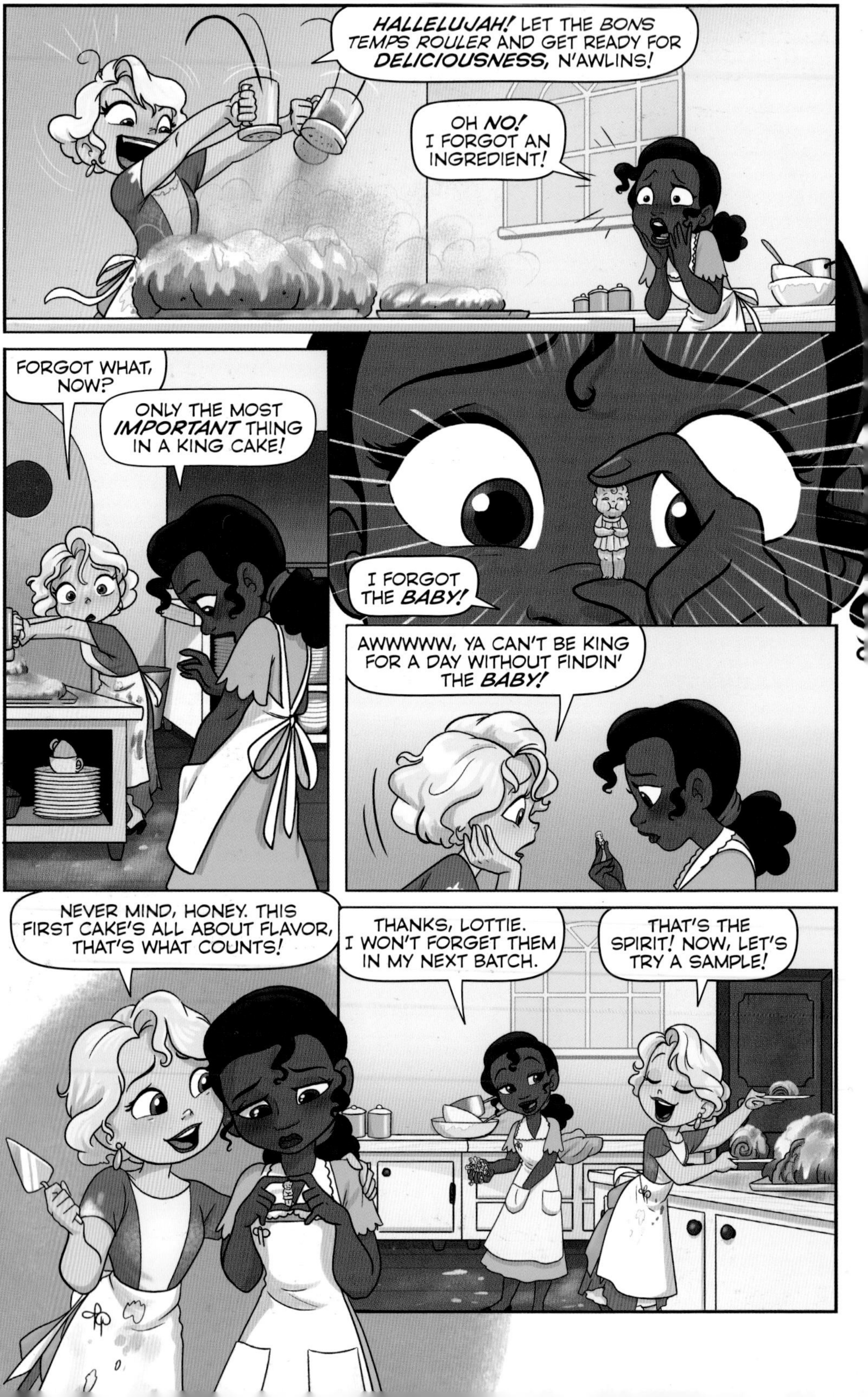
HALLELUJAH! LET THE BONS TEMPS ROULER AND GET READY FOR DELICIOUSNESS, N'AWLINS!
OH NO! I FORGOT AN INGREDIENT!
FORGOT WHAT, NOW?
ONLY THE MOST IMPORTANT THING IN A KING CAKE!
I FORGOT THE BABY!
AWWWWW, YA CAN'T BE KING FOR A DAY WITHOUT FINDIN' THE BABY!
NEVER MIND, HONEY. THIS FIRST CAKE'S ALL ABOUT FLAVOR, THAT'S WHAT COUNTS!
THANKS, LOTTIE. I WON'T FORGET THEM IN MY NEXT BATCH.
THAT'S THE SPIRIT! NOW, LET'S TRY A SAMPLE!

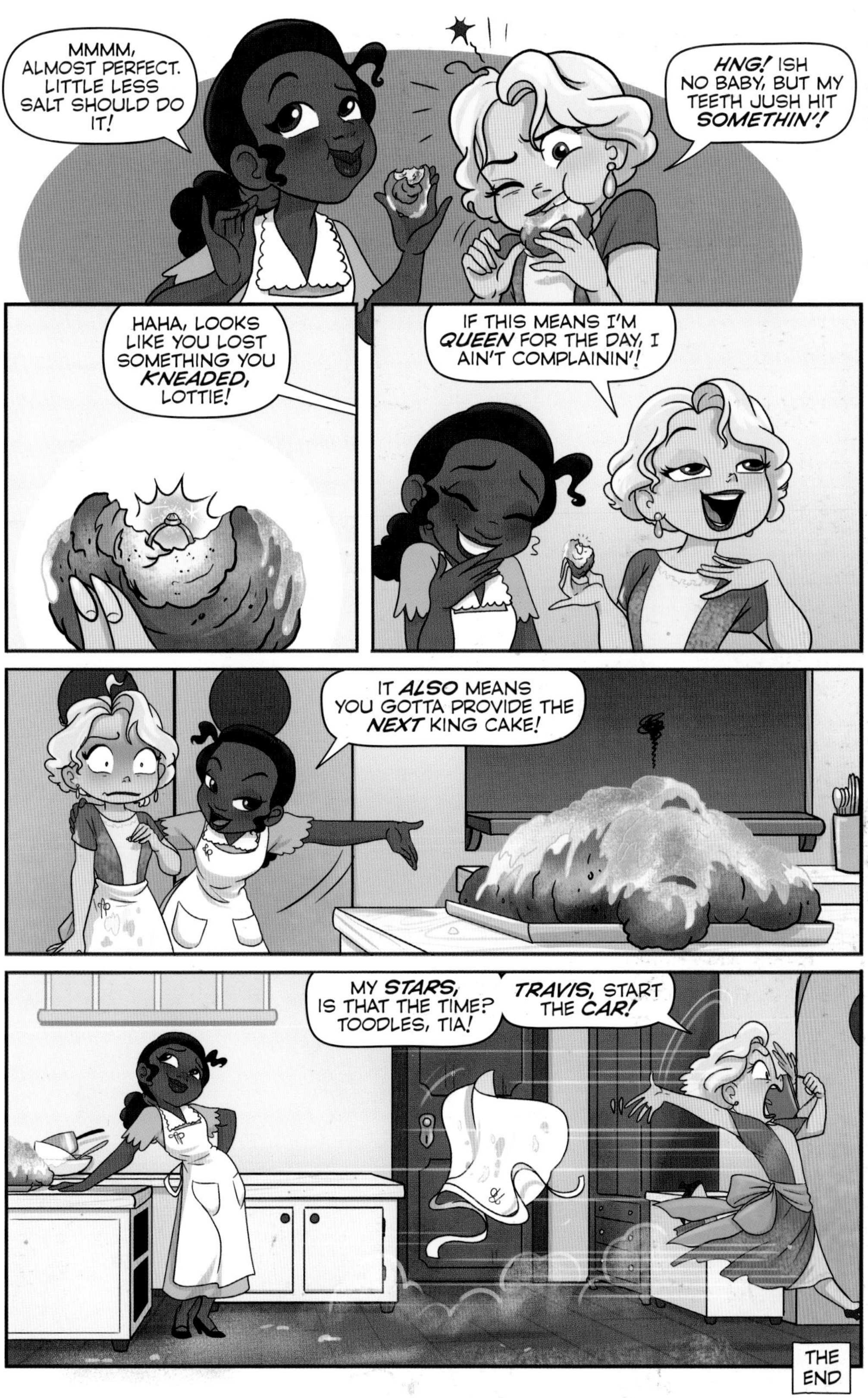
MMMM, ALMOST PERFECT. LITTLE LESS SALT SHOULD DO IT!
HNG! ISH NO BABY, BUT MY TEETH JUSH HIT SOMETHIN'!
HAHA, LOOKS LIKE YOU LOST SOMETHING YOU KNEADED, LOTTIE!
IF THIS MEANS I'M QUEEN FOR THE DAY, I AIN'T COMPLAININ'!
IT ALSO MEANS YOU GOTTA PROVIDE THE NEXT KING CAKE!
MY STARS, IS THAT THE TIME? TOODLES, TIA!
TRAVIS, START THE CAR!
THE END

"BELLE & MAURICE"

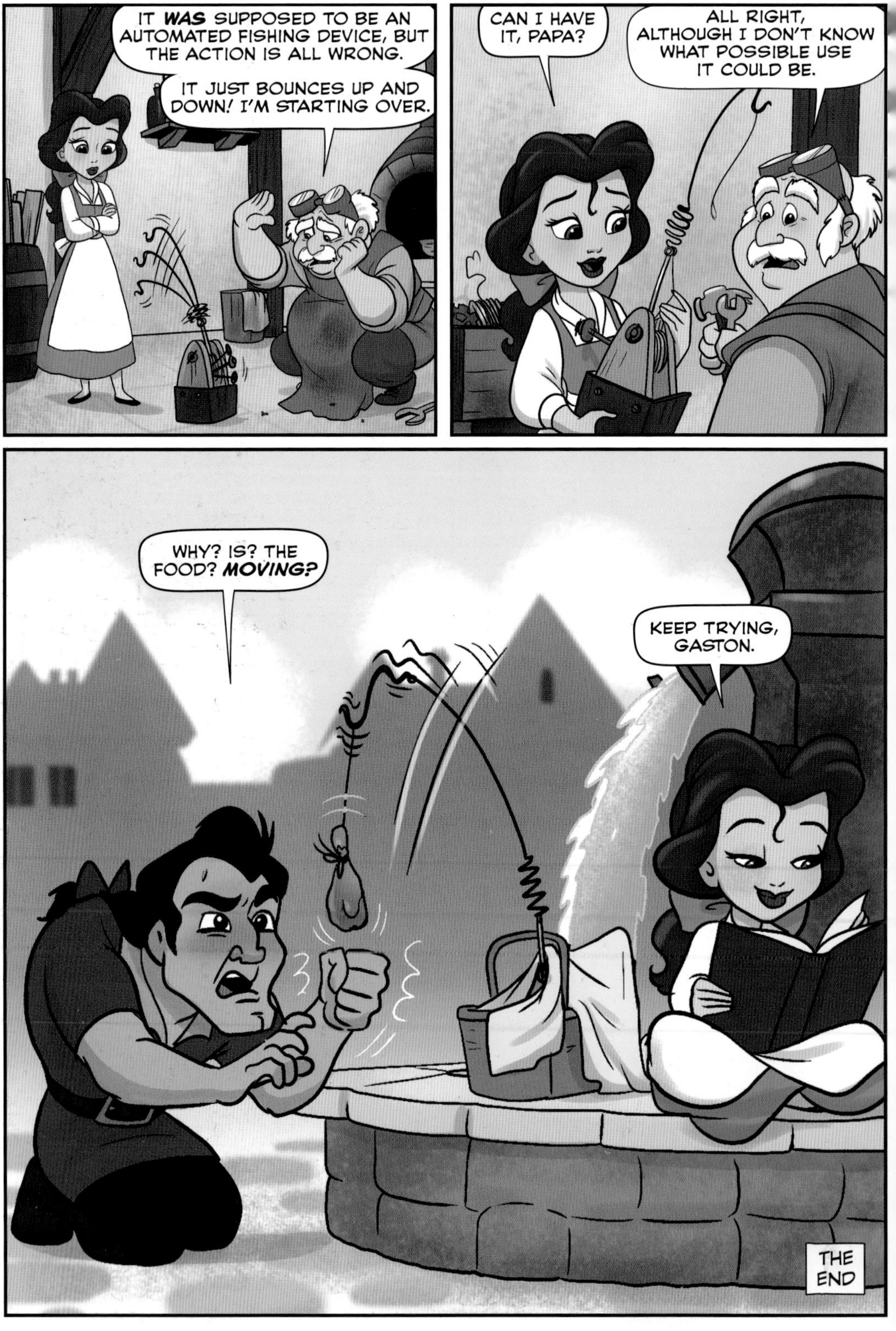
IT WAS SUPPOSED TO BE AN AUTOMATED FISHING DEVICE, BUT THE ACTION IS ALL WRONG.
IT JUST BOUNCES UP AND DOWN! I'M STARTING OVER.
CAN I HAVE IT, PAPA?
ALL RIGHT, ALTHOUGH I DON'T KNOW WHAT POSSIBLE USE IT COULD BE.
WHY? IS? THE FOOD? MOVING?
KEEP TRYING, GASTON.
THE END

"FOLLOWING ME"

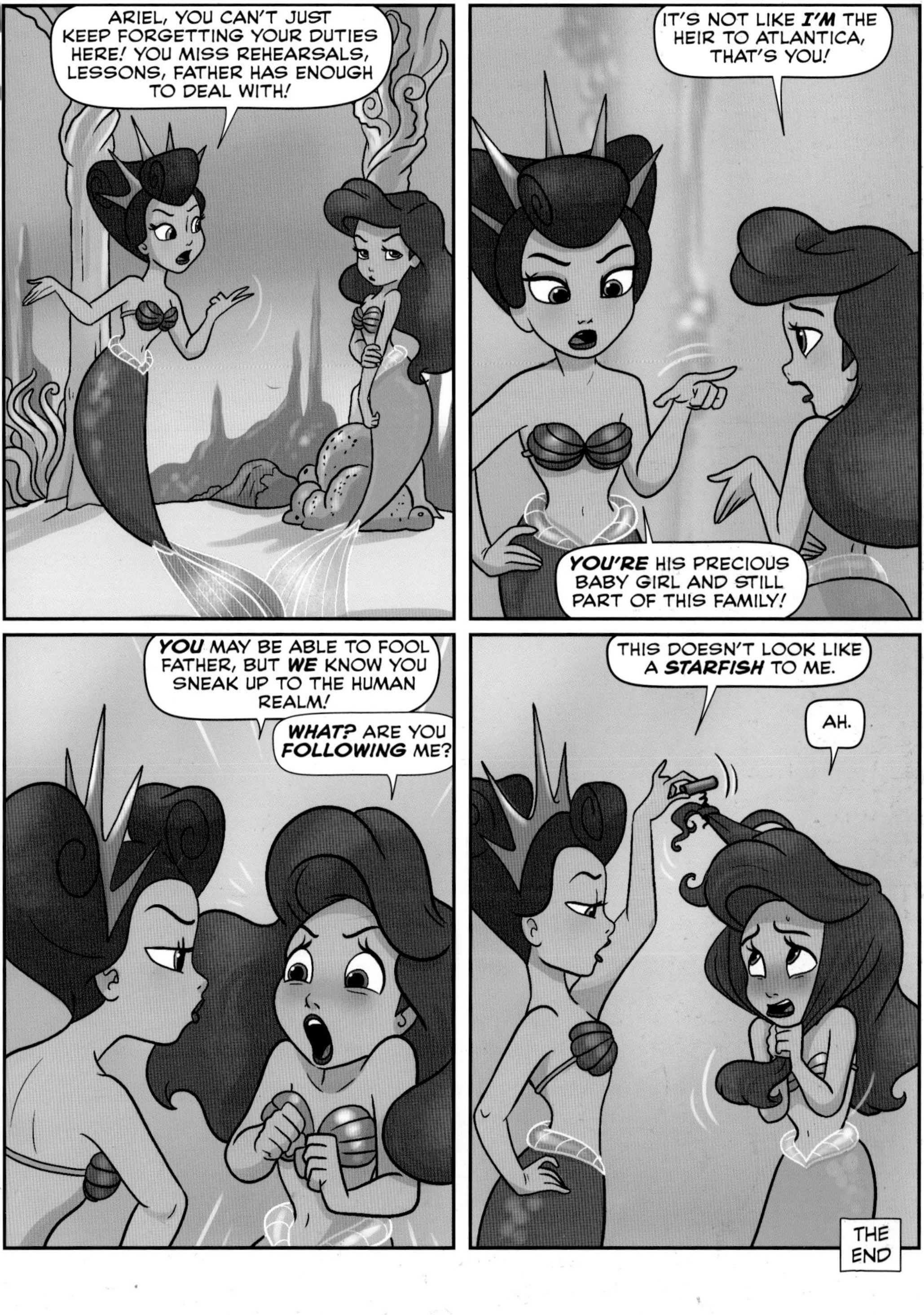
ARIEL, YOU CAN'T JUST KEEP FORGETTING YOUR DUTIES HERE! YOU MISS REHEARSALS, LESSONS, FATHER HAS ENOUGH TO DEAL WITH!
IT'S NOT LIKE ***I'M*** THE HEIR TO ATLANTICA, THAT'S YOU!
YOU'RE HIS PRECIOUS BABY GIRL AND STILL PART OF THIS FAMILY!
YOU MAY BE ABLE TO FOOL FATHER, BUT ***WE*** KNOW YOU SNEAK UP TO THE HUMAN REALM!
WHAT? ARE YOU ***FOLLOWING*** ME?
THIS DOESN'T LOOK LIKE A ***STARFISH*** TO ME.
AH.
THE END

"BEST SEAT IN THE HOUSE"

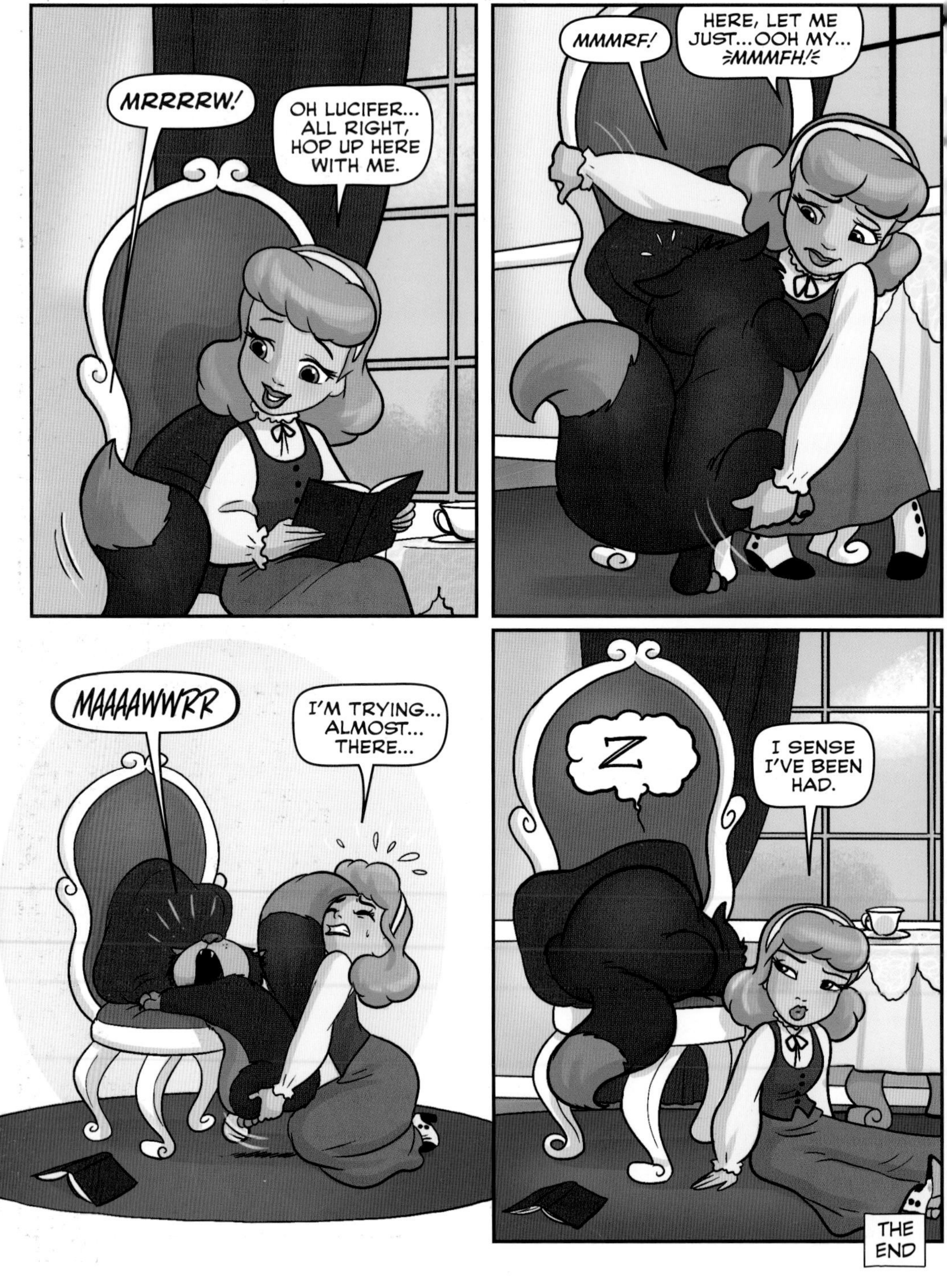
MRRRRW!
OH LUCIFER... ALL RIGHT, HOP UP HERE WITH ME.
MMMRF!
HERE, LET ME JUST...OOH MY... MMMFH!
MAAAAWWRR
I'M TRYING... ALMOST... THERE...
Z
I SENSE I'VE BEEN HAD.
THE END

"ARCHERY FORM"

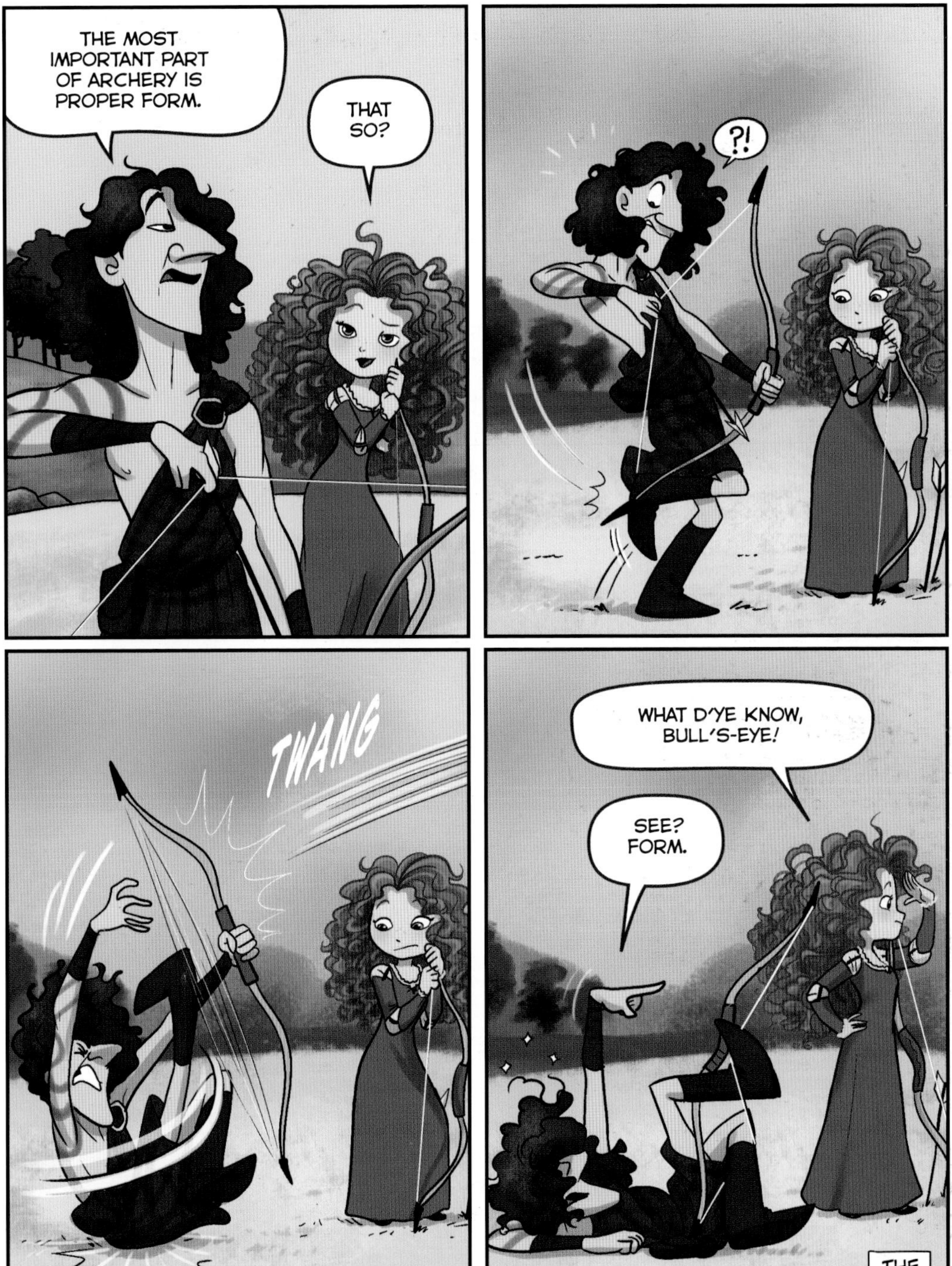
THE MOST IMPORTANT PART OF ARCHERY IS PROPER FORM.
THAT SO?
?!
TWANG
WHAT D'YE KNOW, BULL'S-EYE!
SEE? FORM.
THE END

"FIGHTING UTENSILS"

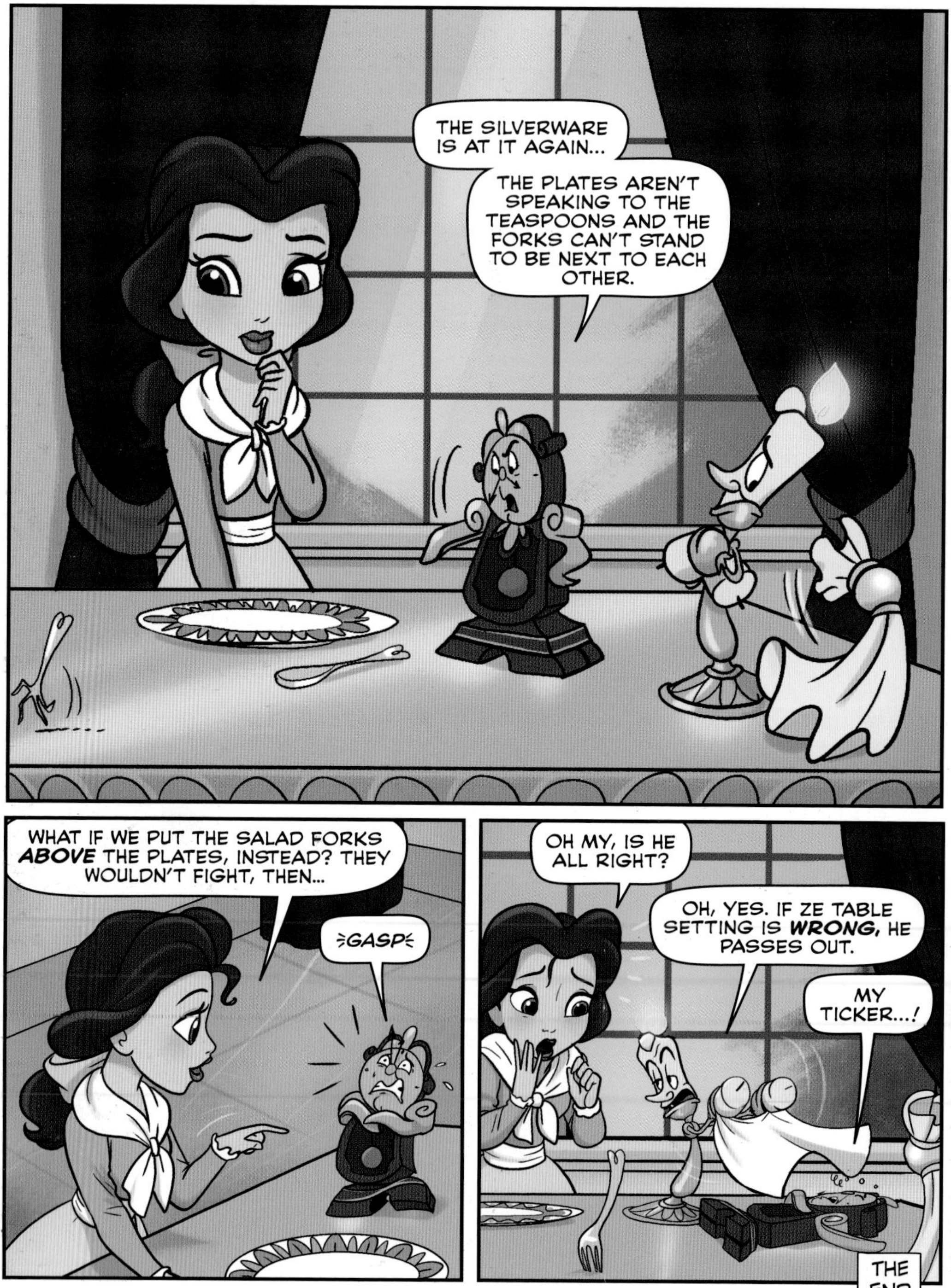
THE SILVERWARE IS AT IT AGAIN...
THE PLATES AREN'T SPEAKING TO THE TEASPOONS AND THE FORKS CAN'T STAND TO BE NEXT TO EACH OTHER.
WHAT IF WE PUT THE SALAD FORKS *ABOVE* THE PLATES, INSTEAD? THEY WOULDN'T FIGHT, THEN...
GASP
OH MY, IS HE ALL RIGHT?
OH, YES. IF ZE TABLE SETTING IS *WRONG,* HE PASSES OUT.
MY TICKER...!
THE END

"BUDDY SYSTEM"

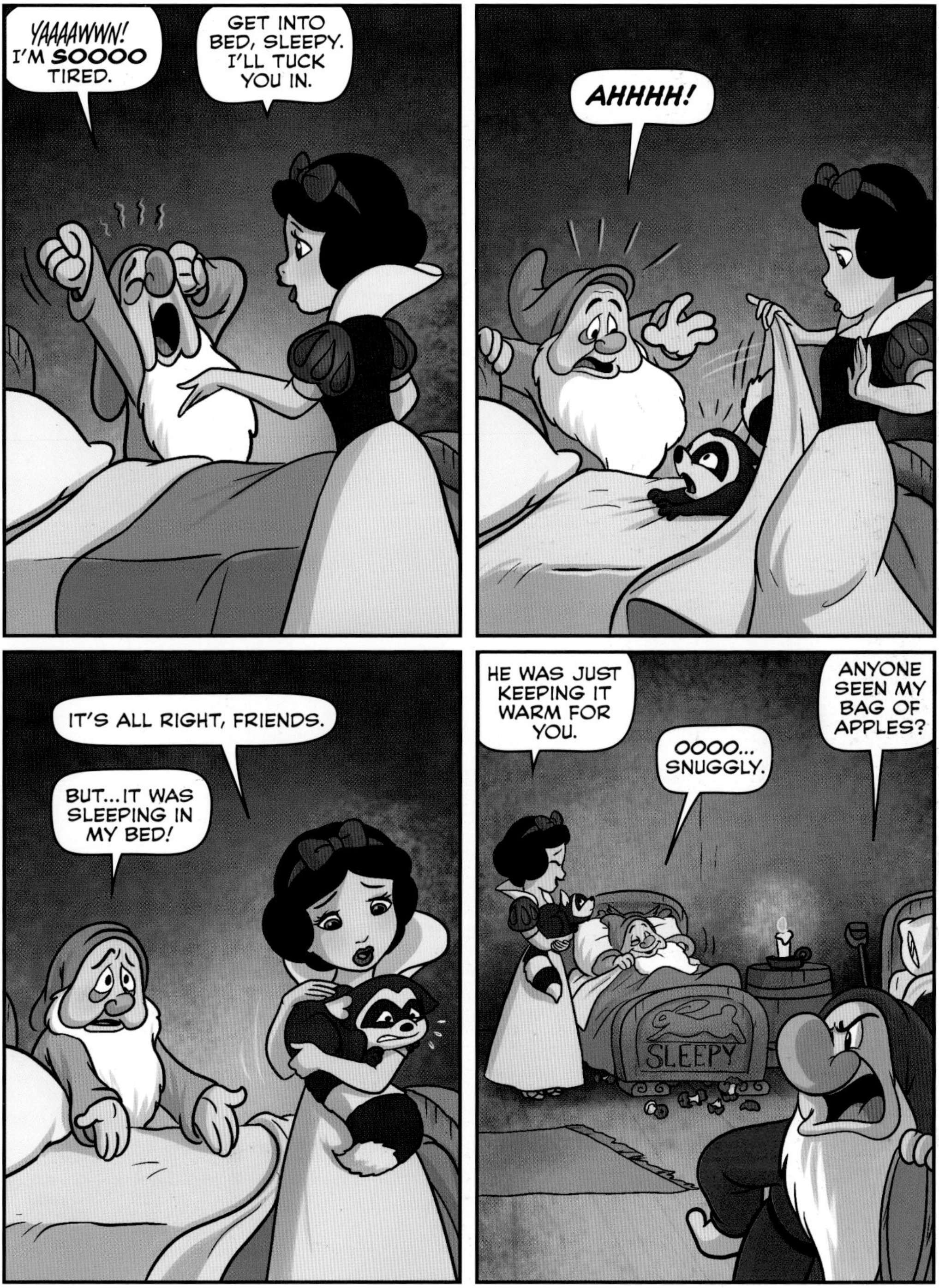

YAAAAWWN! I'M SOOOO TIRED.
GET INTO BED, SLEEPY. I'LL TUCK YOU IN.
AHHHH!
IT'S ALL RIGHT, FRIENDS.
BUT...IT WAS SLEEPING IN MY BED!
HE WAS JUST KEEPING IT WARM FOR YOU.
OOOO... SNUGGLY.
ANYONE SEEN MY BAG OF APPLES?
SLEEPY

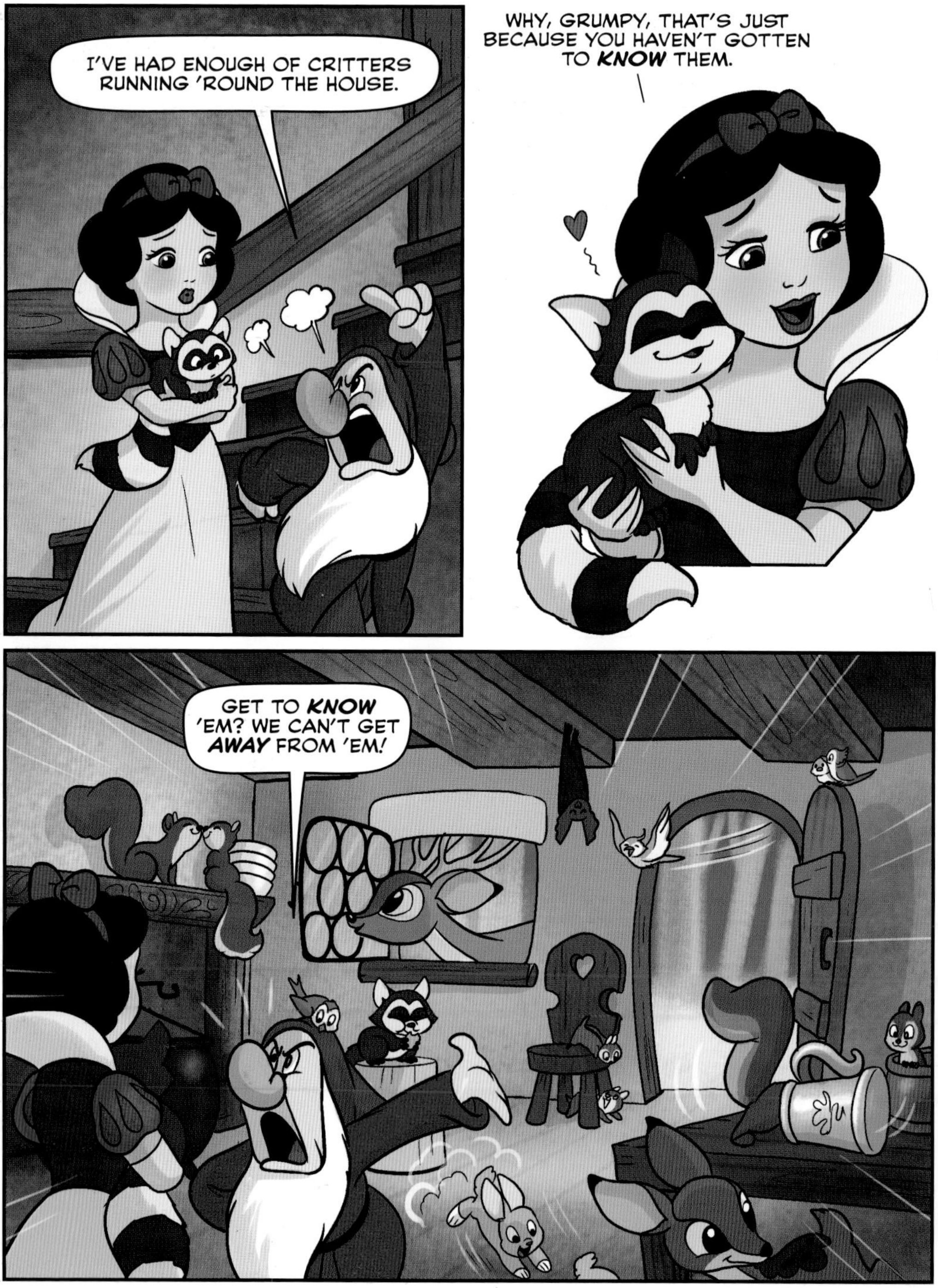
I'VE HAD ENOUGH OF CRITTERS RUNNING 'ROUND THE HOUSE.
WHY, GRUMPY, THAT'S JUST BECAUSE YOU HAVEN'T GOTTEN TO **KNOW** THEM.
GET TO **KNOW** 'EM? WE CAN'T GET **AWAY** FROM 'EM!

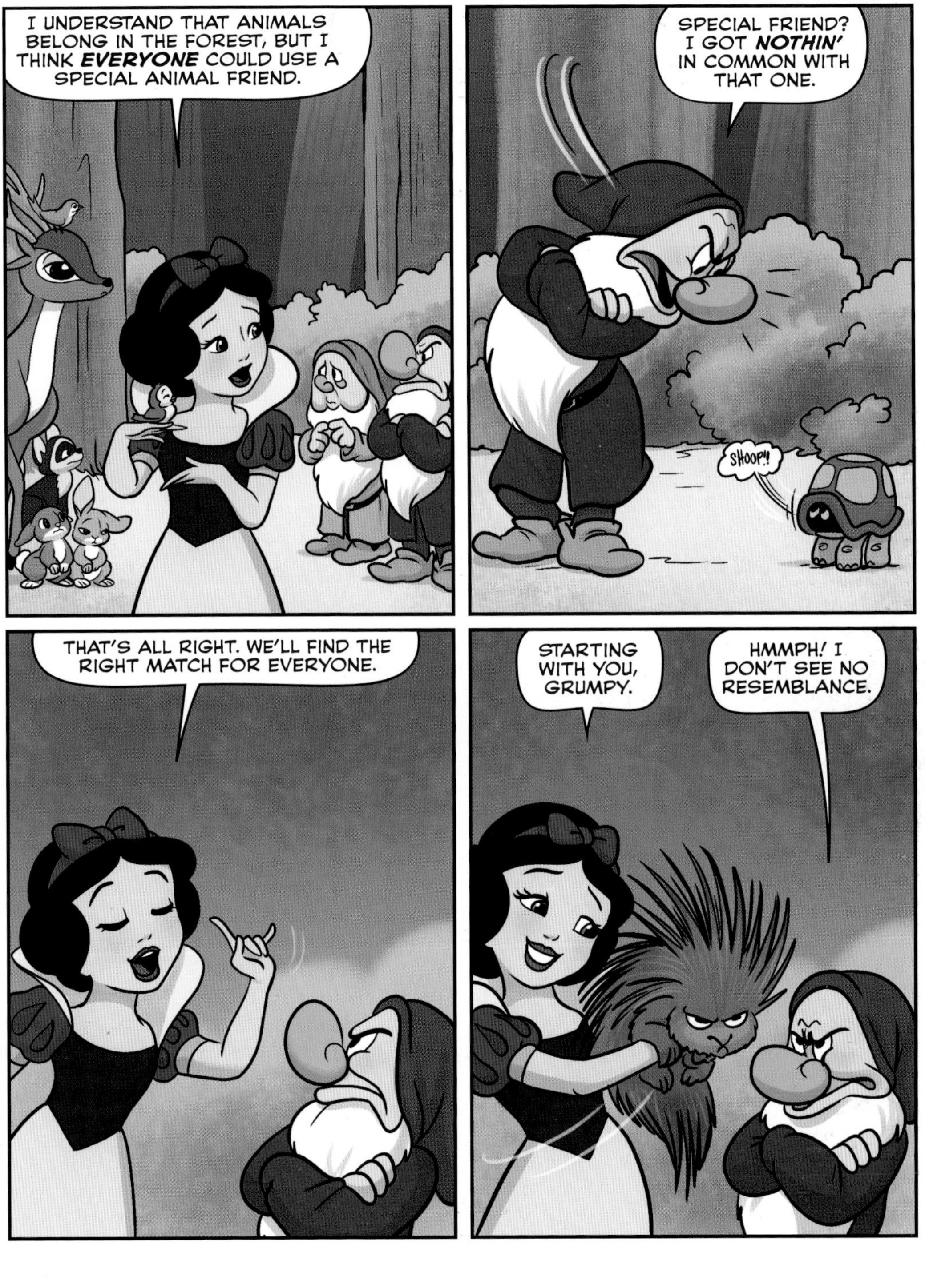
I UNDERSTAND THAT ANIMALS BELONG IN THE FOREST, BUT I THINK ***EVERYONE*** COULD USE A SPECIAL ANIMAL FRIEND.
SPECIAL FRIEND? I GOT ***NOTHIN'*** IN COMMON WITH THAT ONE.
SHOOP!!
THAT'S ALL RIGHT. WE'LL FIND THE RIGHT MATCH FOR EVERYONE.
STARTING WITH YOU, GRUMPY.
HMMPH! I DON'T SEE NO RESEMBLANCE.

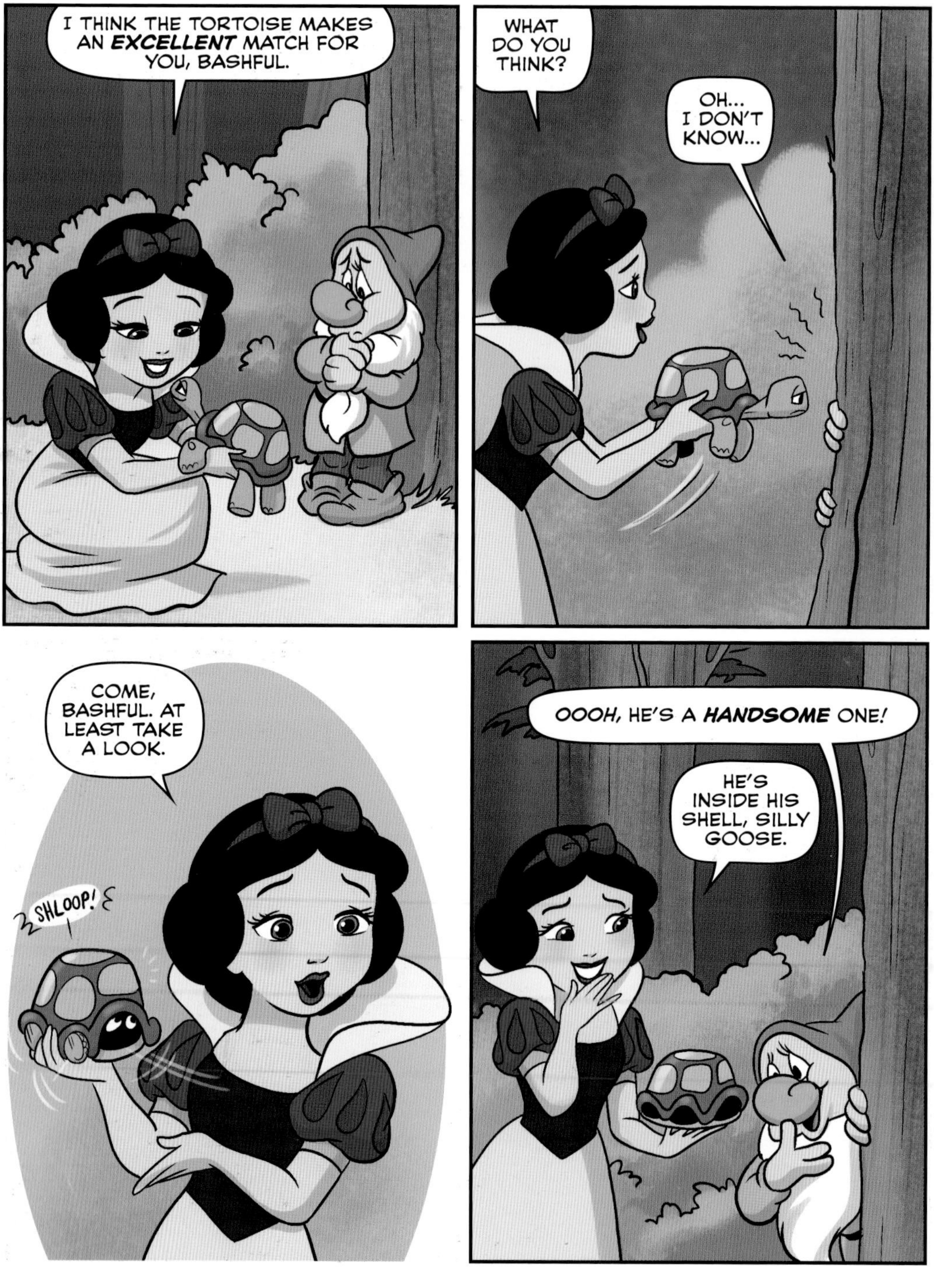
I THINK THE TORTOISE MAKES AN *EXCELLENT* MATCH FOR YOU, BASHFUL.
WHAT DO YOU THINK?
OH... I DON'T KNOW...
COME, BASHFUL. AT LEAST TAKE A LOOK.
SHLOOP!
OOOH, HE'S A ***HANDSOME*** ONE!
HE'S INSIDE HIS SHELL, SILLY GOOSE.

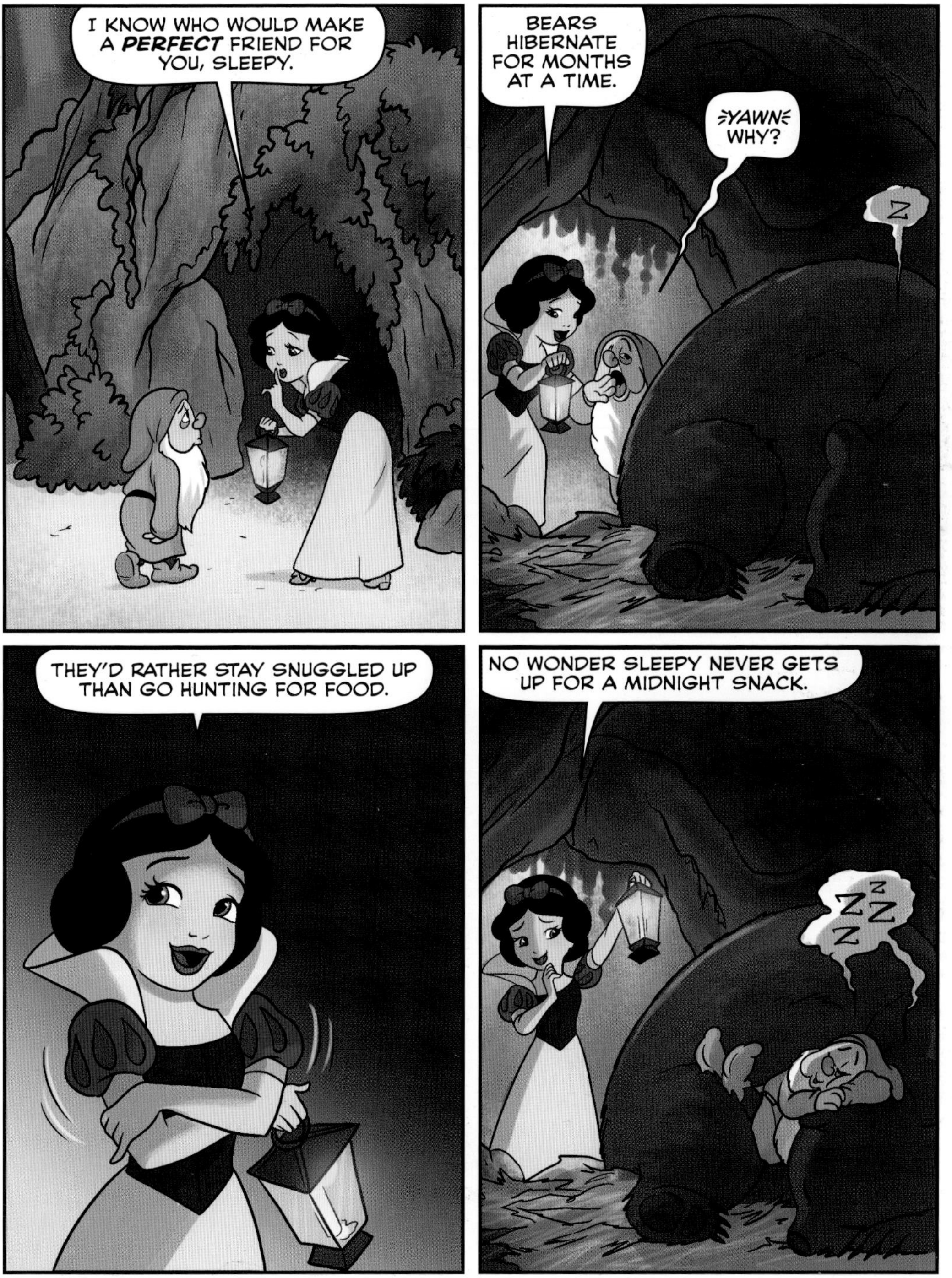
I KNOW WHO WOULD MAKE A ***PERFECT*** FRIEND FOR YOU, SLEEPY.
BEARS HIBERNATE FOR MONTHS AT A TIME.
YAWN WHY?
Z
THEY'D RATHER STAY SNUGGLED UP THAN GO HUNTING FOR FOOD.
NO WONDER SLEEPY NEVER GETS UP FOR A MIDNIGHT SNACK.
Z Z Z

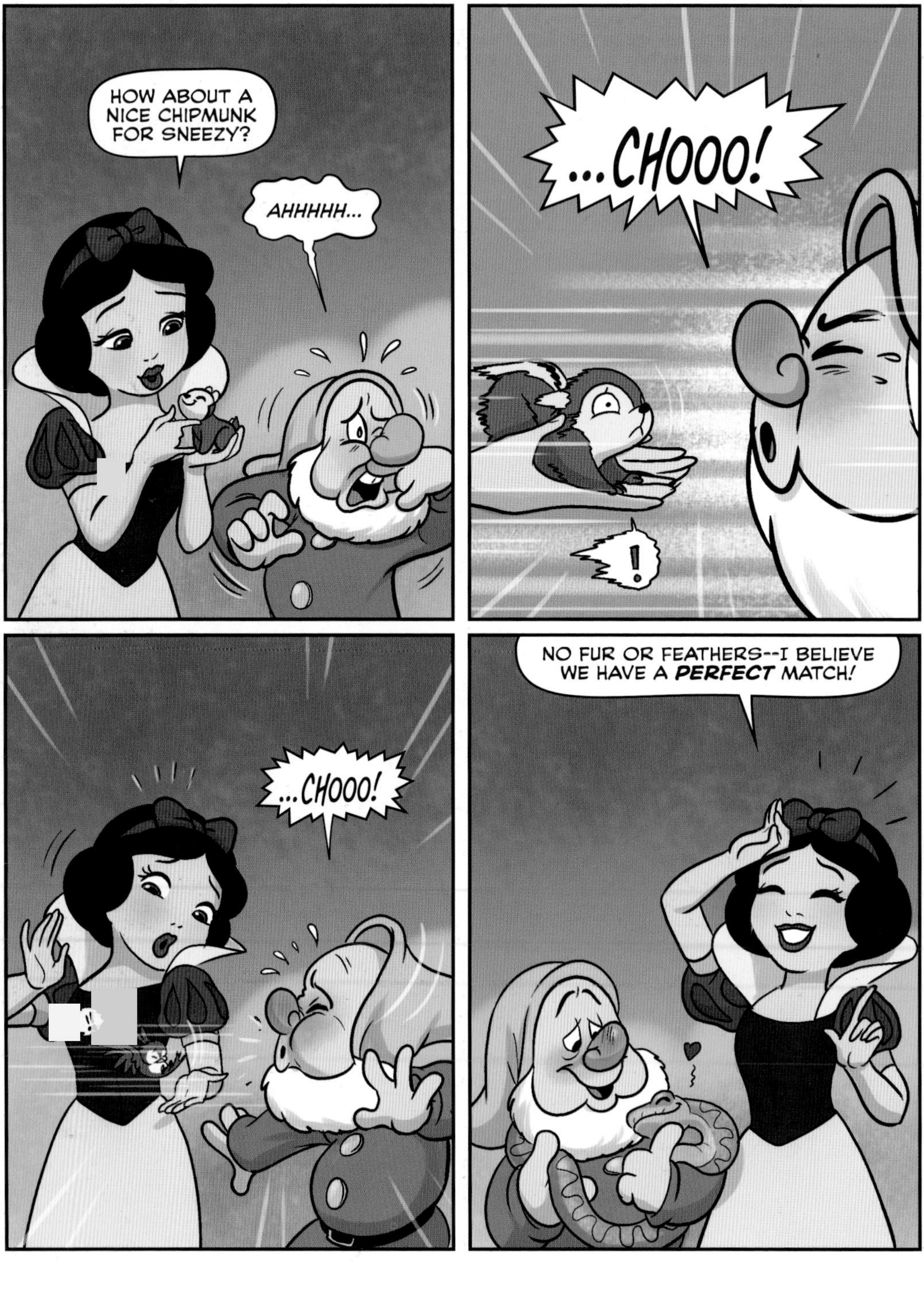
HOW ABOUT A NICE CHIPMUNK FOR SNEEZY?
AHHHHH...
...CHOOO!
!
...CHOOO!
NO FUR OR FEATHERS--I BELIEVE WE HAVE A **PERFECT** MATCH!

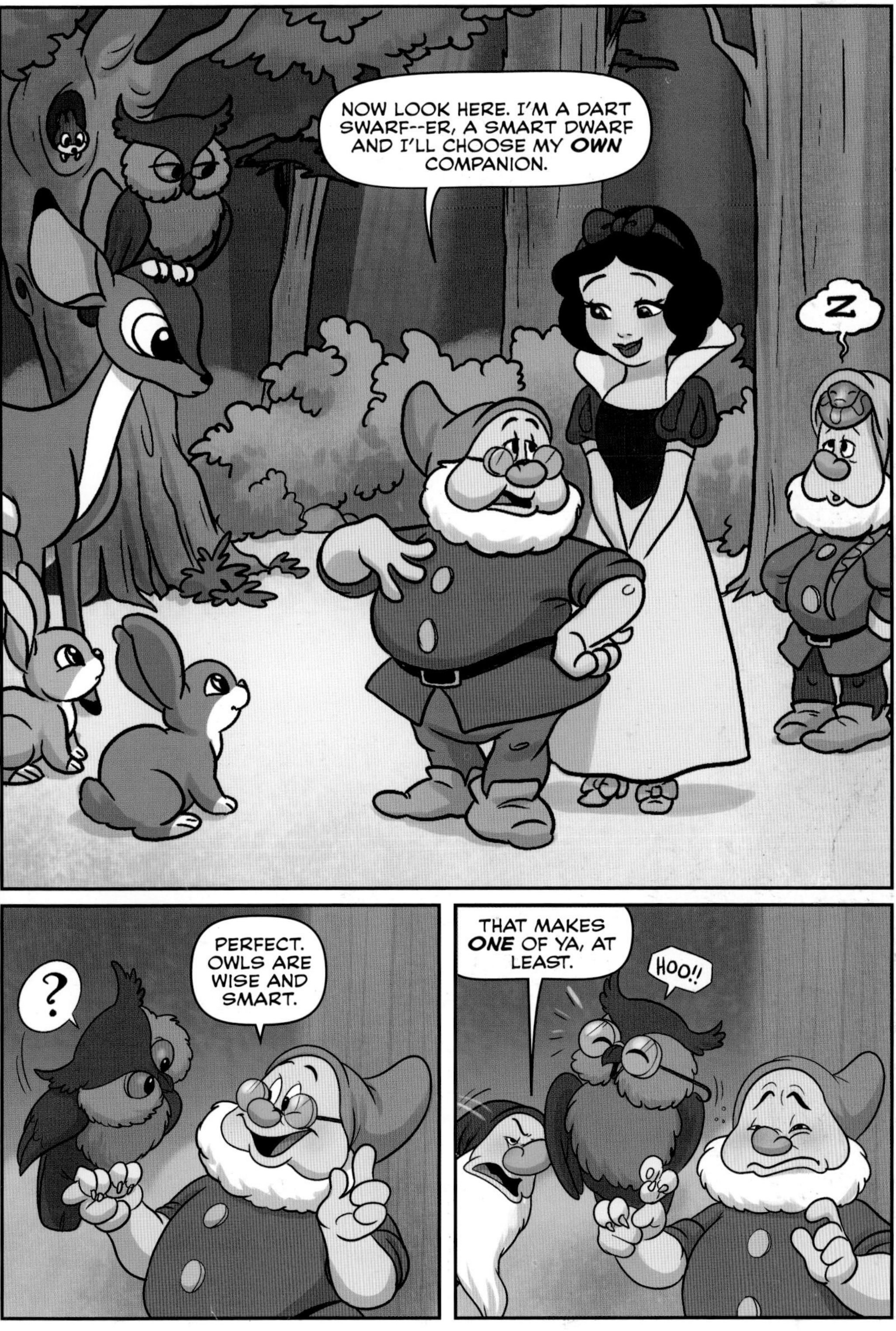
NOW LOOK HERE. I'M A DART SWARF--ER, A SMART DWARF AND I'LL CHOOSE MY *OWN* COMPANION.
Z
?
PERFECT. OWLS ARE WISE AND SMART.
THAT MAKES *ONE* OF YA, AT LEAST.
HOO!!

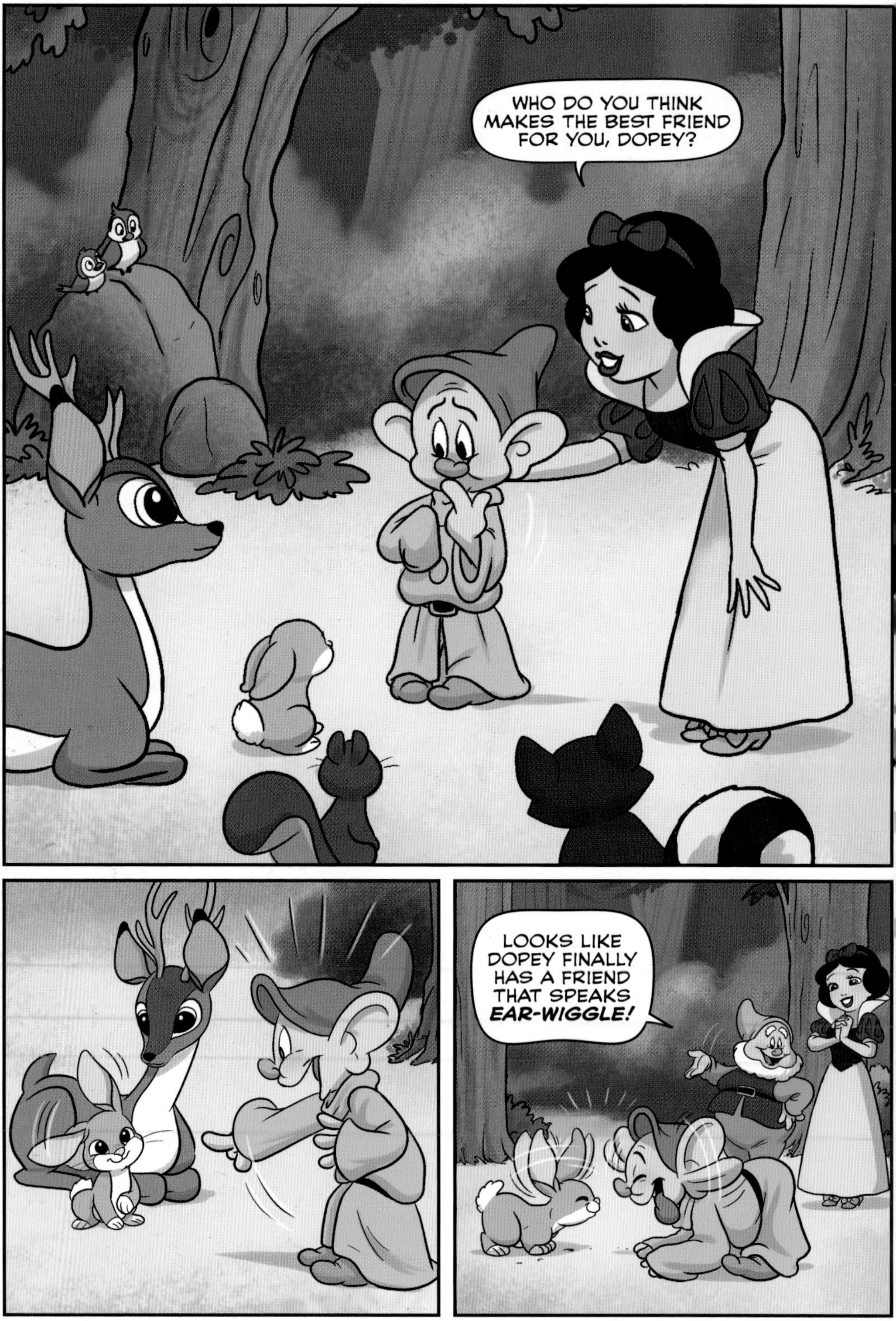
WHO DO YOU THINK MAKES THE BEST FRIEND FOR YOU, DOPEY?
LOOKS LIKE DOPEY FINALLY HAS A FRIEND THAT SPEAKS ***EAR-WIGGLE!***

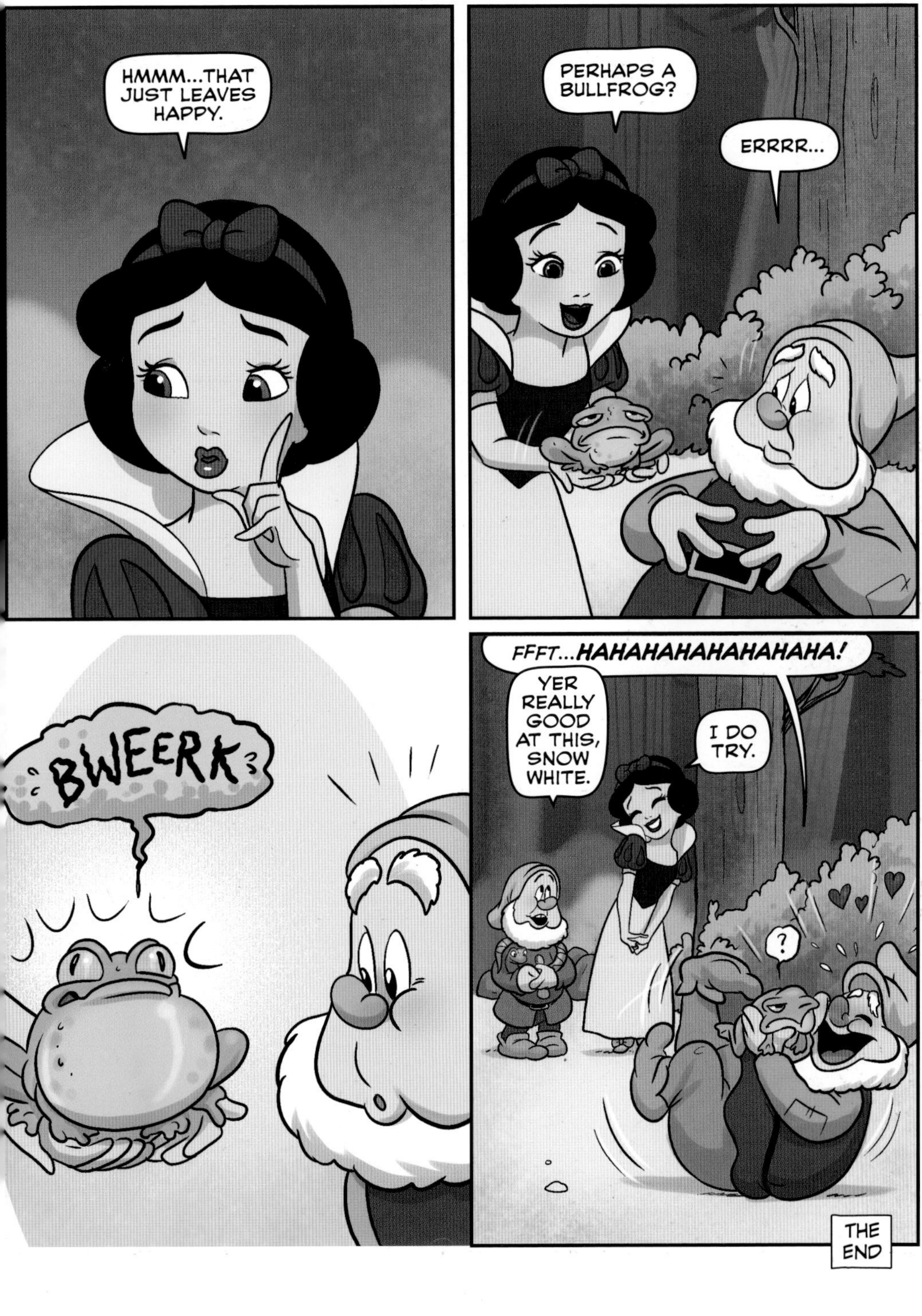
HMMM...THAT JUST LEAVES HAPPY.
PERHAPS A BULLFROG?
ERRRR...
BWEERK
FFFT...HAHAHAHAHAHAHAHA!
YER REALLY GOOD AT THIS, SNOW WHITE.
I DO TRY.
?
THE END

"UNWIND"

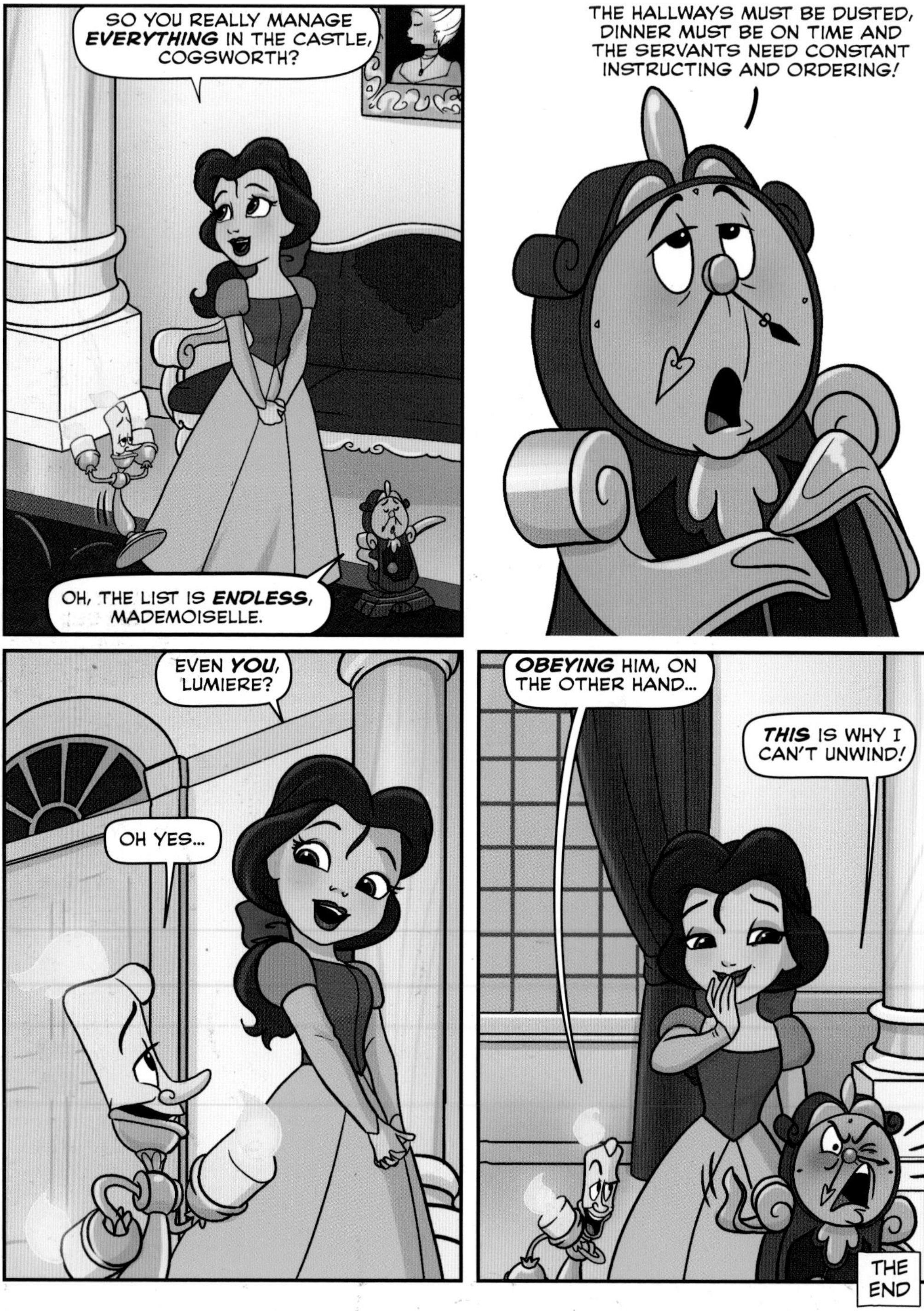

SO YOU REALLY MANAGE *EVERYTHING* IN THE CASTLE, COGSWORTH?
OH, THE LIST IS *ENDLESS*, MADEMOISELLE.
THE HALLWAYS MUST BE DUSTED, DINNER MUST BE ON TIME AND THE SERVANTS NEED CONSTANT INSTRUCTING AND ORDERING!
EVEN *YOU*, LUMIERE?
OH YES...
OBEYING HIM, ON THE OTHER HAND...
THIS IS WHY I CAN'T UNWIND!
THE END

"GOLDI-LOCKED!"

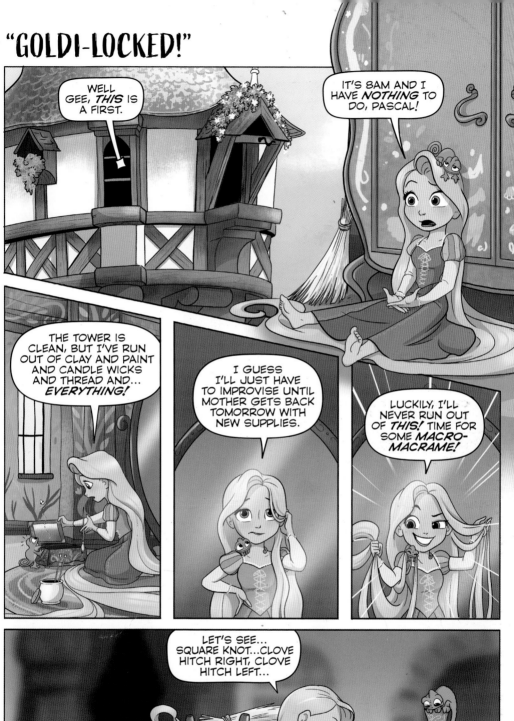

WELL GEE, *THIS* IS A FIRST.

IT'S 8AM AND I HAVE *NOTHING* TO DO, PASCAL!

THE TOWER IS CLEAN, BUT I'VE RUN OUT OF CLAY AND PAINT AND CANDLE WICKS AND THREAD AND... *EVERYTHING!*

I GUESS I'LL JUST HAVE TO IMPROVISE UNTIL MOTHER GETS BACK TOMORROW WITH NEW SUPPLIES.

LUCKILY, I'LL NEVER RUN OUT OF *THIS!* TIME FOR SOME *MACRO-MACRAME!*

LET'S SEE... SQUARE KNOT...CLOVE HITCH RIGHT, CLOVE HITCH LEFT...

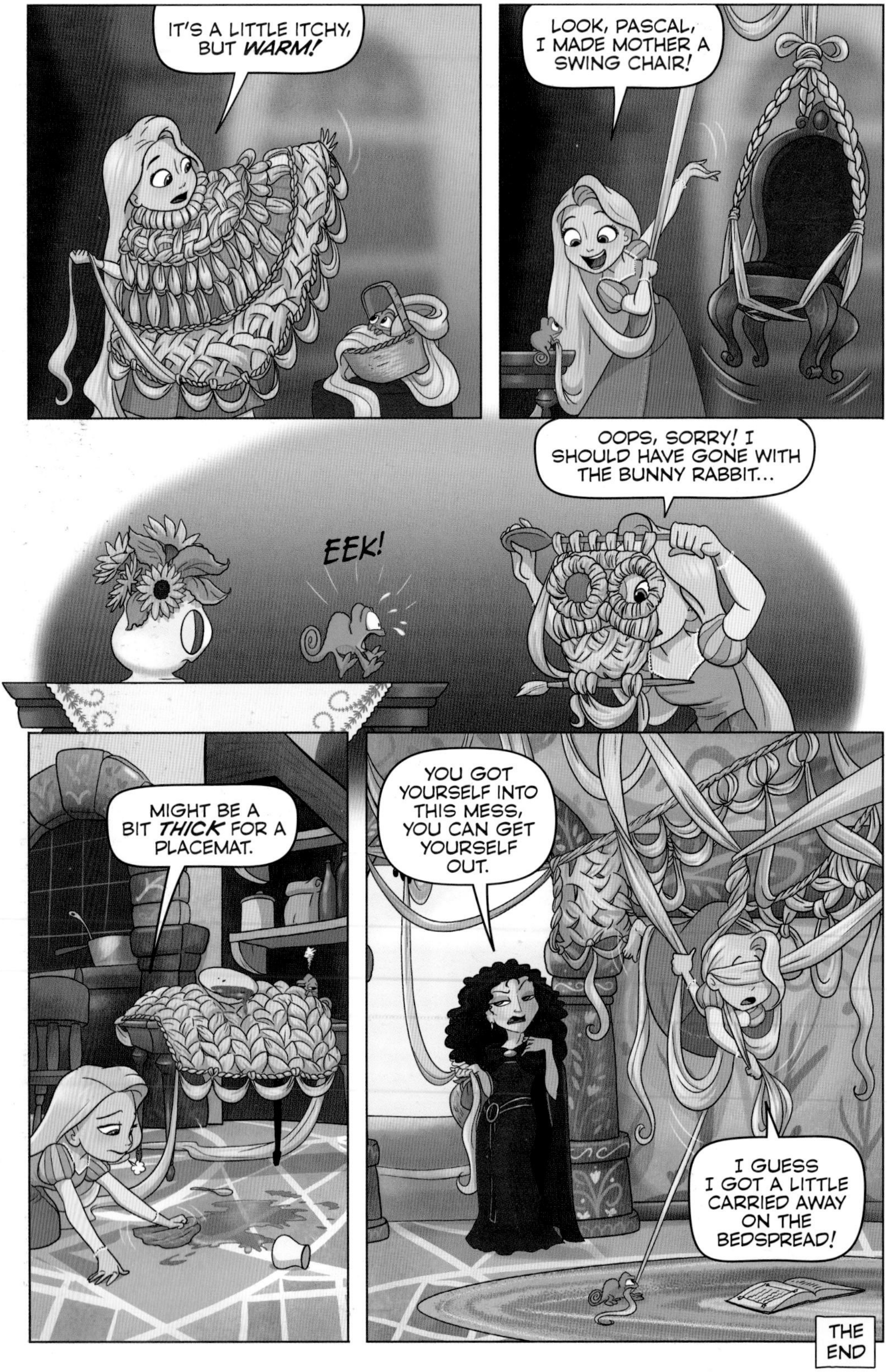
IT'S A LITTLE ITCHY, BUT *WARM!*
LOOK, PASCAL, I MADE MOTHER A SWING CHAIR!
EEK!
OOPS, SORRY! I SHOULD HAVE GONE WITH THE BUNNY RABBIT...
MIGHT BE A BIT *THICK* FOR A PLACEMAT.
YOU GOT YOURSELF INTO THIS MESS, YOU CAN GET YOURSELF OUT.
I GUESS I GOT A LITTLE CARRIED AWAY ON THE BEDSPREAD!
THE END

"ARCHERY TRAINING"

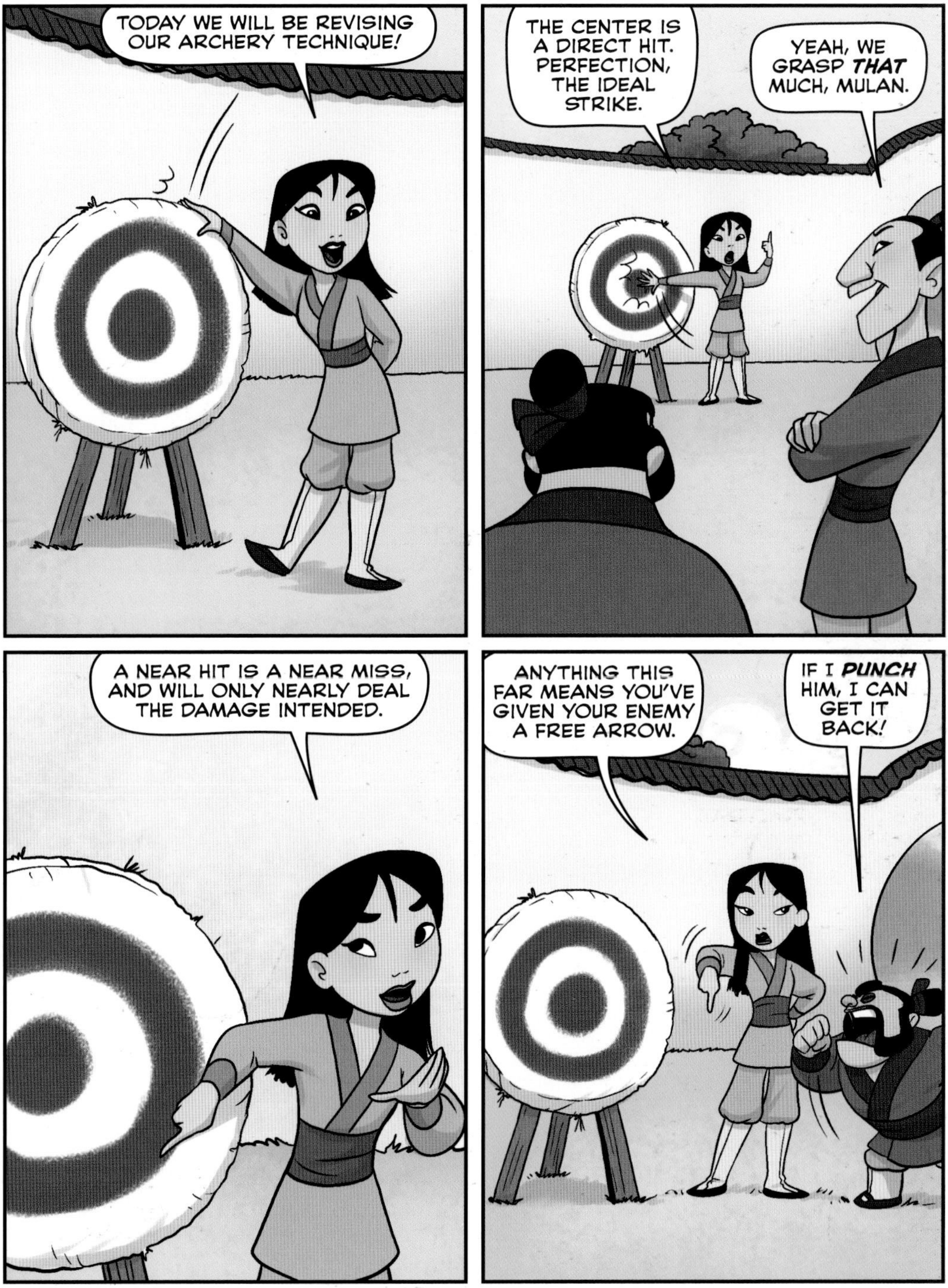

TODAY WE WILL BE REVISING OUR ARCHERY TECHNIQUE!
THE CENTER IS A DIRECT HIT. PERFECTION, THE IDEAL STRIKE.
YEAH, WE GRASP *THAT* MUCH, MULAN.
A NEAR HIT IS A NEAR MISS, AND WILL ONLY NEARLY DEAL THE DAMAGE INTENDED.
ANYTHING THIS FAR MEANS YOU'VE GIVEN YOUR ENEMY A FREE ARROW.
IF I *PUNCH* HIM, I CAN GET IT BACK!

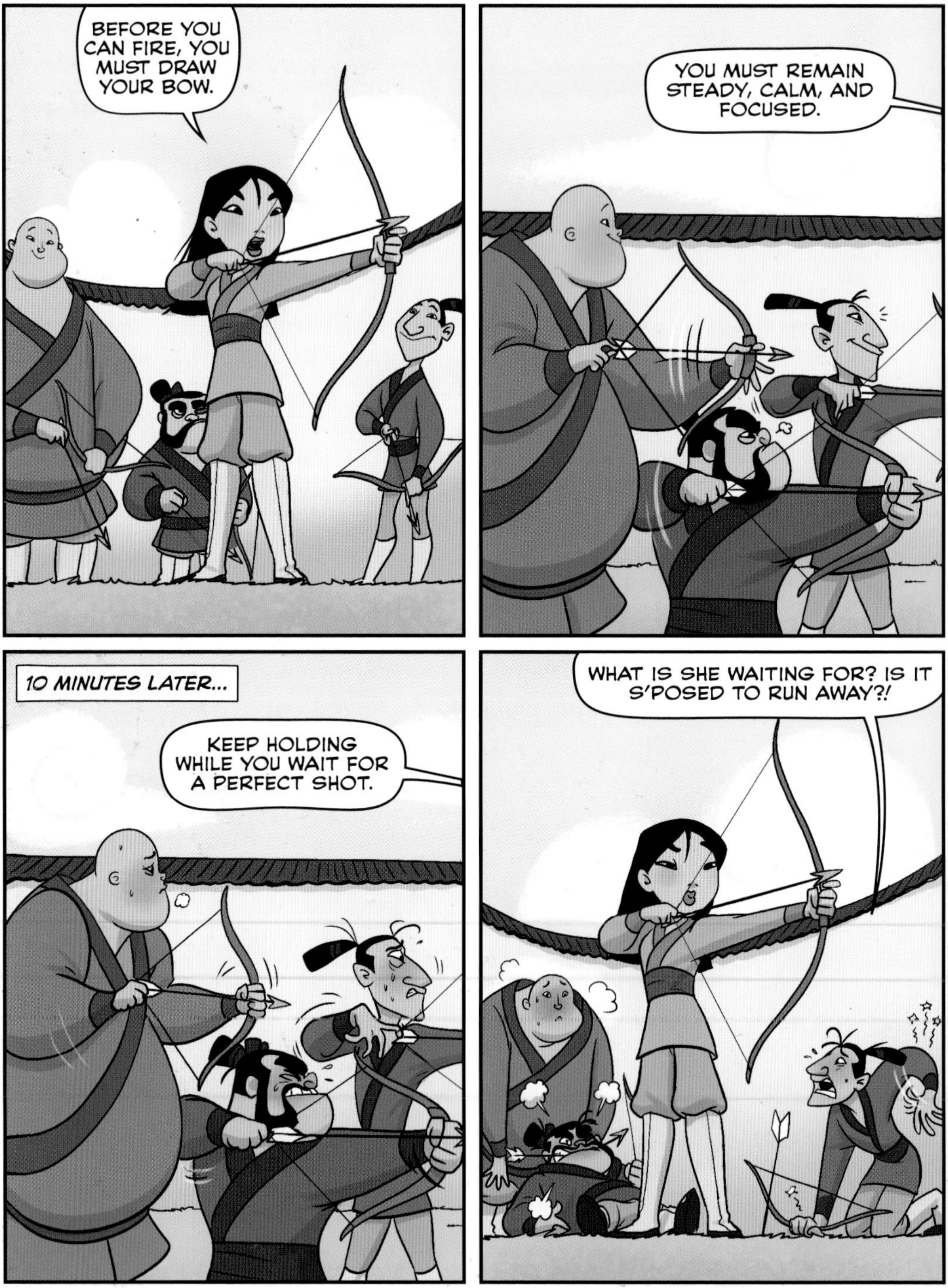
BEFORE YOU CAN FIRE, YOU MUST DRAW YOUR BOW.
YOU MUST REMAIN STEADY, CALM, AND FOCUSED.
10 MINUTES LATER...
KEEP HOLDING WHILE YOU WAIT FOR A PERFECT SHOT.
WHAT IS SHE WAITING FOR? IS IT S'POSED TO RUN AWAY?!

TRICK SHOT TIME!

THIS ISN'T REALLY THE POINT OF TRAINING.

PHTOOM!

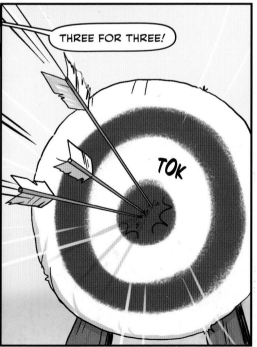

THREE FOR THREE!

TOK

I PREFER CLOSE COMBAT!

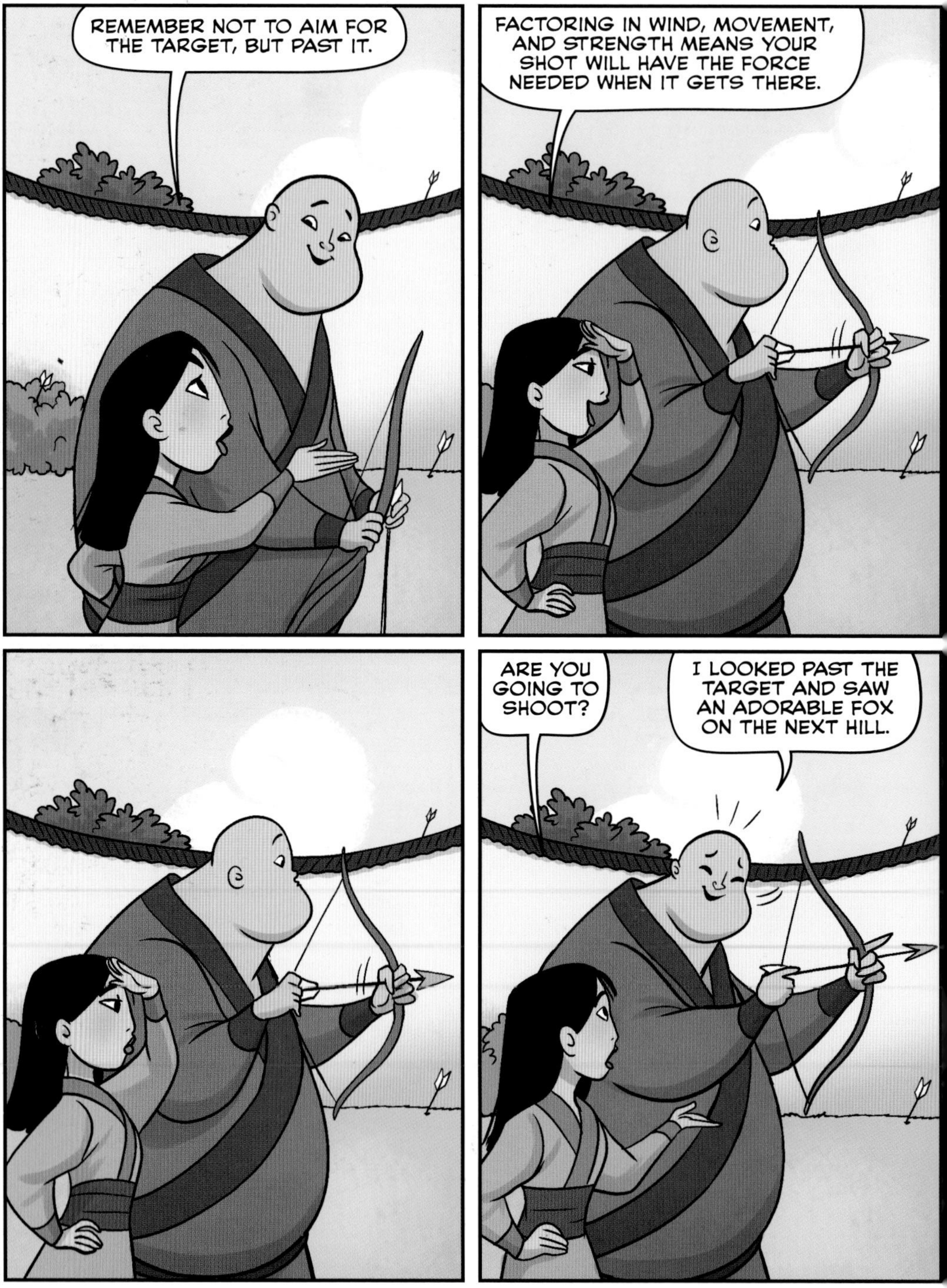
REMEMBER NOT TO AIM FOR THE TARGET, BUT PAST IT.
FACTORING IN WIND, MOVEMENT, AND STRENGTH MEANS YOUR SHOT WILL HAVE THE FORCE NEEDED WHEN IT GETS THERE.
ARE YOU GOING TO SHOOT?
I LOOKED PAST THE TARGET AND SAW AN ADORABLE FOX ON THE NEXT HILL.

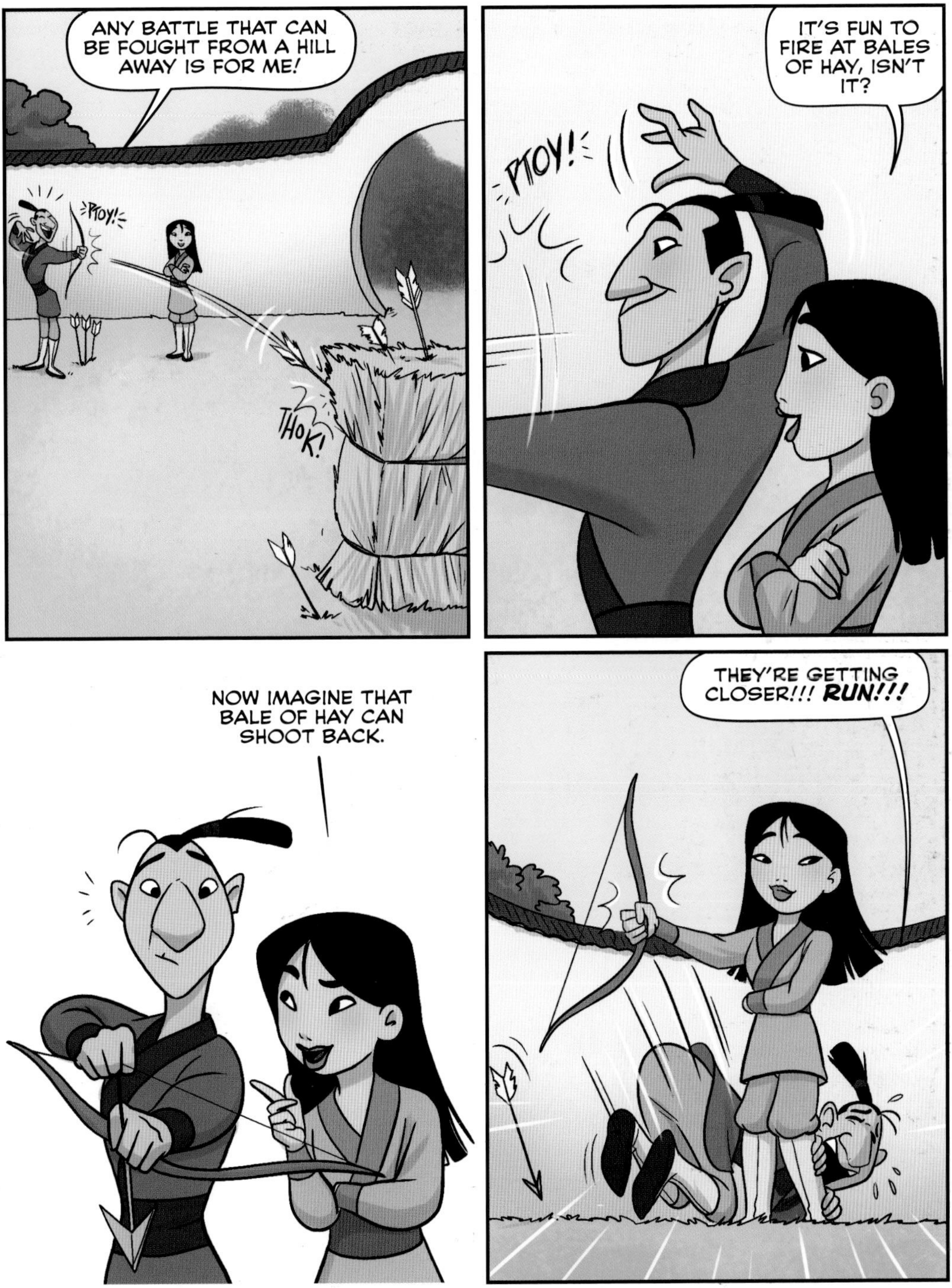
ANY BATTLE THAT CAN BE FOUGHT FROM A HILL AWAY IS FOR ME!
PTOY!
THOK!
IT'S FUN TO FIRE AT BALES OF HAY, ISN'T IT?
PTOY!
NOW IMAGINE THAT BALE OF HAY CAN SHOOT BACK.
THEY'RE GETTING CLOSER!!! RUN!!!

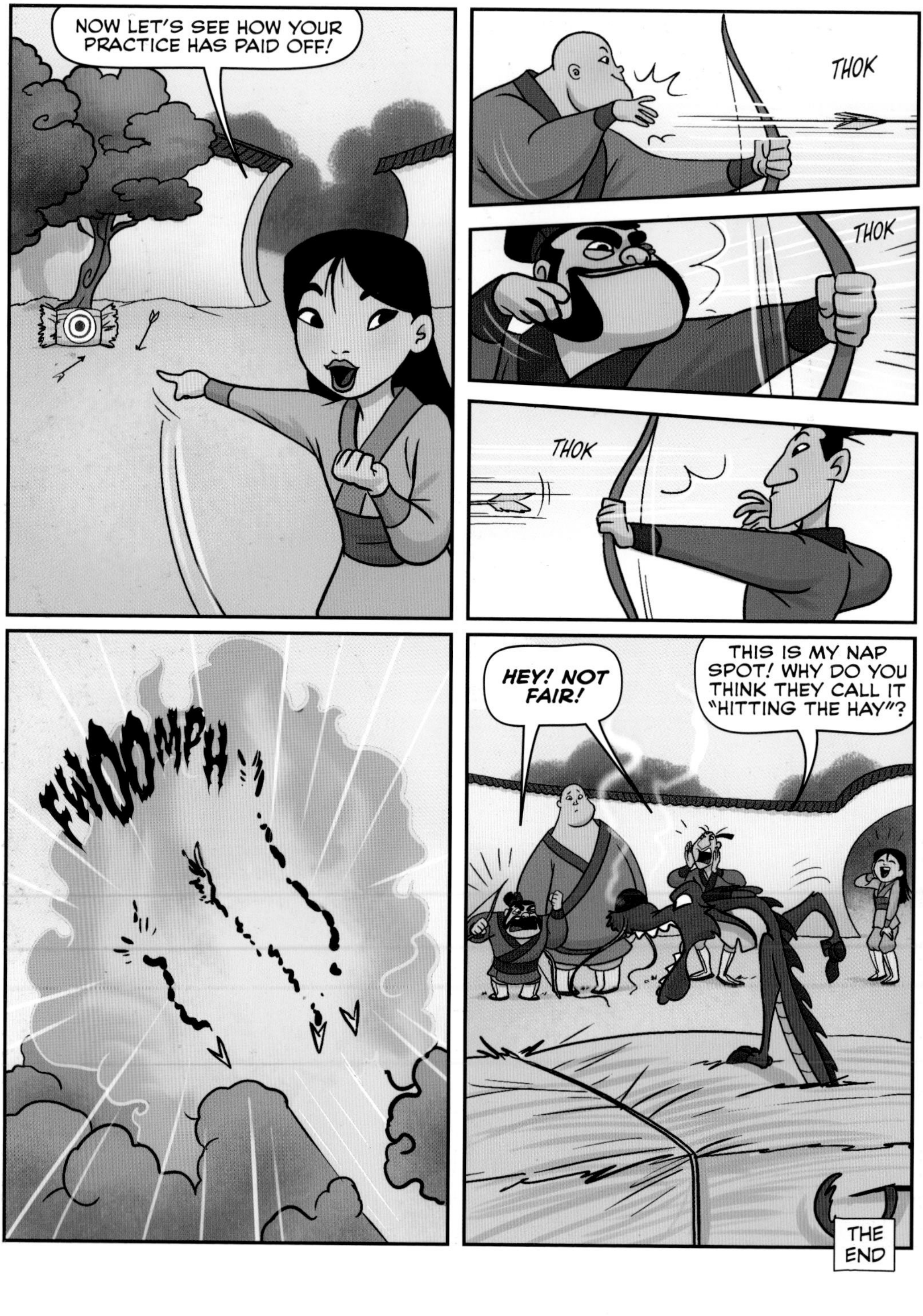
NOW LET'S SEE HOW YOUR PRACTICE HAS PAID OFF!
THOK
THOK
THOK
FWOOMPH
HEY! NOT FAIR!
THIS IS MY NAP SPOT! WHY DO YOU THINK THEY CALL IT "HITTING THE HAY"?
THE END

"GUMBO"

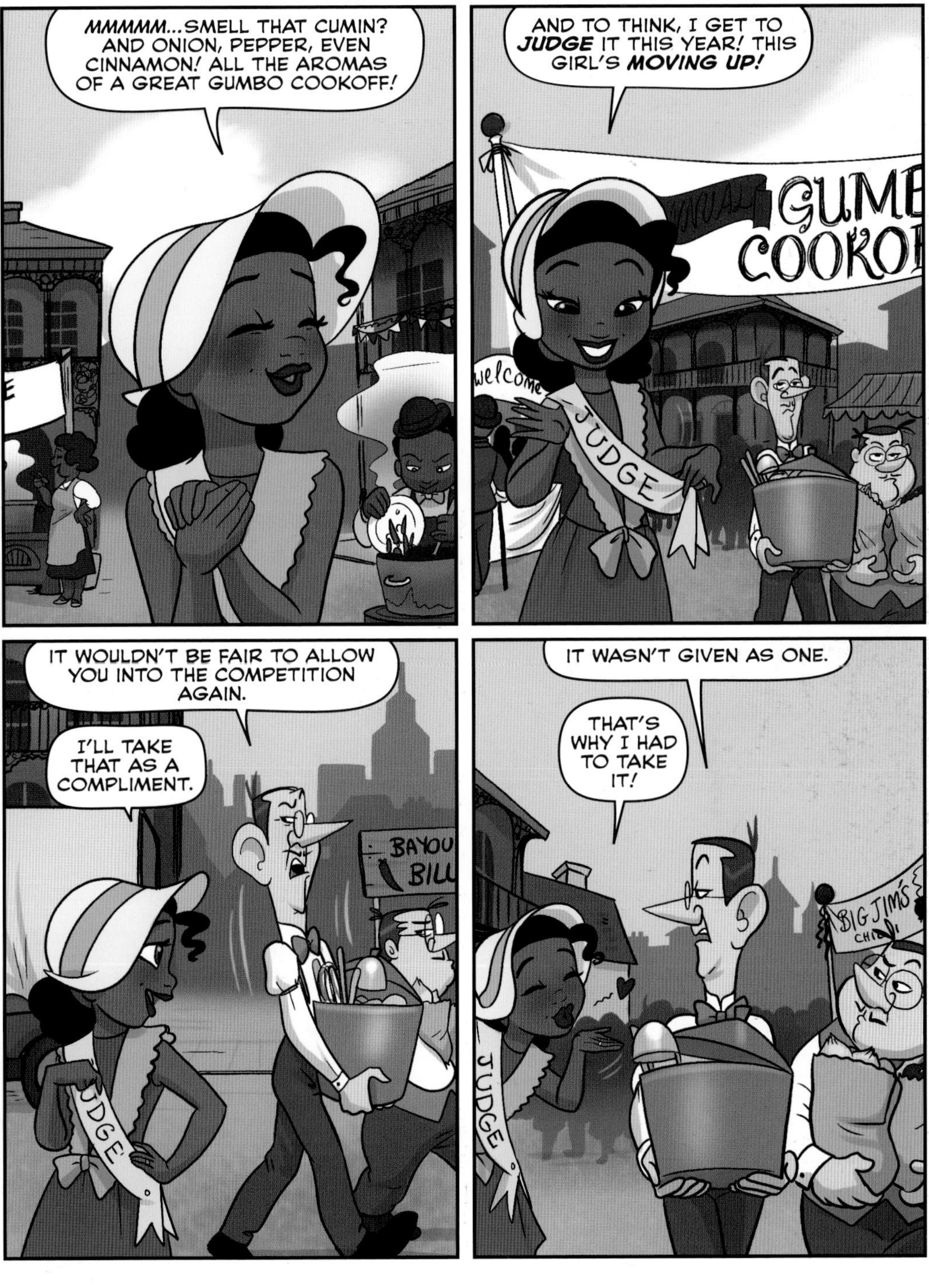
MMMMM...SMELL THAT CUMIN? AND ONION, PEPPER, EVEN CINNAMON! ALL THE AROMAS OF A GREAT GUMBO COOKOFF!
AND TO THINK, I GET TO JUDGE IT THIS YEAR! THIS GIRL'S MOVING UP!
GUMB COOKOF
WELCOME
JUDGE
IT WOULDN'T BE FAIR TO ALLOW YOU INTO THE COMPETITION AGAIN.
I'LL TAKE THAT AS A COMPLIMENT.
BAYOU BILL
JUDGE
IT WASN'T GIVEN AS ONE.
THAT'S WHY I HAD TO TAKE IT!
BIG JIM'S CHILI
JUDGE

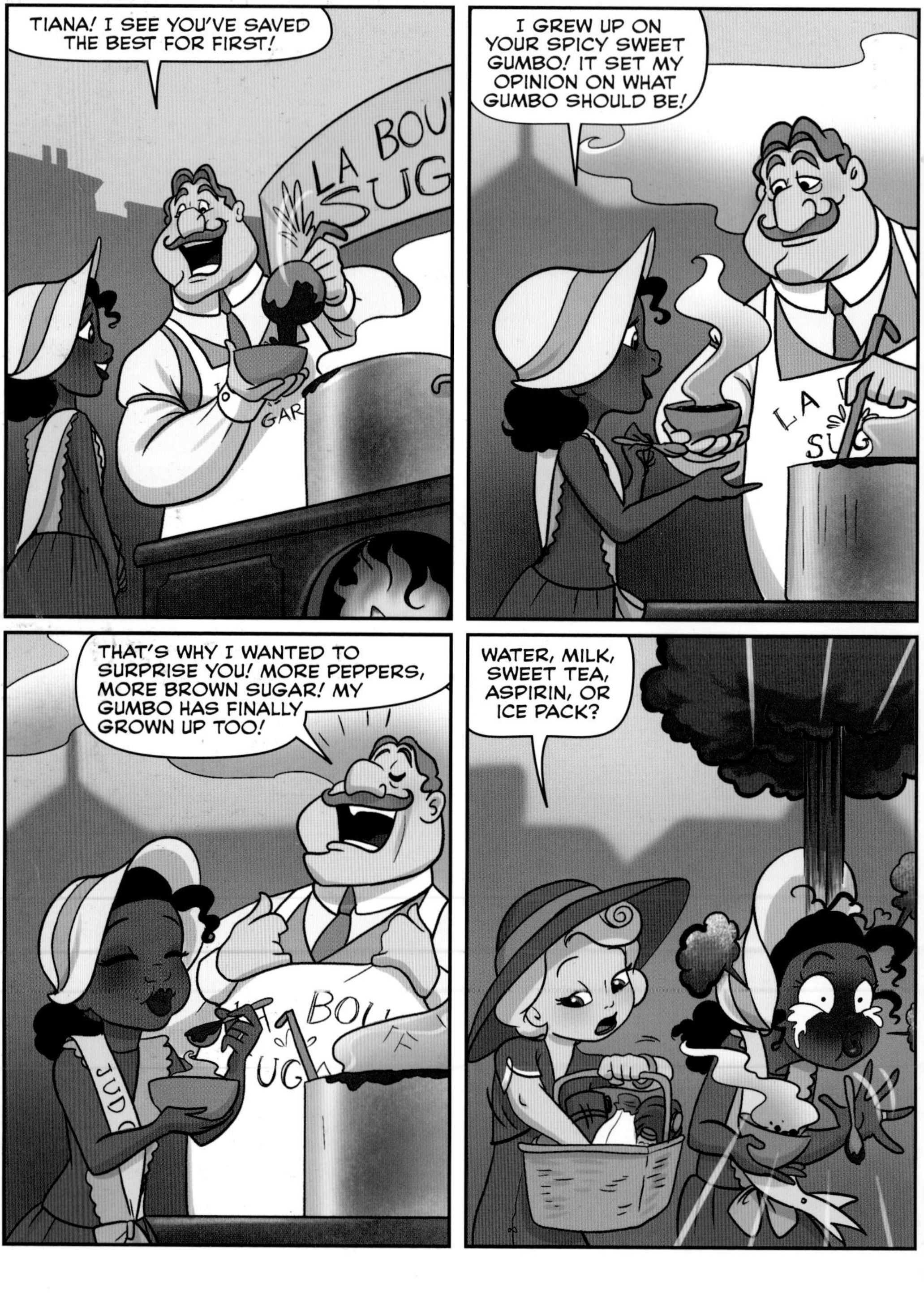
TIANA! I SEE YOU'VE SAVED THE BEST FOR FIRST!
I GREW UP ON YOUR SPICY SWEET GUMBO! IT SET MY OPINION ON WHAT GUMBO SHOULD BE!
THAT'S WHY I WANTED TO SURPRISE YOU! MORE PEPPERS, MORE BROWN SUGAR! MY GUMBO HAS FINALLY GROWN UP TOO!
WATER, MILK, SWEET TEA, ASPIRIN, OR ICE PACK?

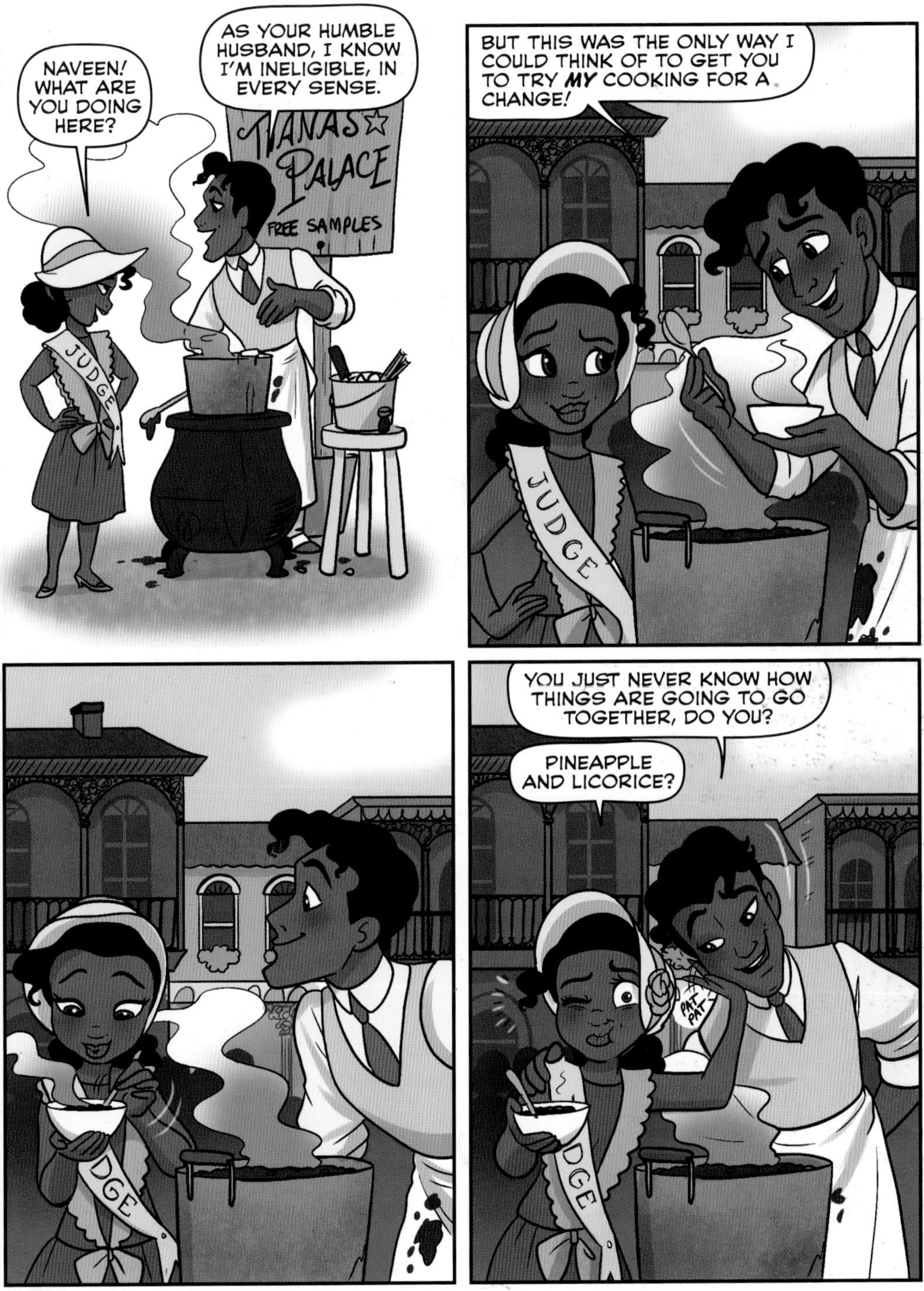
NAVEEN! WHAT ARE YOU DOING HERE?
AS YOUR HUMBLE HUSBAND, I KNOW I'M INELIGIBLE, IN EVERY SENSE.
TIANAS PALACE
FREE SAMPLES
JUDGE
BUT THIS WAS THE ONLY WAY I COULD THINK OF TO GET YOU TO TRY *MY* COOKING FOR A CHANGE!
JUDGE
YOU JUST NEVER KNOW HOW THINGS ARE GOING TO GO TOGETHER, DO YOU?
PINEAPPLE AND LICORICE?
PAT PAT

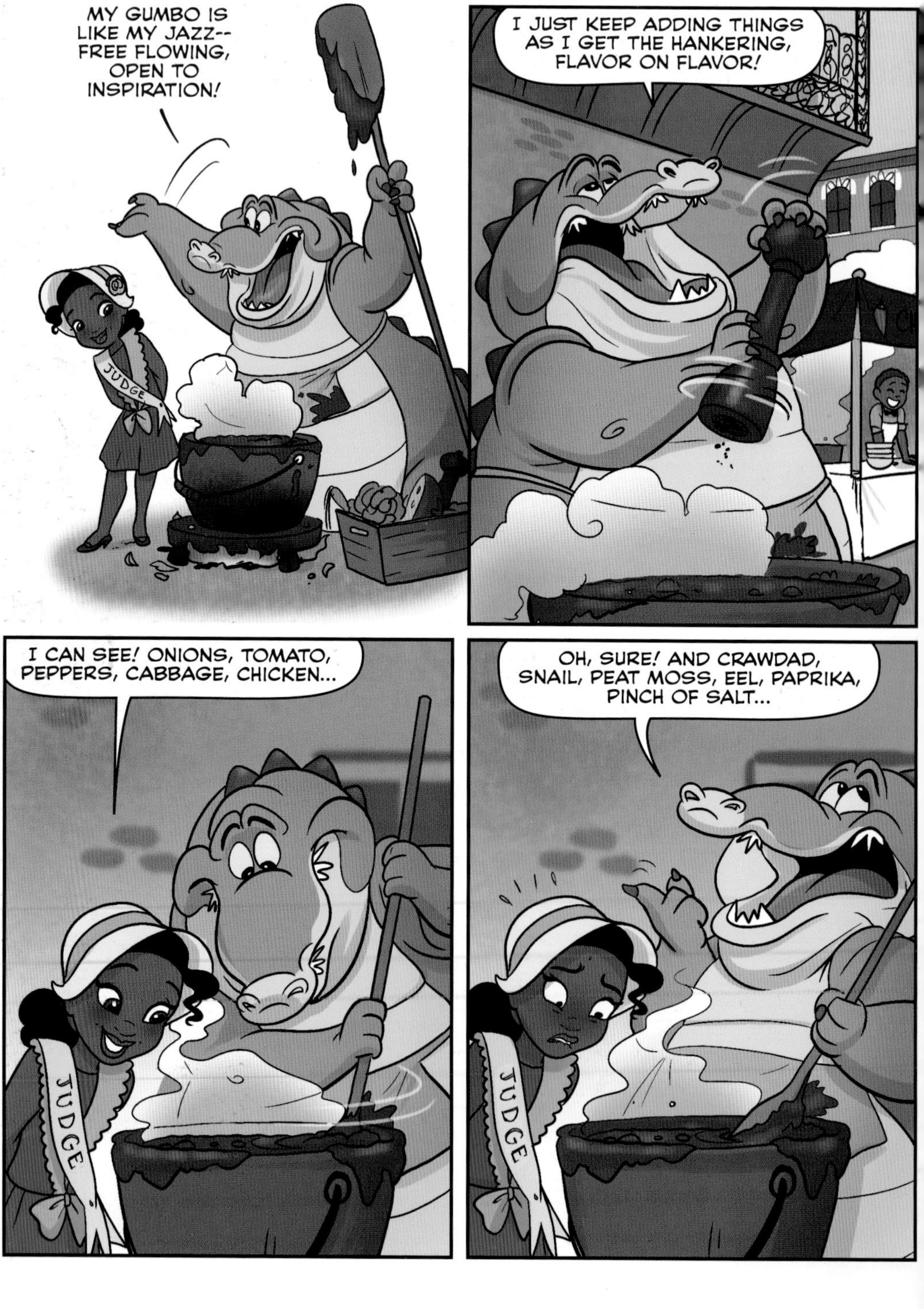
MY GUMBO IS LIKE MY JAZZ-- FREE FLOWING, OPEN TO INSPIRATION!
JUDGE
I JUST KEEP ADDING THINGS AS I GET THE HANKERING, FLAVOR ON FLAVOR!
I CAN SEE! ONIONS, TOMATO, PEPPERS, CABBAGE, CHICKEN...
JUDGE
OH, SURE! AND CRAWDAD, SNAIL, PEAT MOSS, EEL, PAPRIKA, PINCH OF SALT...
JUDGE

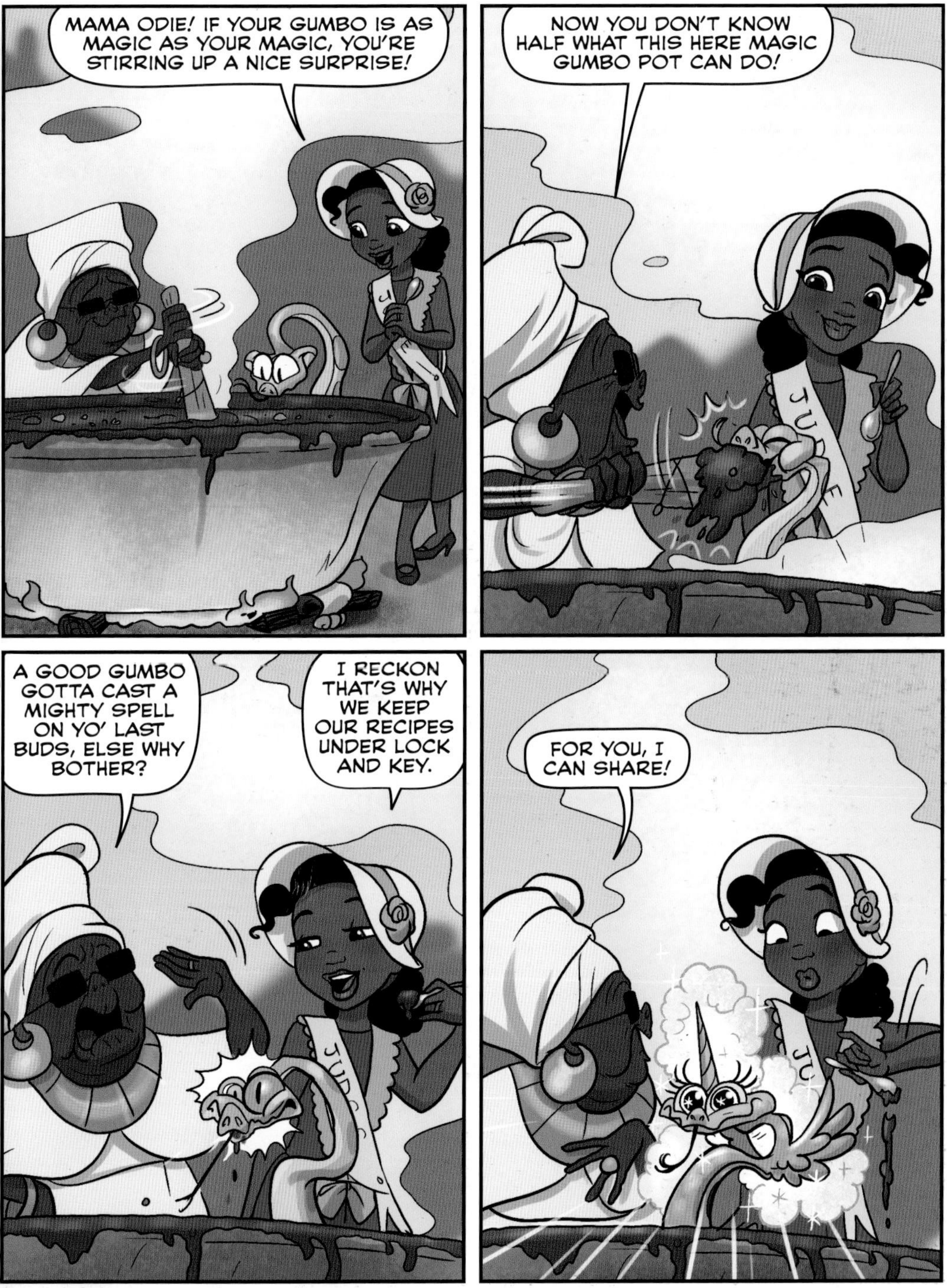
MAMA ODIE! IF YOUR GUMBO IS AS MAGIC AS YOUR MAGIC, YOU'RE STIRRING UP A NICE SURPRISE!
NOW YOU DON'T KNOW HALF WHAT THIS HERE MAGIC GUMBO POT CAN DO!
A GOOD GUMBO GOTTA CAST A MIGHTY SPELL ON YO' LAST BUDS, ELSE WHY BOTHER?
I RECKON THAT'S WHY WE KEEP OUR RECIPES UNDER LOCK AND KEY.
FOR YOU, I CAN SHARE!

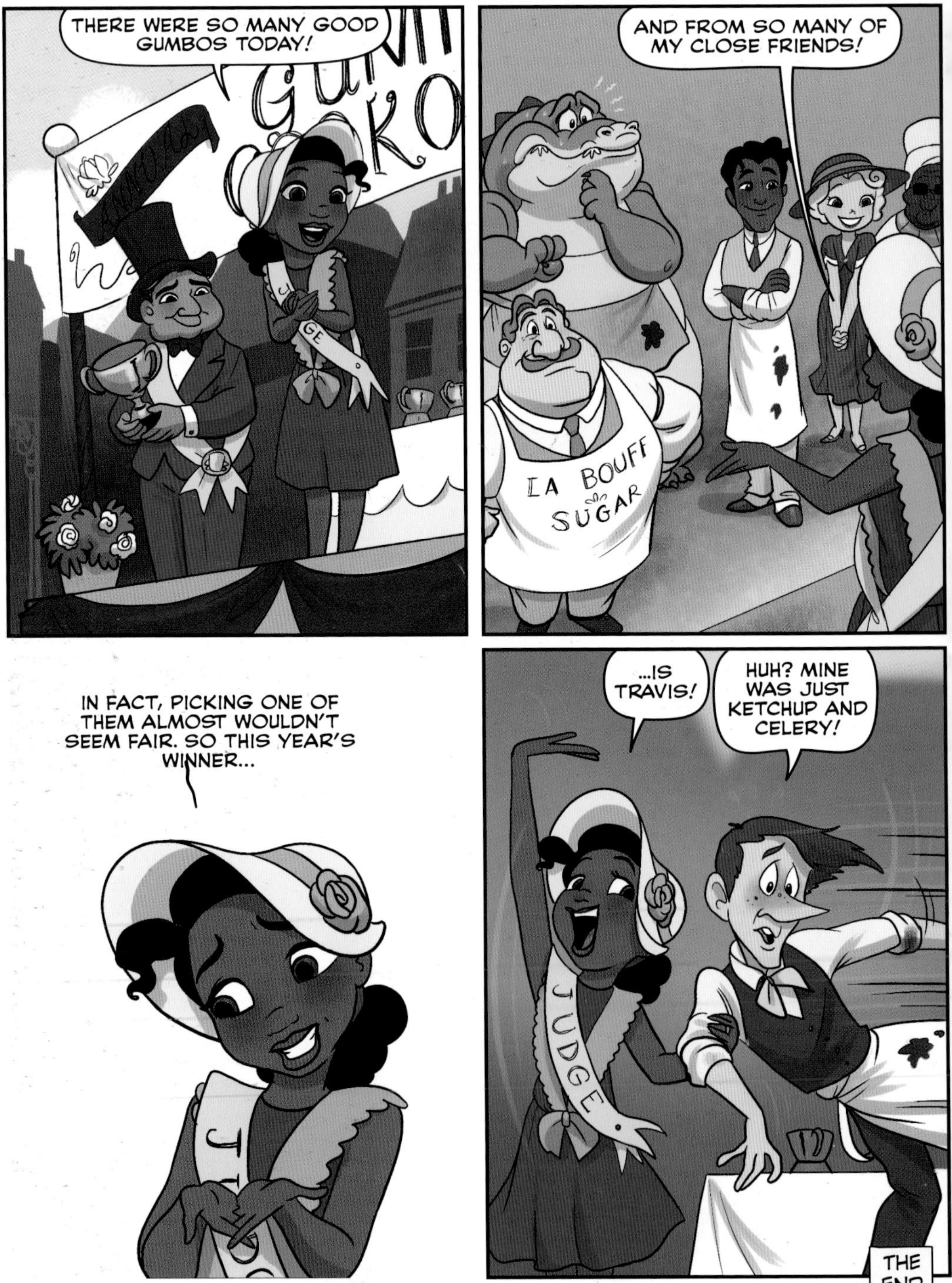
THERE WERE SO MANY GOOD GUMBOS TODAY!
AND FROM SO MANY OF MY CLOSE FRIENDS!
LA BOUFF SUGAR
IN FACT, PICKING ONE OF THEM ALMOST WOULDN'T SEEM FAIR. SO THIS YEAR'S WINNER...
...IS TRAVIS!
HUH? MINE WAS JUST KETCHUP AND CELERY!
JUDGE
THE END

"MY FATHER"

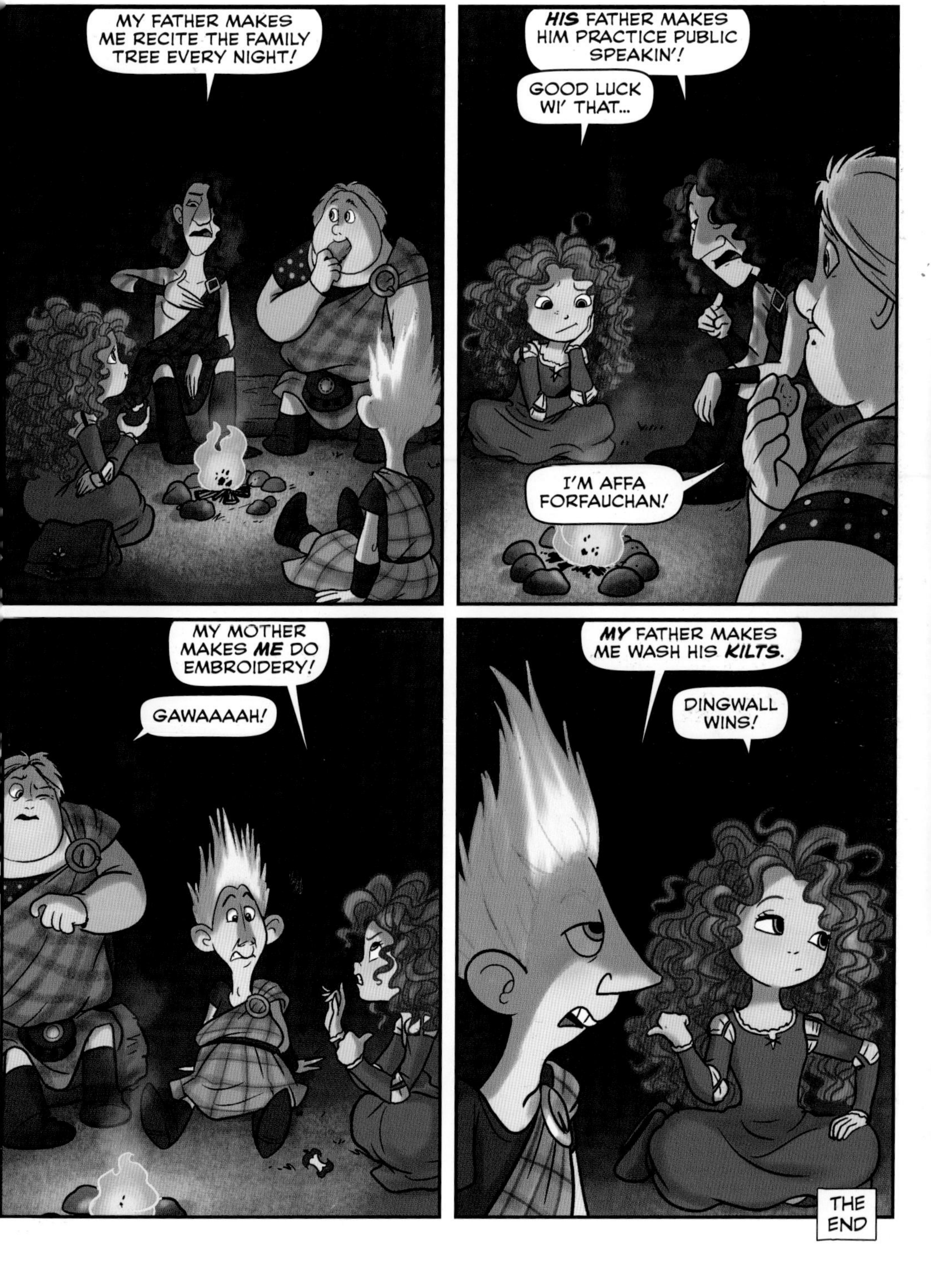

MY FATHER MAKES ME RECITE THE FAMILY TREE EVERY NIGHT!
HIS FATHER MAKES HIM PRACTICE PUBLIC SPEAKIN'!
GOOD LUCK WI' THAT...
I'M AFFA FORFAUCHAN!
MY MOTHER MAKES ME DO EMBROIDERY!
GAWAAAAH!
MY FATHER MAKES ME WASH HIS KILTS.
DINGWALL WINS!
THE END

"HUMAN MAPS"

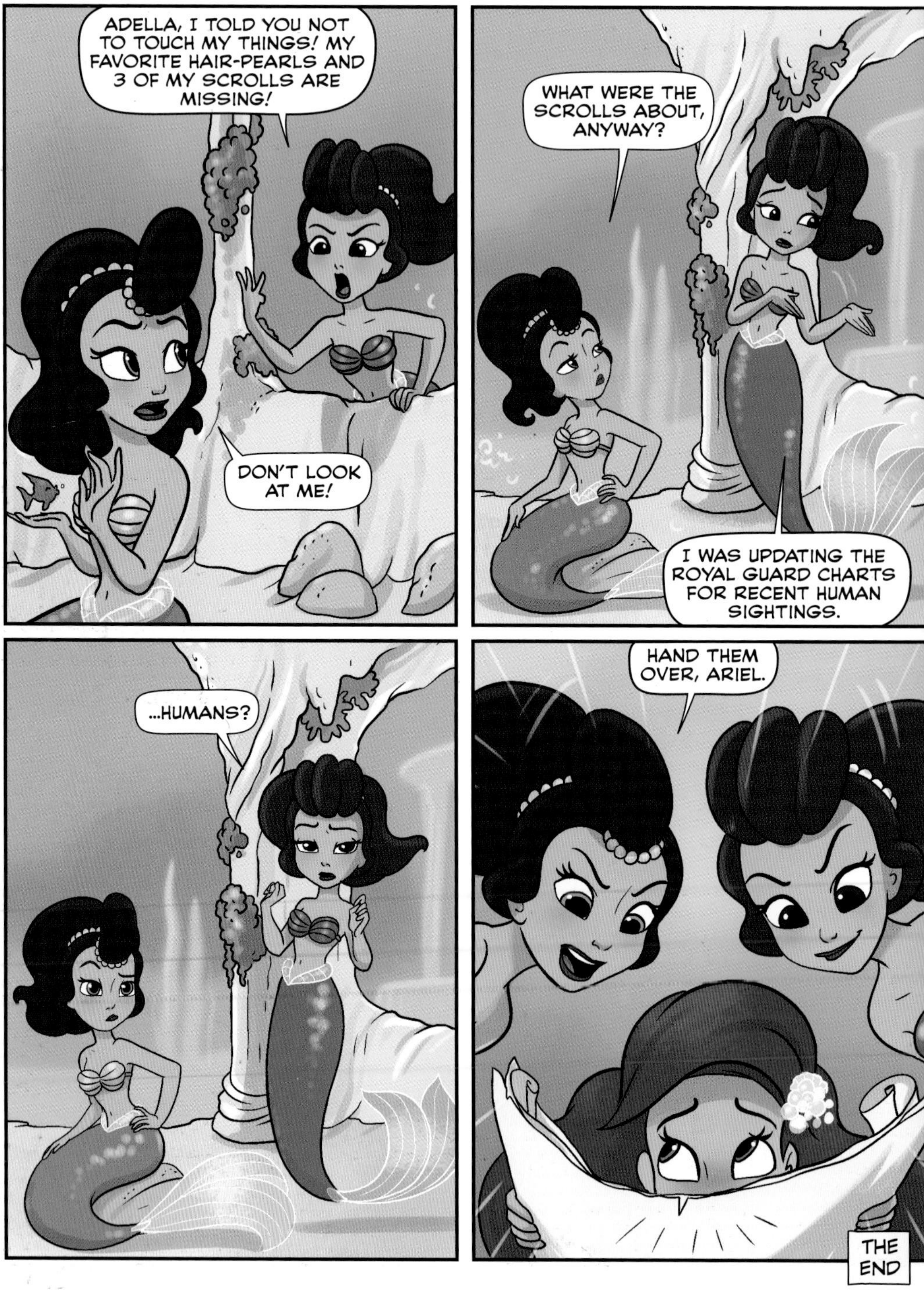
ADELLA, I TOLD YOU NOT TO TOUCH MY THINGS! MY FAVORITE HAIR-PEARLS AND 3 OF MY SCROLLS ARE MISSING!
DON'T LOOK AT ME!
WHAT WERE THE SCROLLS ABOUT, ANYWAY?
I WAS UPDATING THE ROYAL GUARD CHARTS FOR RECENT HUMAN SIGHTINGS.
...HUMANS?
HAND THEM OVER, ARIEL.
THE END

"BEAST POETRY"

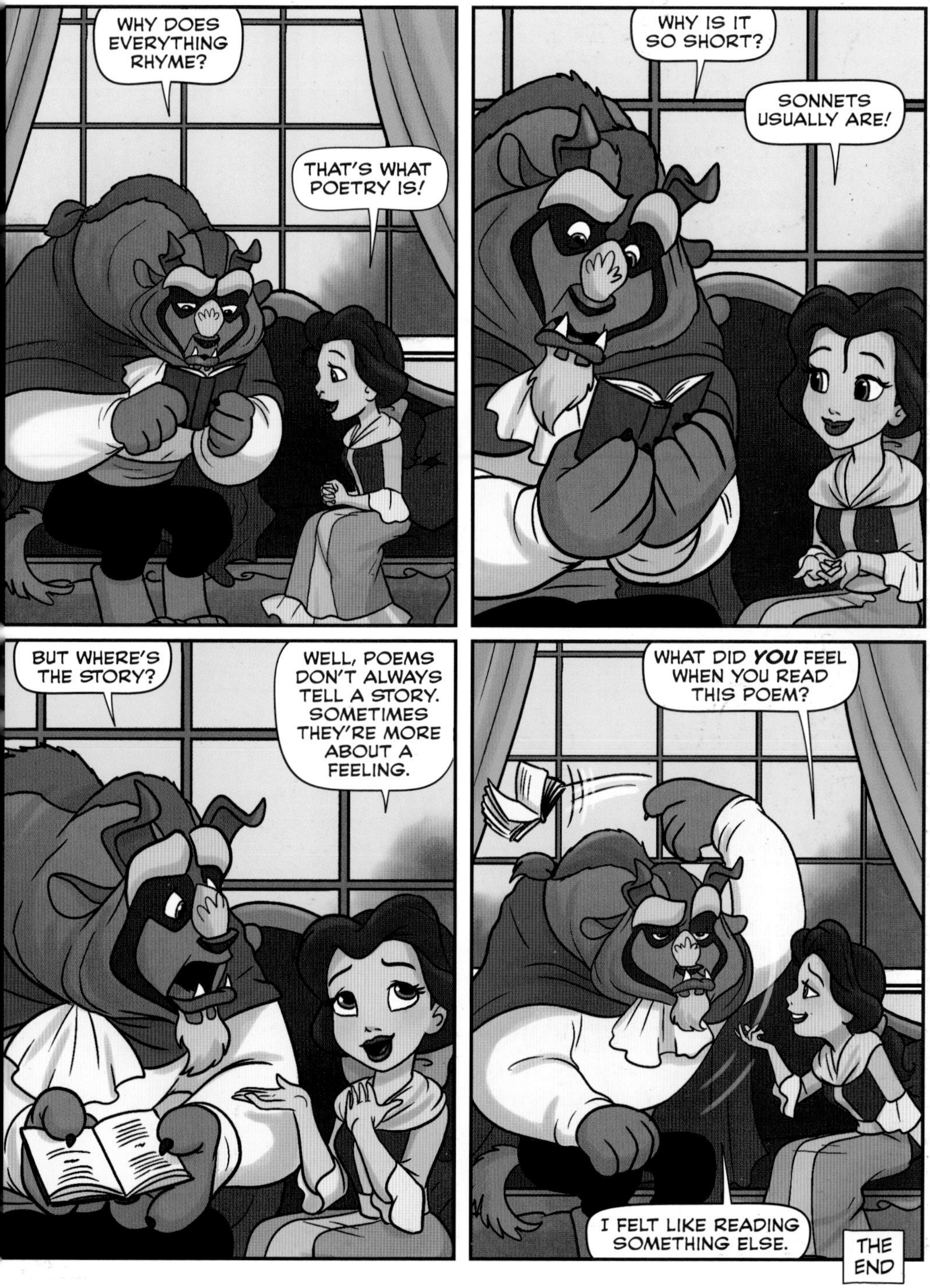
WHY DOES EVERYTHING RHYME?
THAT'S WHAT POETRY IS!
WHY IS IT SO SHORT?
SONNETS USUALLY ARE!
BUT WHERE'S THE STORY?
WELL, POEMS DON'T ALWAYS TELL A STORY. SOMETIMES THEY'RE MORE ABOUT A FEELING.
WHAT DID *YOU* FEEL WHEN YOU READ THIS POEM?
I FELT LIKE READING SOMETHING ELSE.
THE END

"MICE"

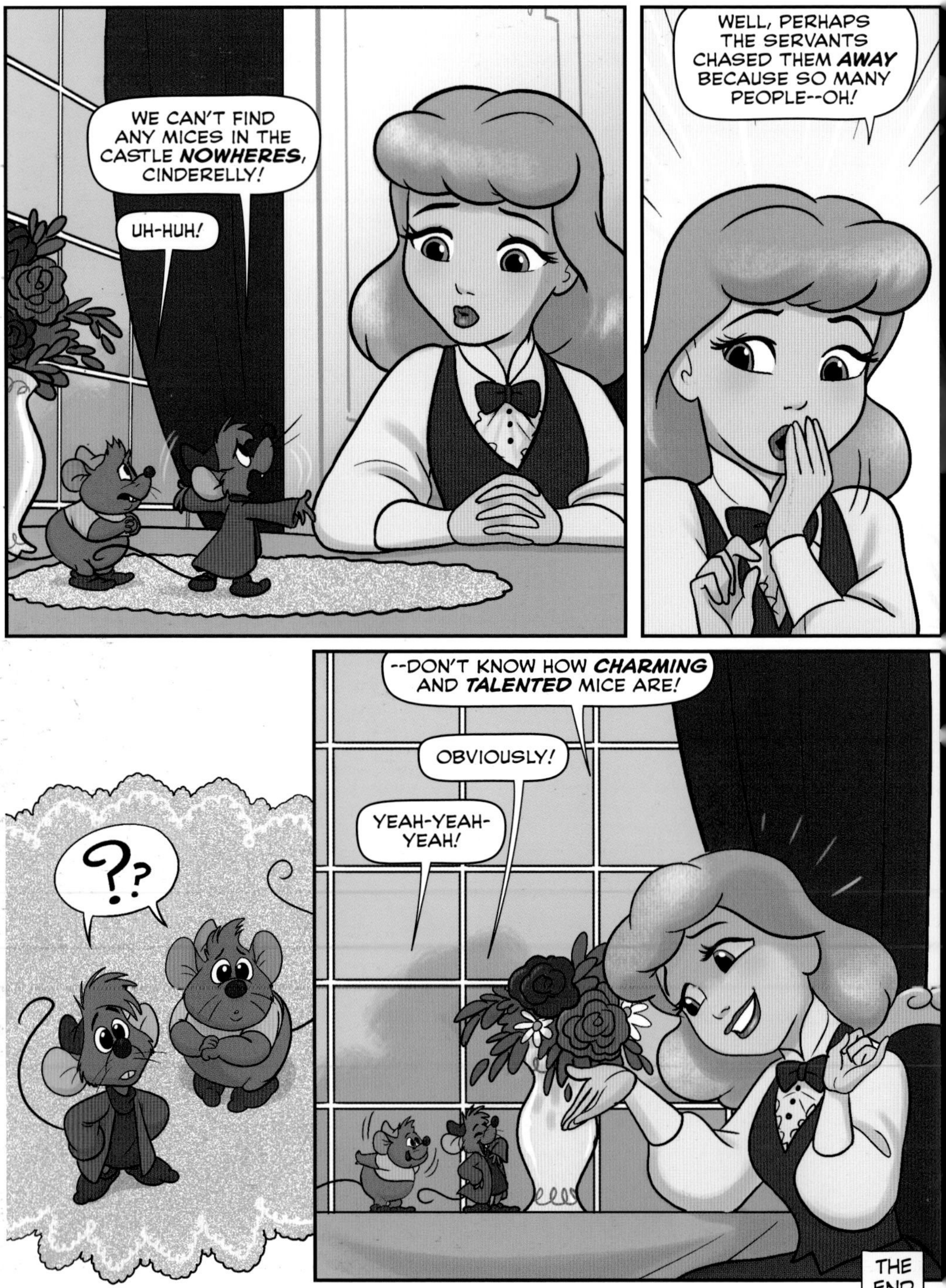

WE CAN'T FIND ANY MICES IN THE CASTLE NOWHERES, CINDERELLY!
UH-HUH!
WELL, PERHAPS THE SERVANTS CHASED THEM AWAY BECAUSE SO MANY PEOPLE--OH!
??
--DON'T KNOW HOW CHARMING AND TALENTED MICE ARE!
OBVIOUSLY!
YEAH-YEAH-YEAH!
THE END

"HIDE AND SEEK"

WE HAVE THE DAY ALL TO OURSELVES, WHAT SHALL WE DO?

HMMM...

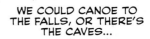

WE COULD CANOE TO THE FALLS, OR THERE'S THE CAVES...

OR... POCAHONTAS? OH NO...

WE ARE *NOT* PLAYING HIDE AND SEEK, YOU KNOW I'M TERRIBLE AT IT!

TOO LATE!

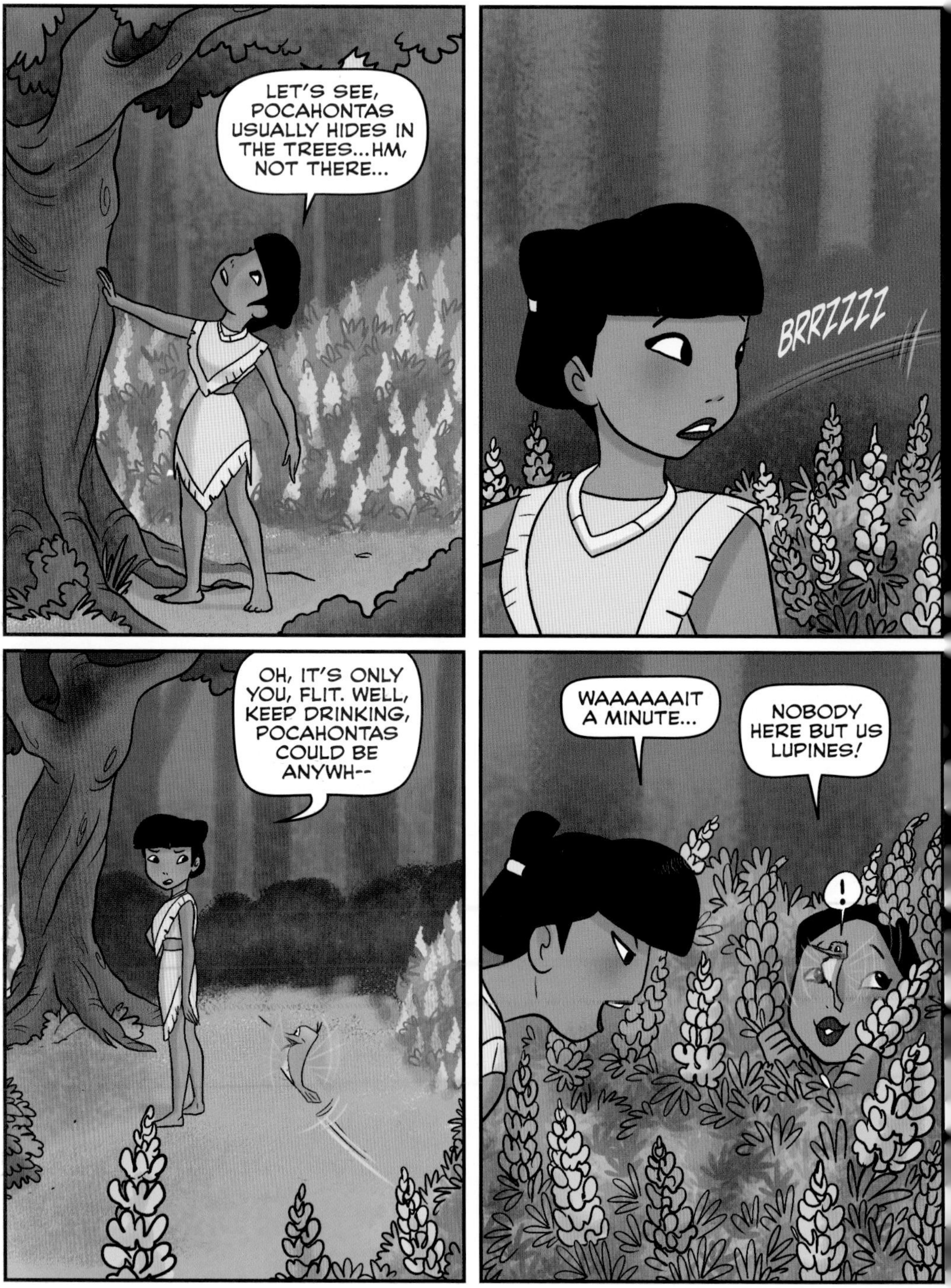
LET'S SEE, POCAHONTAS USUALLY HIDES IN THE TREES...HM, NOT THERE...
BRRZZZZ
OH, IT'S ONLY YOU, FLIT. WELL, KEEP DRINKING, POCAHONTAS COULD BE ANYWH--
WAAAAAAIT A MINUTE...
NOBODY HERE BUT US LUPINES!
!

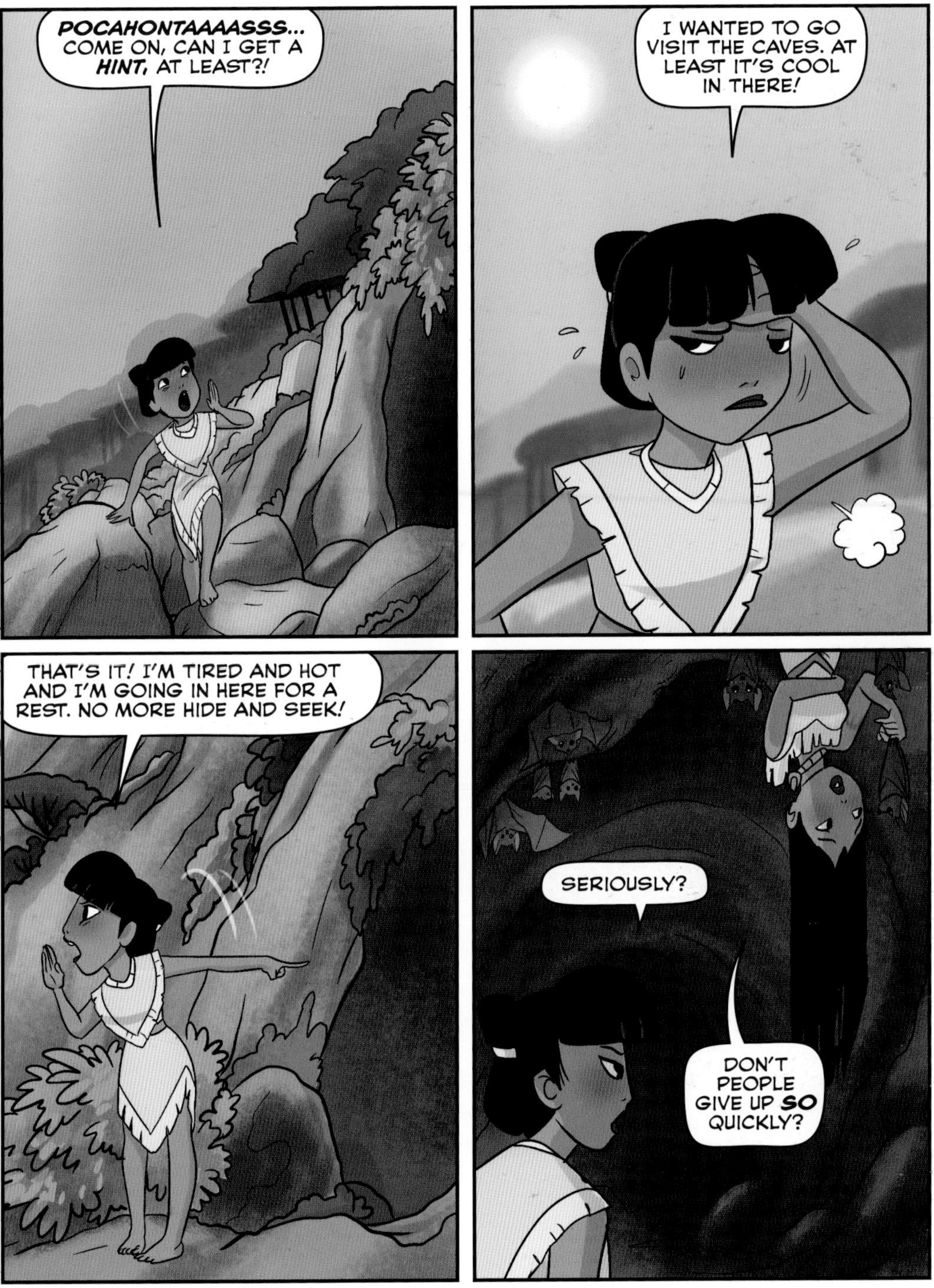
POCAHONTAAAASSS... COME ON, CAN I GET A HINT, AT LEAST?!
I WANTED TO GO VISIT THE CAVES. AT LEAST IT'S COOL IN THERE!
THAT'S IT! I'M TIRED AND HOT AND I'M GOING IN HERE FOR A REST. NO MORE HIDE AND SEEK!
SERIOUSLY?
DON'T PEOPLE GIVE UP SO QUICKLY?

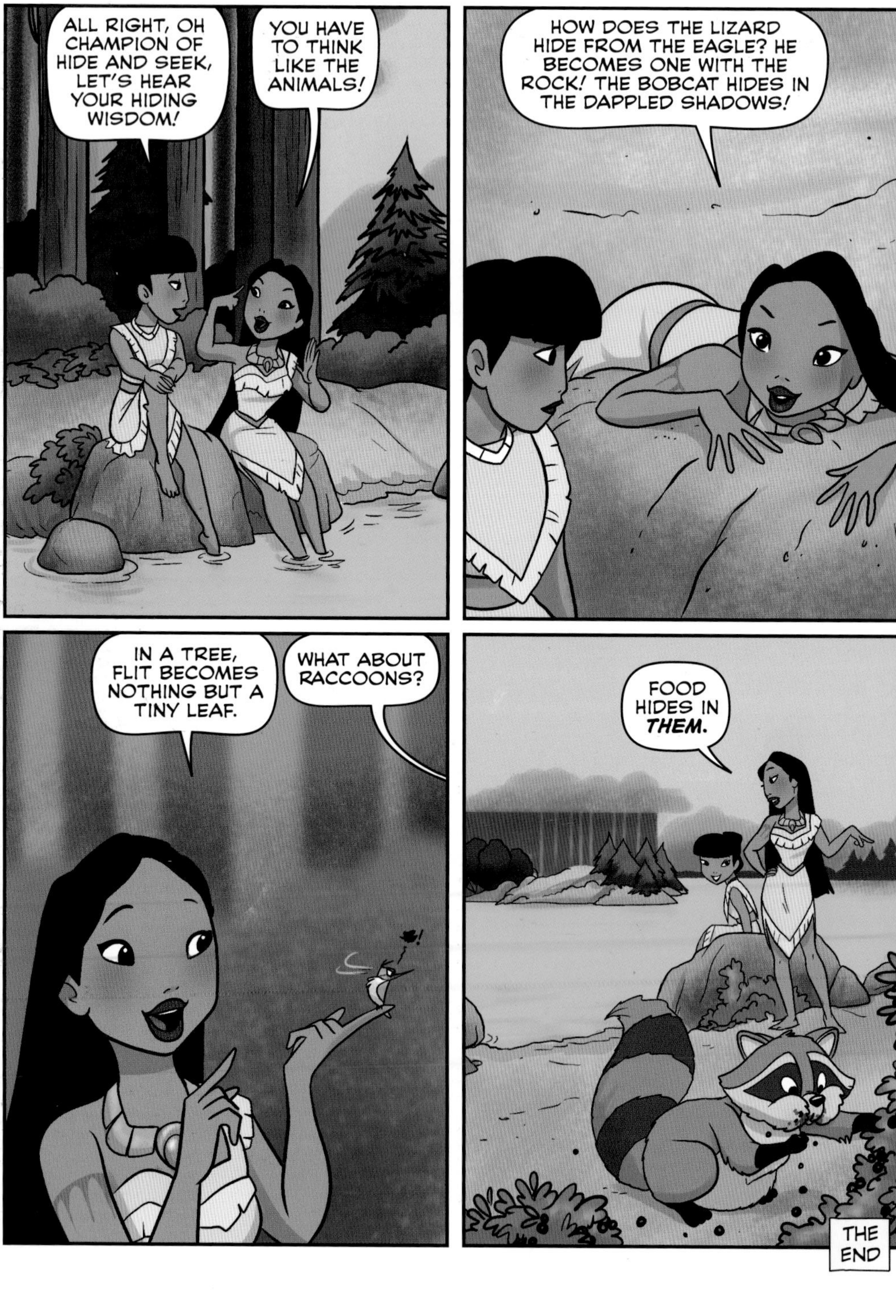
ALL RIGHT, OH CHAMPION OF HIDE AND SEEK, LET'S HEAR YOUR HIDING WISDOM!
YOU HAVE TO THINK LIKE THE ANIMALS!
HOW DOES THE LIZARD HIDE FROM THE EAGLE? HE BECOMES ONE WITH THE ROCK! THE BOBCAT HIDES IN THE DAPPLED SHADOWS!
IN A TREE, FLIT BECOMES NOTHING BUT A TINY LEAF.
WHAT ABOUT RACCOONS?
FOOD HIDES IN *THEM*.
THE END

"TRAVEL CAT"

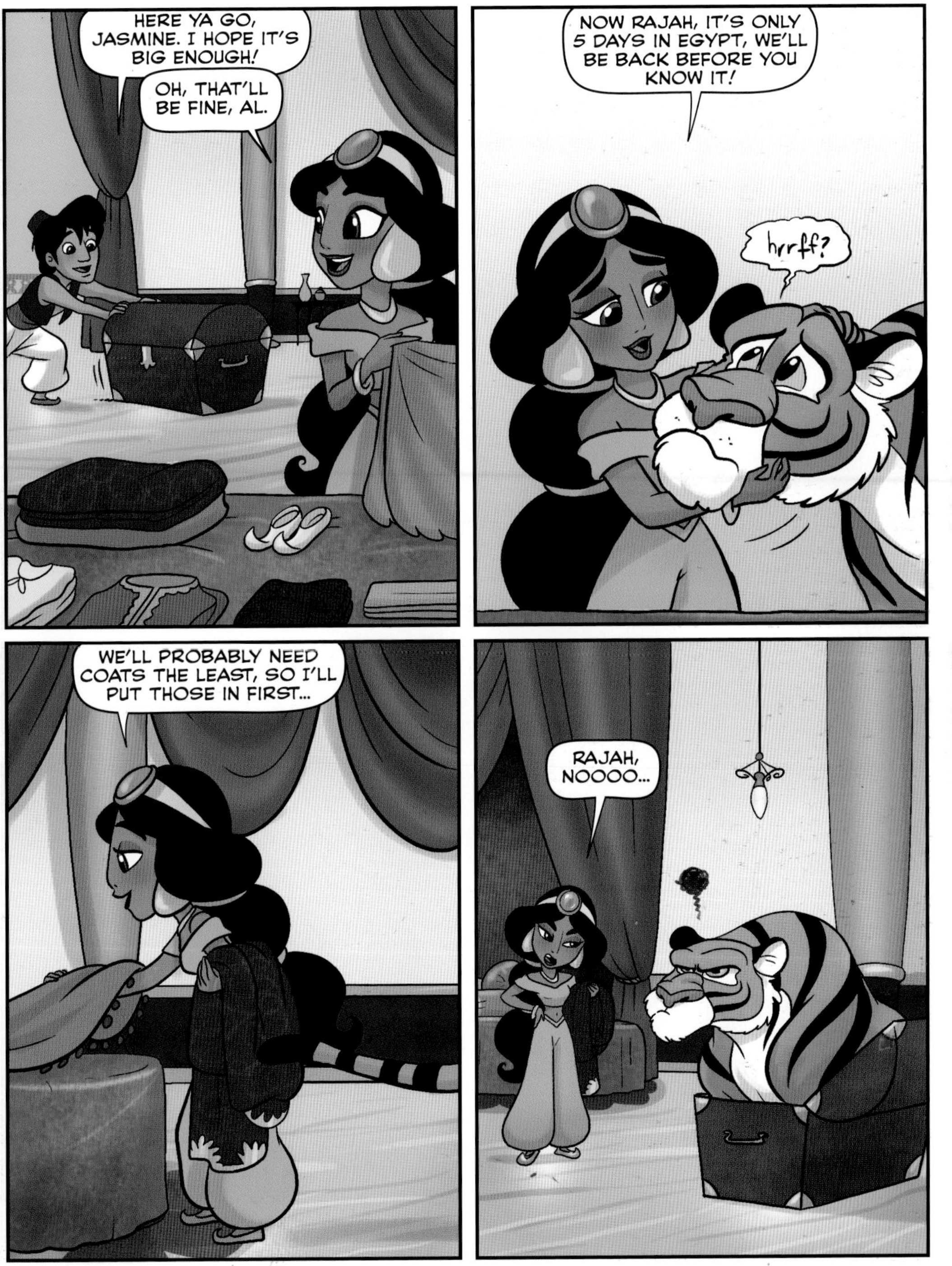
HERE YA GO, JASMINE. I HOPE IT'S BIG ENOUGH!
OH, THAT'LL BE FINE, AL.
NOW RAJAH, IT'S ONLY 5 DAYS IN EGYPT, WE'LL BE BACK BEFORE YOU KNOW IT!
hrrff?
WE'LL PROBABLY NEED COATS THE LEAST, SO I'LL PUT THOSE IN FIRST...
RAJAH, NOOOO...

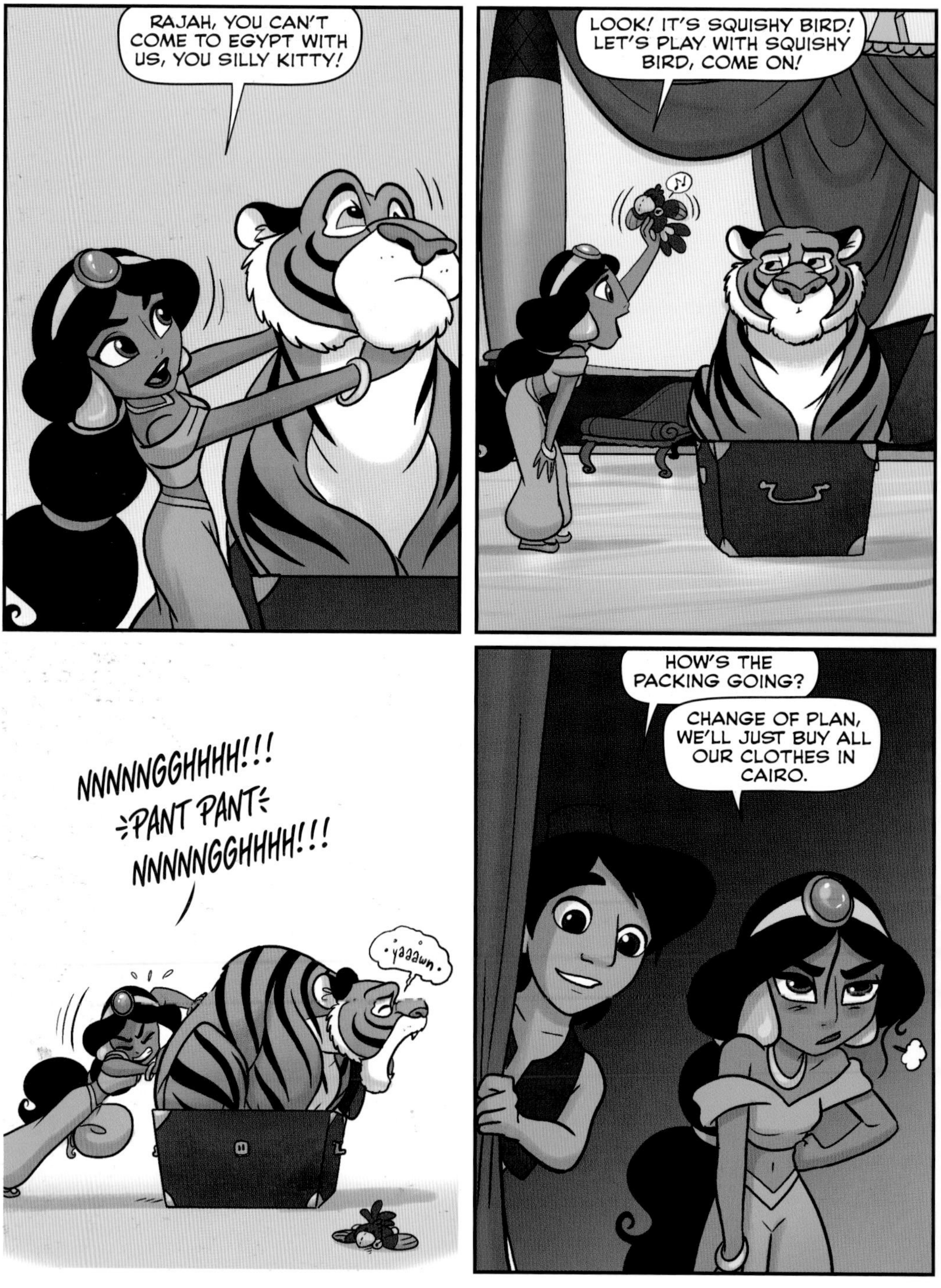
RAJAH, YOU CAN'T COME TO EGYPT WITH US, YOU SILLY KITTY!
LOOK! IT'S SQUISHY BIRD! LET'S PLAY WITH SQUISHY BIRD, COME ON!
NNNNNGGHHHH!!!
PANT PANT
NNNNNGGHHHH!!!
yaaawn
HOW'S THE PACKING GOING?
CHANGE OF PLAN, WE'LL JUST BUY ALL OUR CLOTHES IN CAIRO.

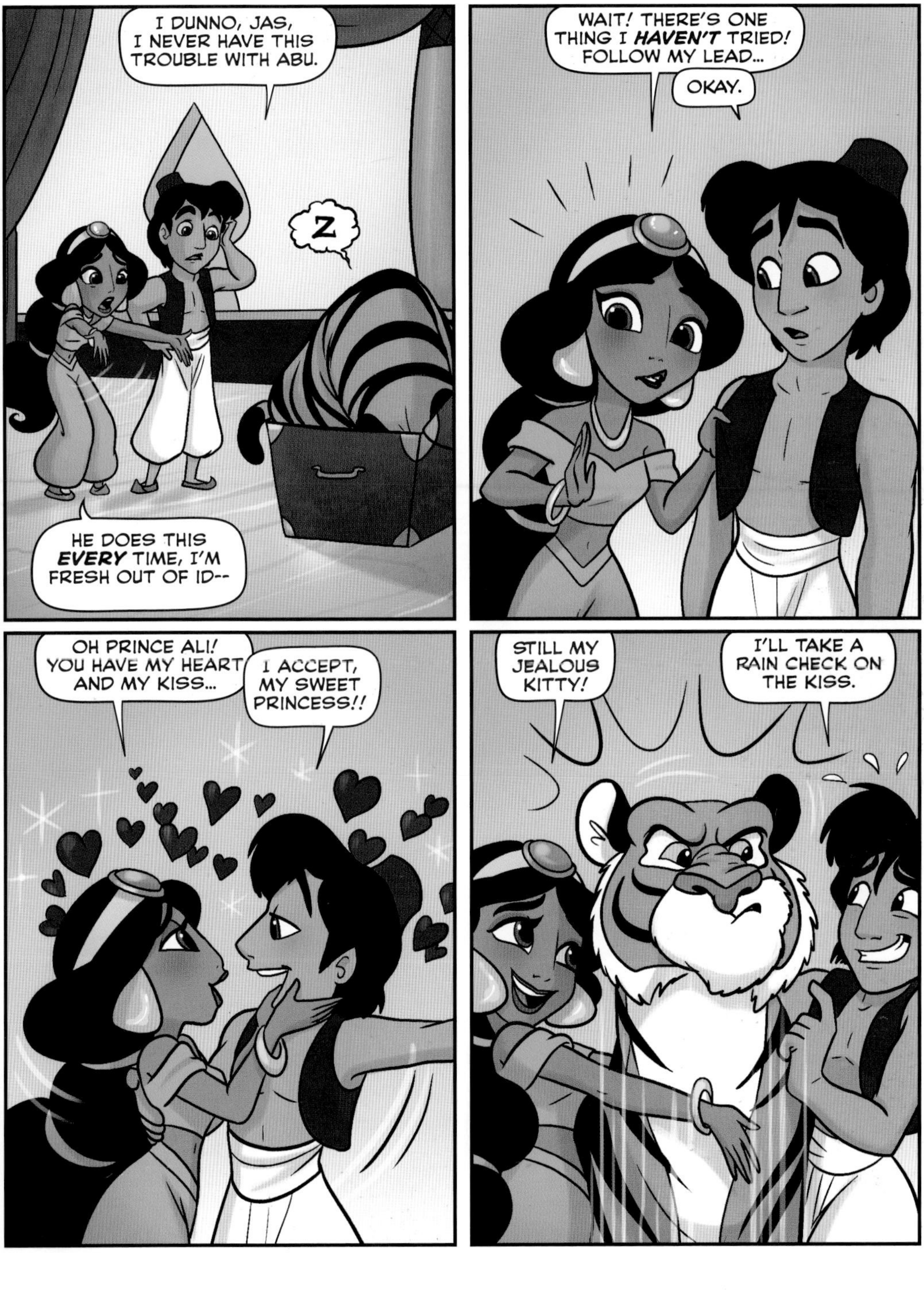
I DUNNO, JAS, I NEVER HAVE THIS TROUBLE WITH ABU.
Z
HE DOES THIS **EVERY** TIME, I'M FRESH OUT OF ID--
WAIT! THERE'S ONE THING I ***HAVEN'T*** TRIED! FOLLOW MY LEAD...
OKAY.
OH PRINCE ALI! YOU HAVE MY HEART AND MY KISS...
I ACCEPT, MY SWEET PRINCESS!!
STILL MY JEALOUS KITTY!
I'LL TAKE A RAIN CHECK ON THE KISS.

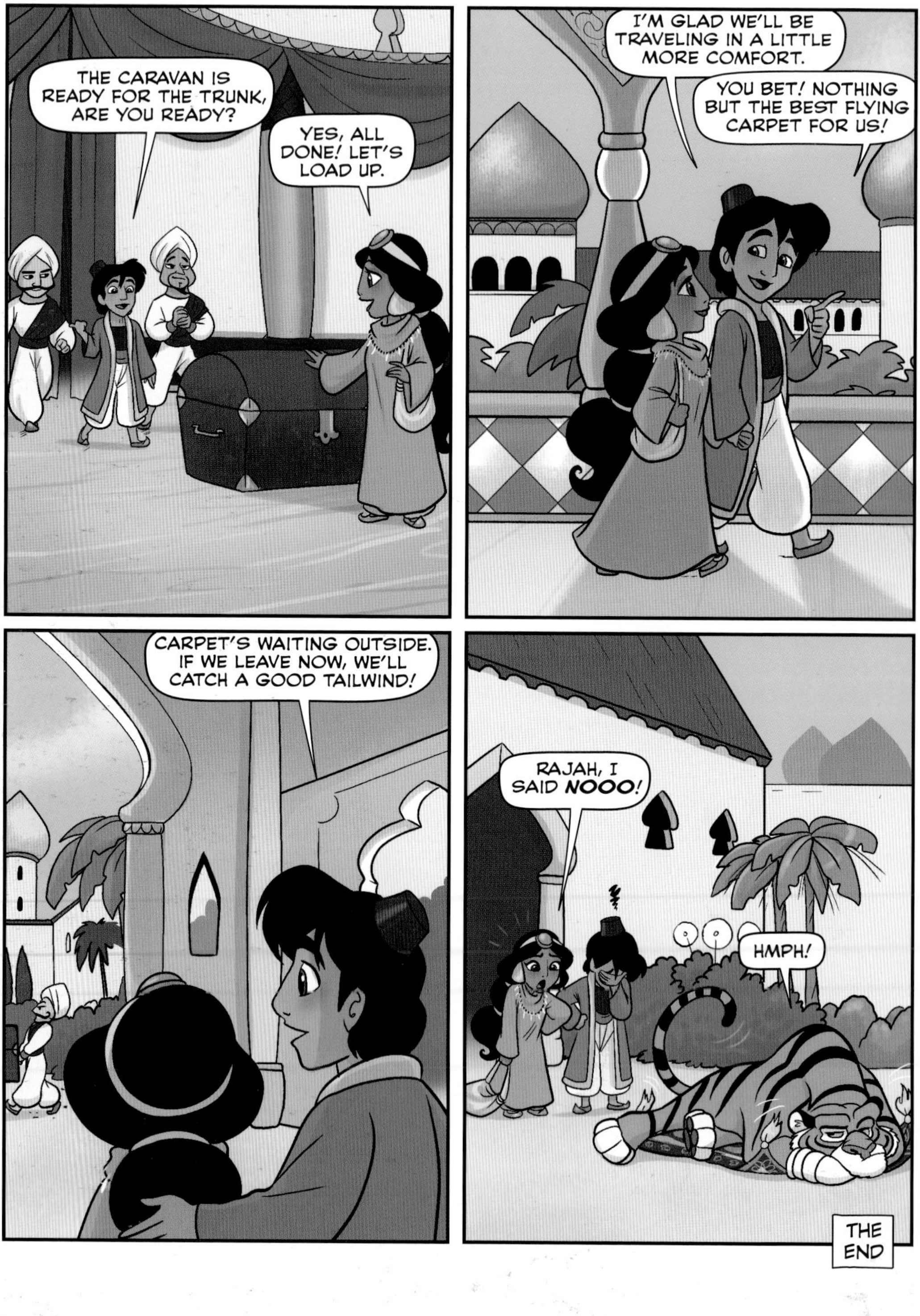
THE CARAVAN IS READY FOR THE TRUNK, ARE YOU READY?
YES, ALL DONE! LET'S LOAD UP.
I'M GLAD WE'LL BE TRAVELING IN A LITTLE MORE COMFORT.
YOU BET! NOTHING BUT THE BEST FLYING CARPET FOR US!
CARPET'S WAITING OUTSIDE. IF WE LEAVE NOW, WE'LL CATCH A GOOD TAILWIND!
RAJAH, I SAID NOOO!
HMPH!
THE END

"STEPSISTERS"

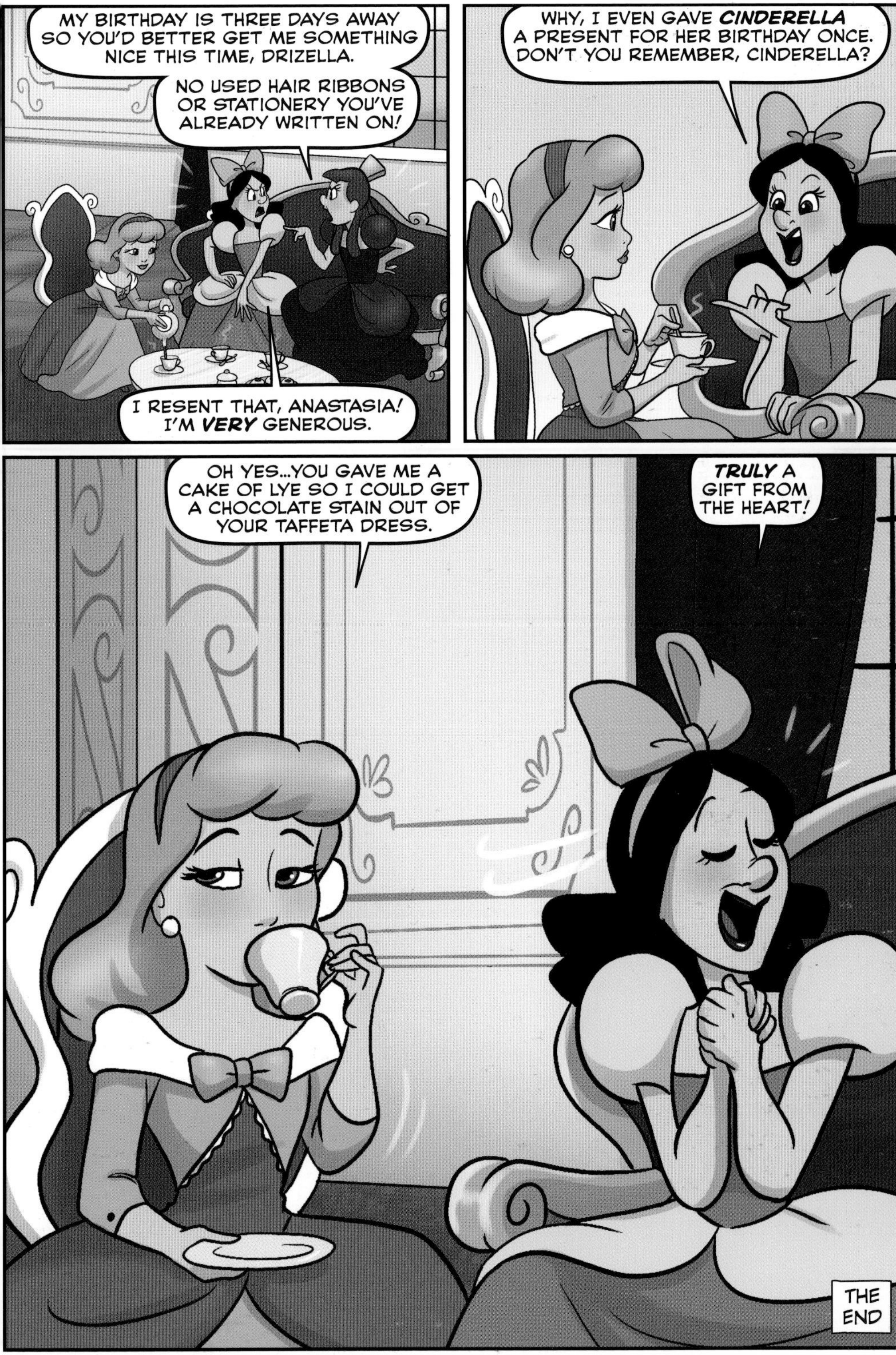

MY BIRTHDAY IS THREE DAYS AWAY SO YOU'D BETTER GET ME SOMETHING NICE THIS TIME, DRIZELLA.
NO USED HAIR RIBBONS OR STATIONERY YOU'VE ALREADY WRITTEN ON!
I RESENT THAT, ANASTASIA! I'M VERY GENEROUS.
WHY, I EVEN GAVE CINDERELLA A PRESENT FOR HER BIRTHDAY ONCE. DON'T YOU REMEMBER, CINDERELLA?
OH YES...YOU GAVE ME A CAKE OF LYE SO I COULD GET A CHOCOLATE STAIN OUT OF YOUR TAFFETA DRESS.
TRULY A GIFT FROM THE HEART!
THE END

"BACK TO NATURE"

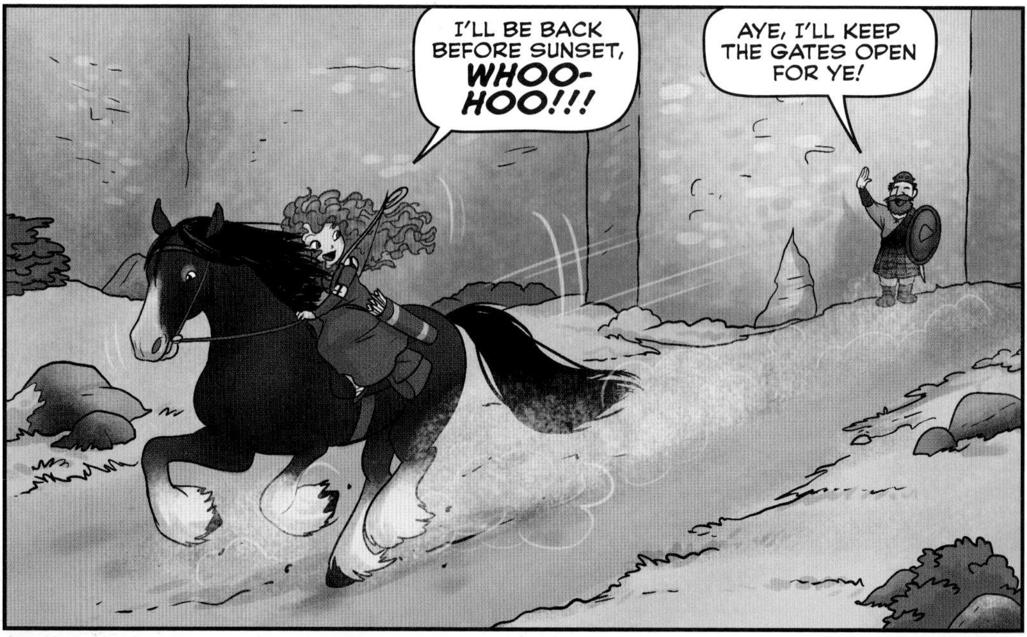
I'LL BE BACK BEFORE SUNSET, WHOO-HOO!!!
AYE, I'LL KEEP THE GATES OPEN FOR YE!

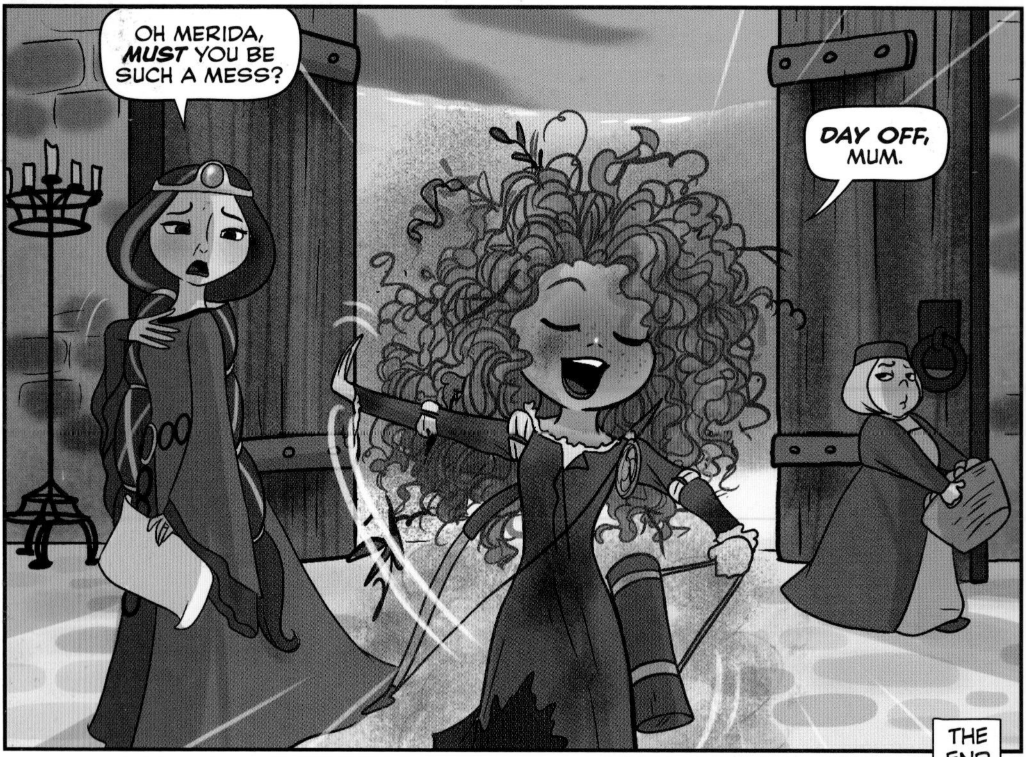
OH MERIDA, MUST YOU BE SUCH A MESS?
DAY OFF, MUM.
THE END

"RAP-STALLION"

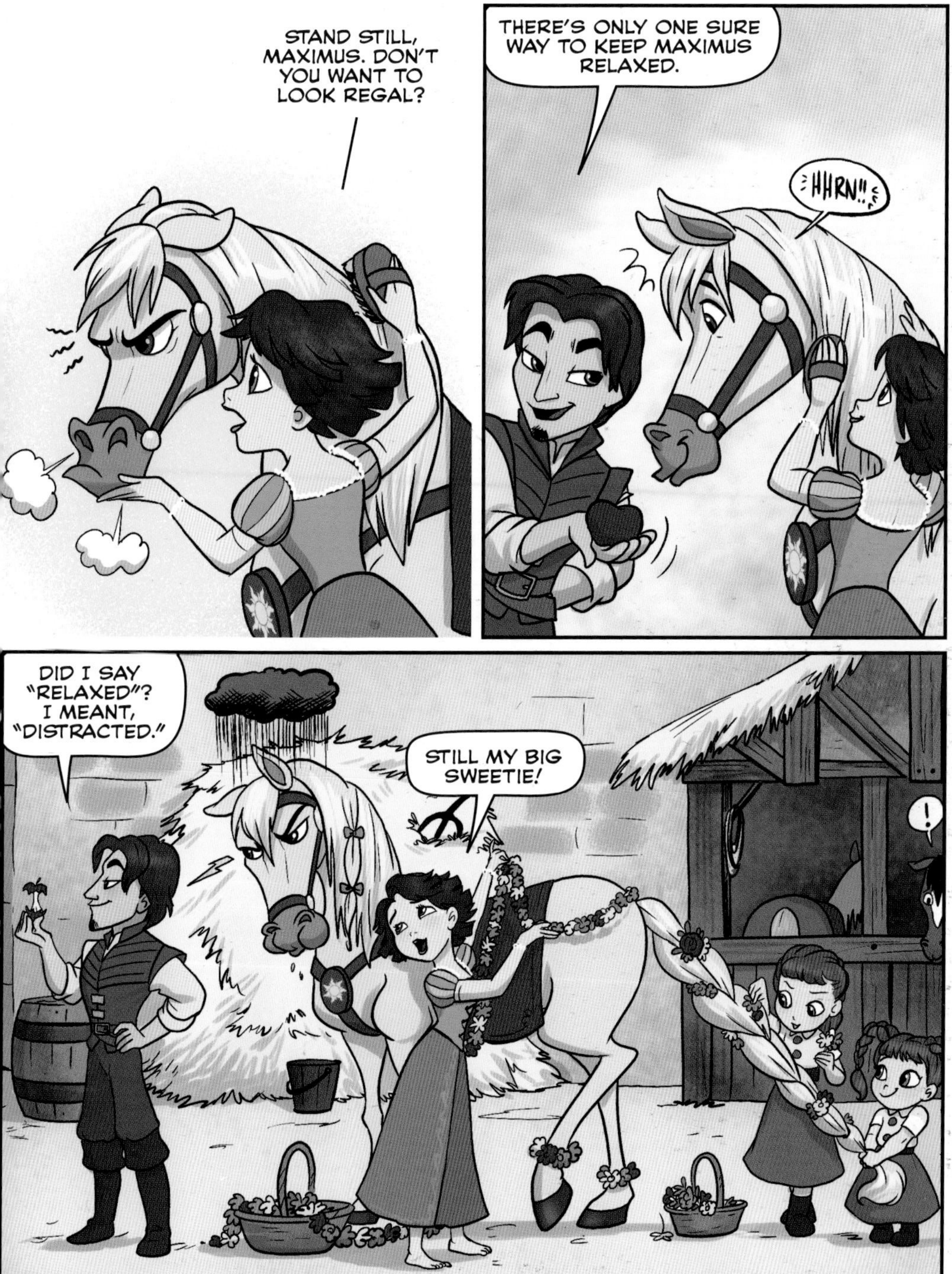
STAND STILL, MAXIMUS. DON'T YOU WANT TO LOOK REGAL?
THERE'S ONLY ONE SURE WAY TO KEEP MAXIMUS RELAXED.
HHRN!!
DID I SAY "RELAXED"? I MEANT, "DISTRACTED."
STILL MY BIG SWEETIE!
!

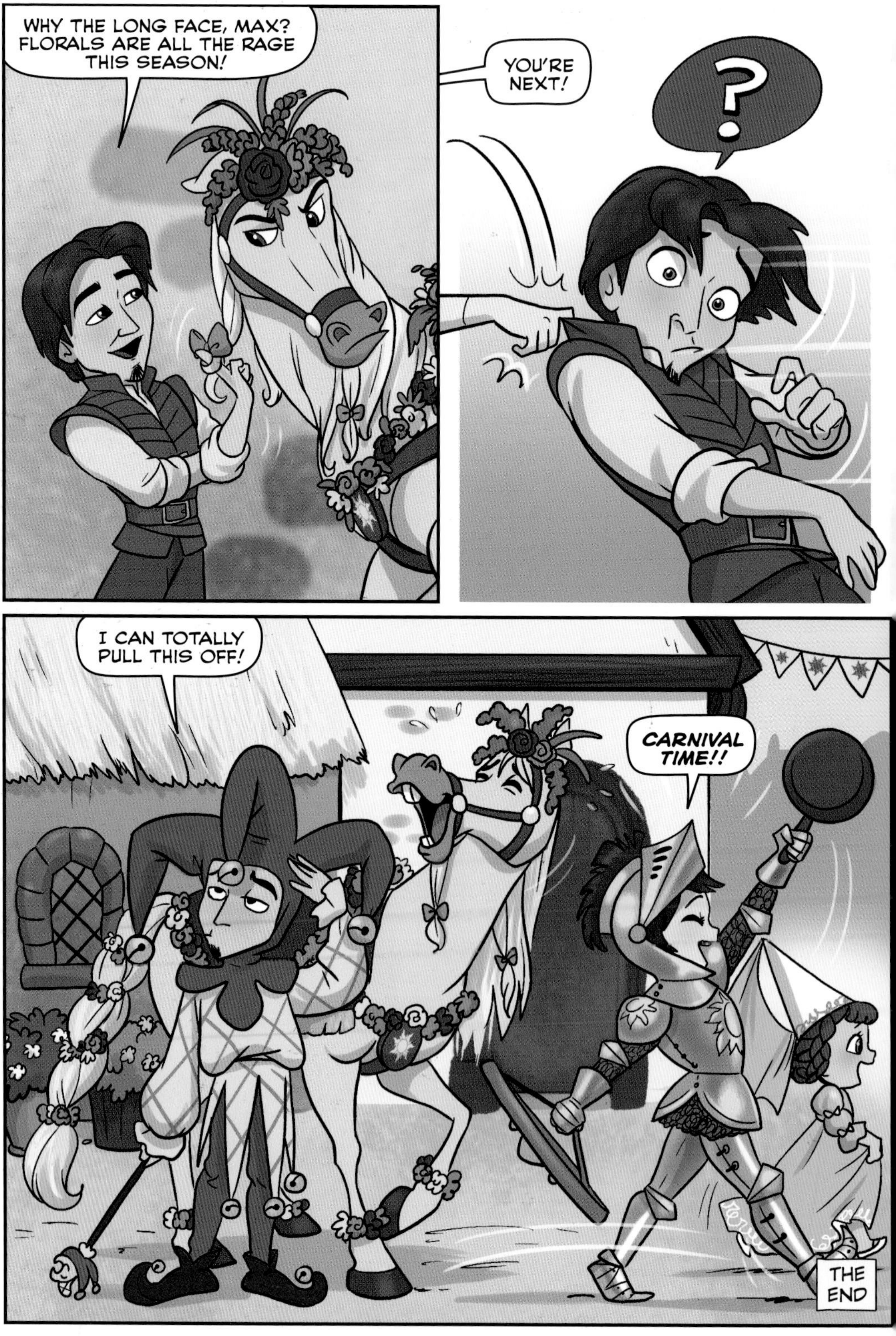
WHY THE LONG FACE, MAX? FLORALS ARE ALL THE RAGE THIS SEASON!
YOU'RE NEXT!
?
I CAN TOTALLY PULL THIS OFF!
CARNIVAL TIME!!
THE END

"BEAUTY AND THE BOOKS"

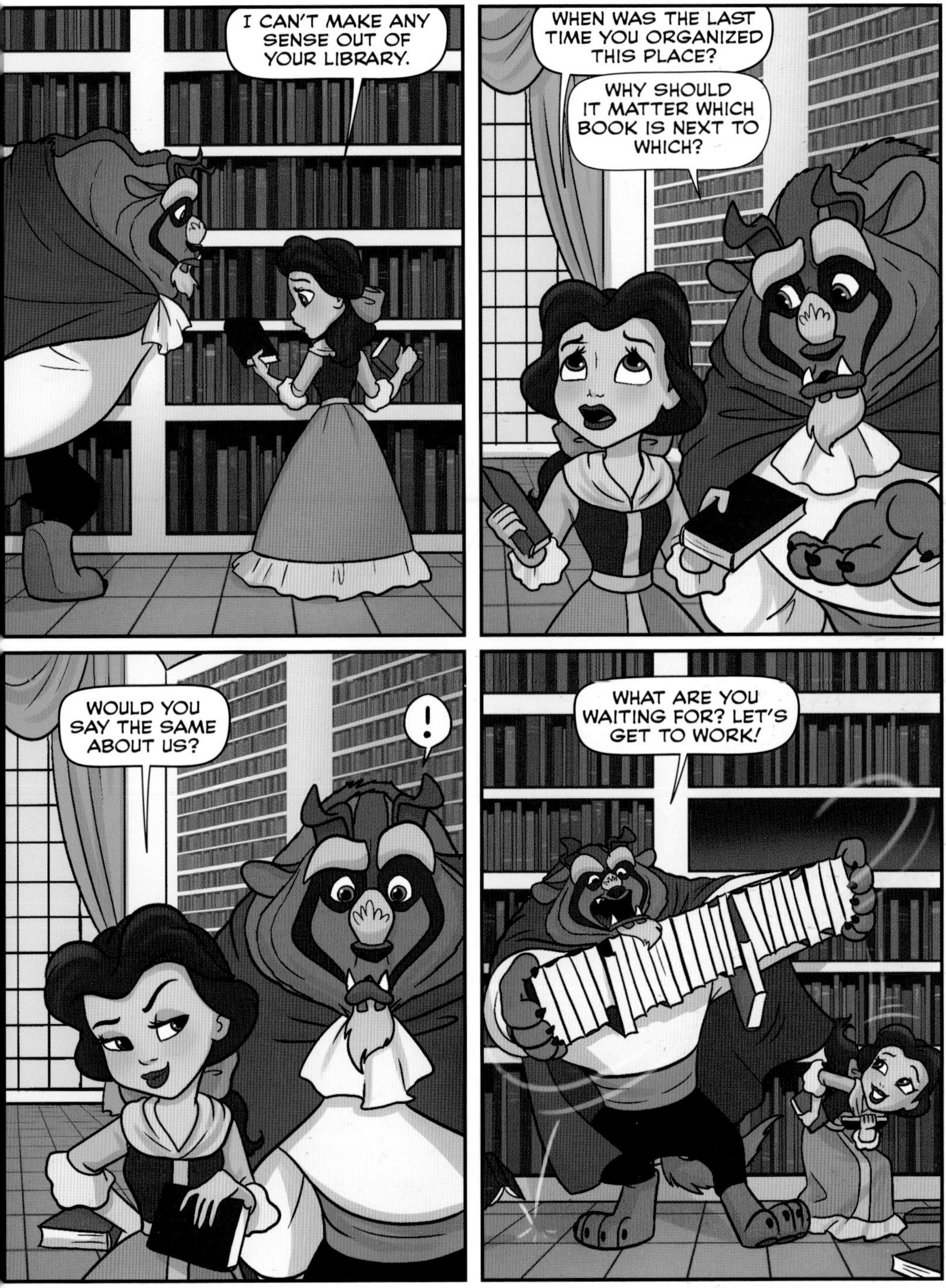
I CAN'T MAKE ANY SENSE OUT OF YOUR LIBRARY.
WHEN WAS THE LAST TIME YOU ORGANIZED THIS PLACE?
WHY SHOULD IT MATTER WHICH BOOK IS NEXT TO WHICH?
WOULD YOU SAY THE SAME ABOUT US?
!
WHAT ARE YOU WAITING FOR? LET'S GET TO WORK!

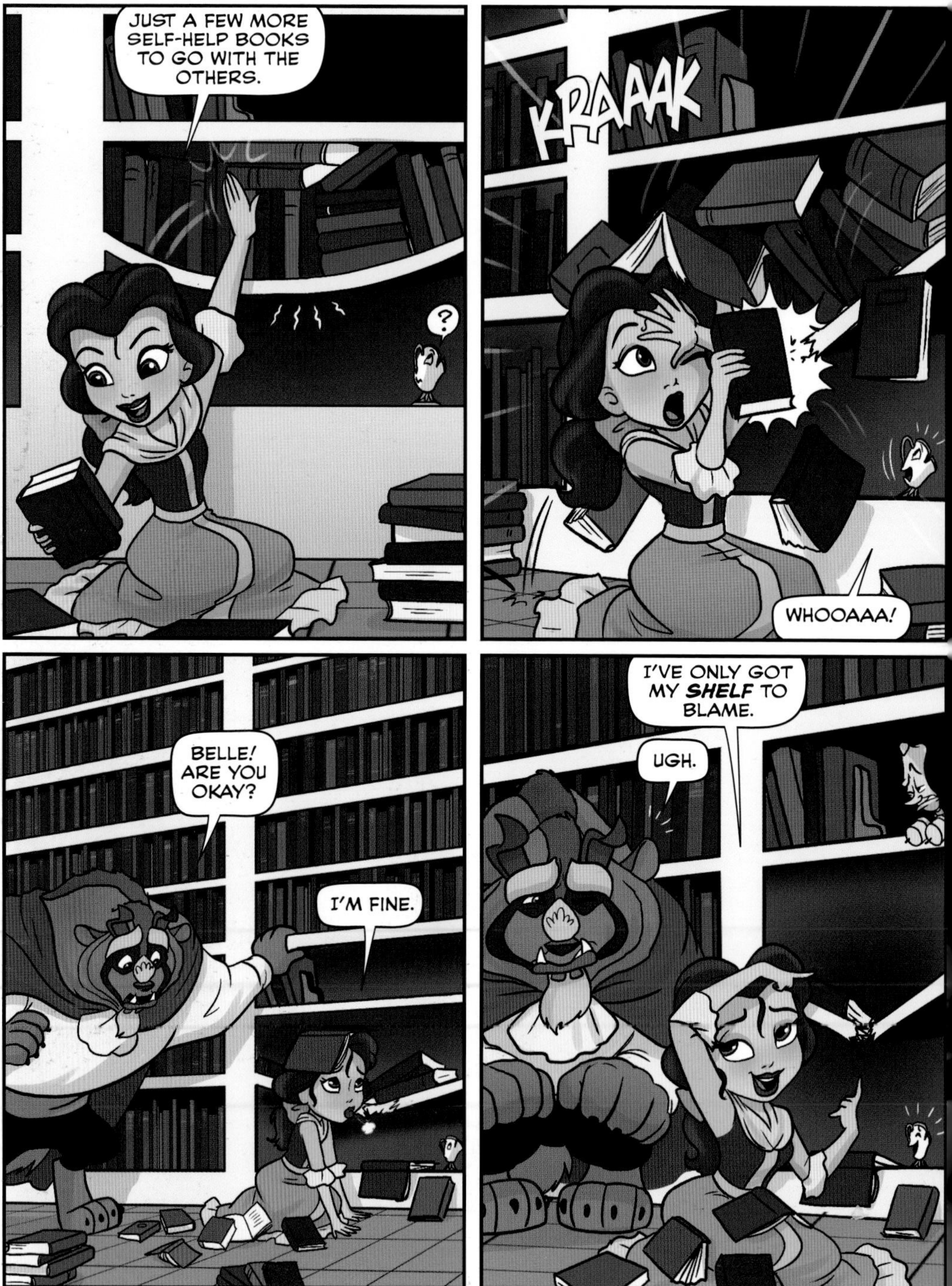
JUST A FEW MORE SELF-HELP BOOKS TO GO WITH THE OTHERS.
?
KRAAAK
WHOOAAA!
BELLE! ARE YOU OKAY?
I'M FINE.
I'VE ONLY GOT MY ***SHELF*** TO BLAME.
UGH.

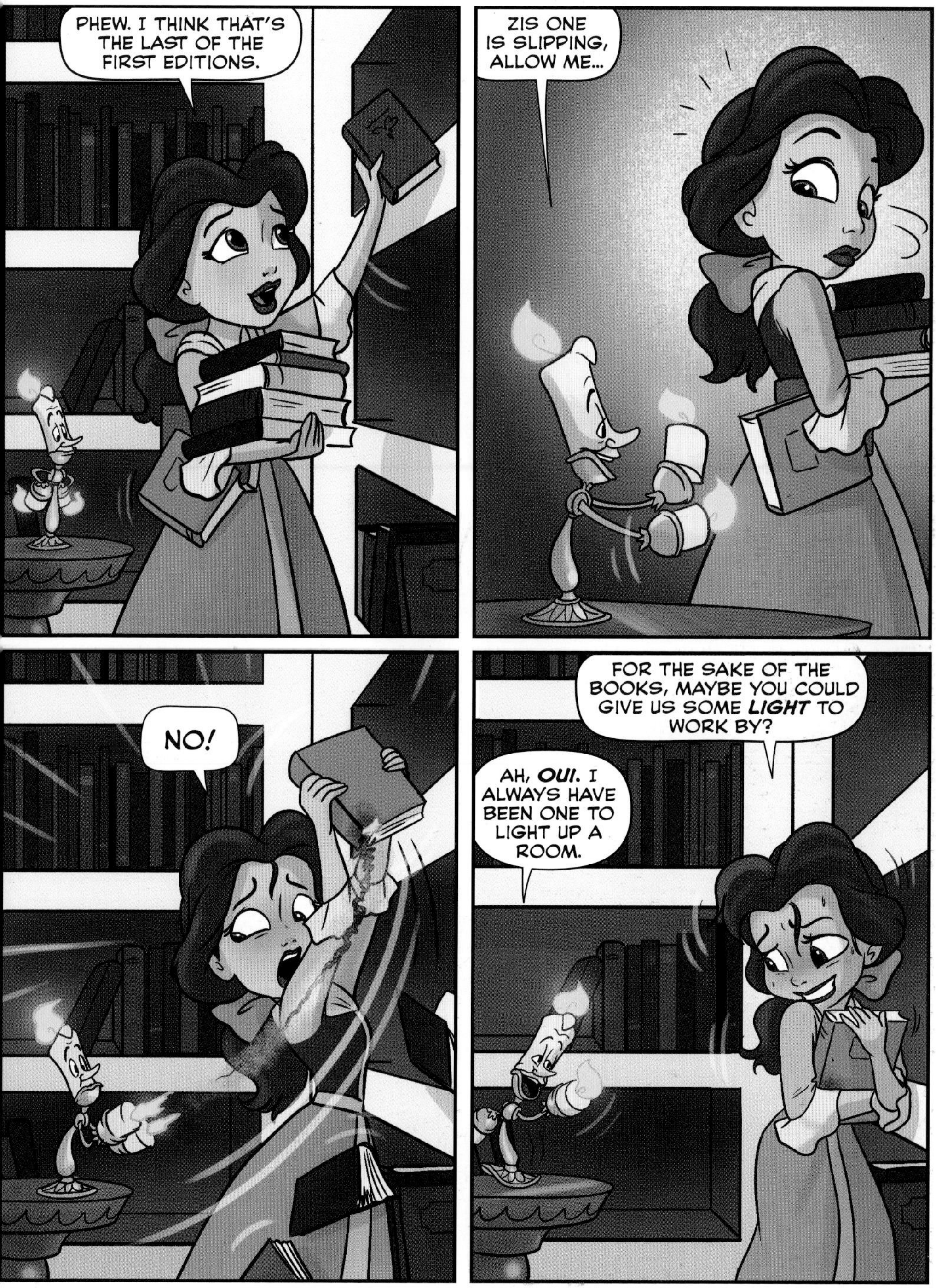
PHEW. I THINK THAT'S THE LAST OF THE FIRST EDITIONS.
ZIS ONE IS SLIPPING, ALLOW ME...
NO!
FOR THE SAKE OF THE BOOKS, MAYBE YOU COULD GIVE US SOME ***LIGHT*** TO WORK BY?
AH, ***OUI***. I ALWAYS HAVE BEEN ONE TO LIGHT UP A ROOM.

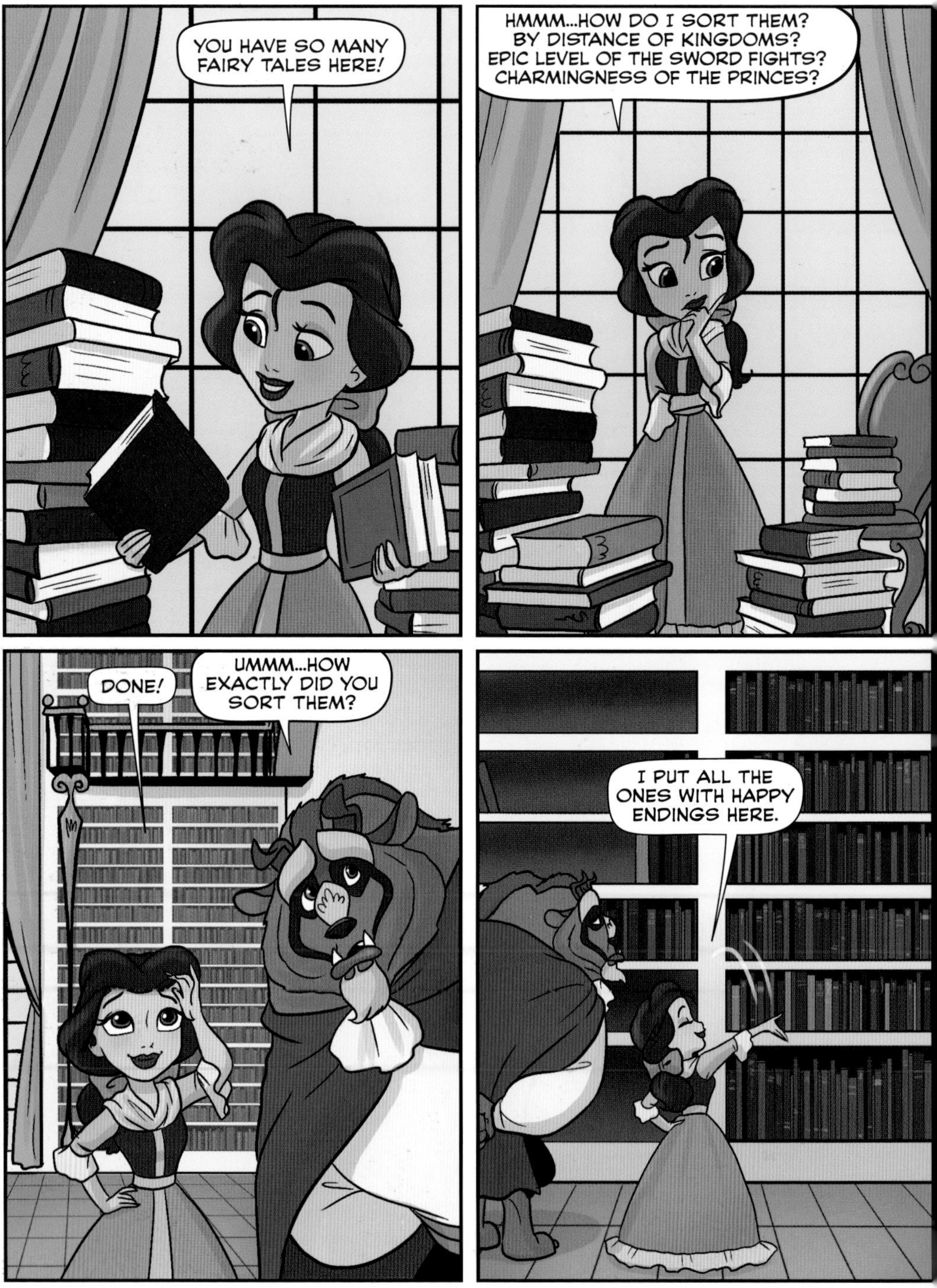
YOU HAVE SO MANY FAIRY TALES HERE!
HMMM...HOW DO I SORT THEM? BY DISTANCE OF KINGDOMS? EPIC LEVEL OF THE SWORD FIGHTS? CHARMINGNESS OF THE PRINCES?
DONE!
UMMM...HOW EXACTLY DID YOU SORT THEM?
I PUT ALL THE ONES WITH HAPPY ENDINGS HERE.

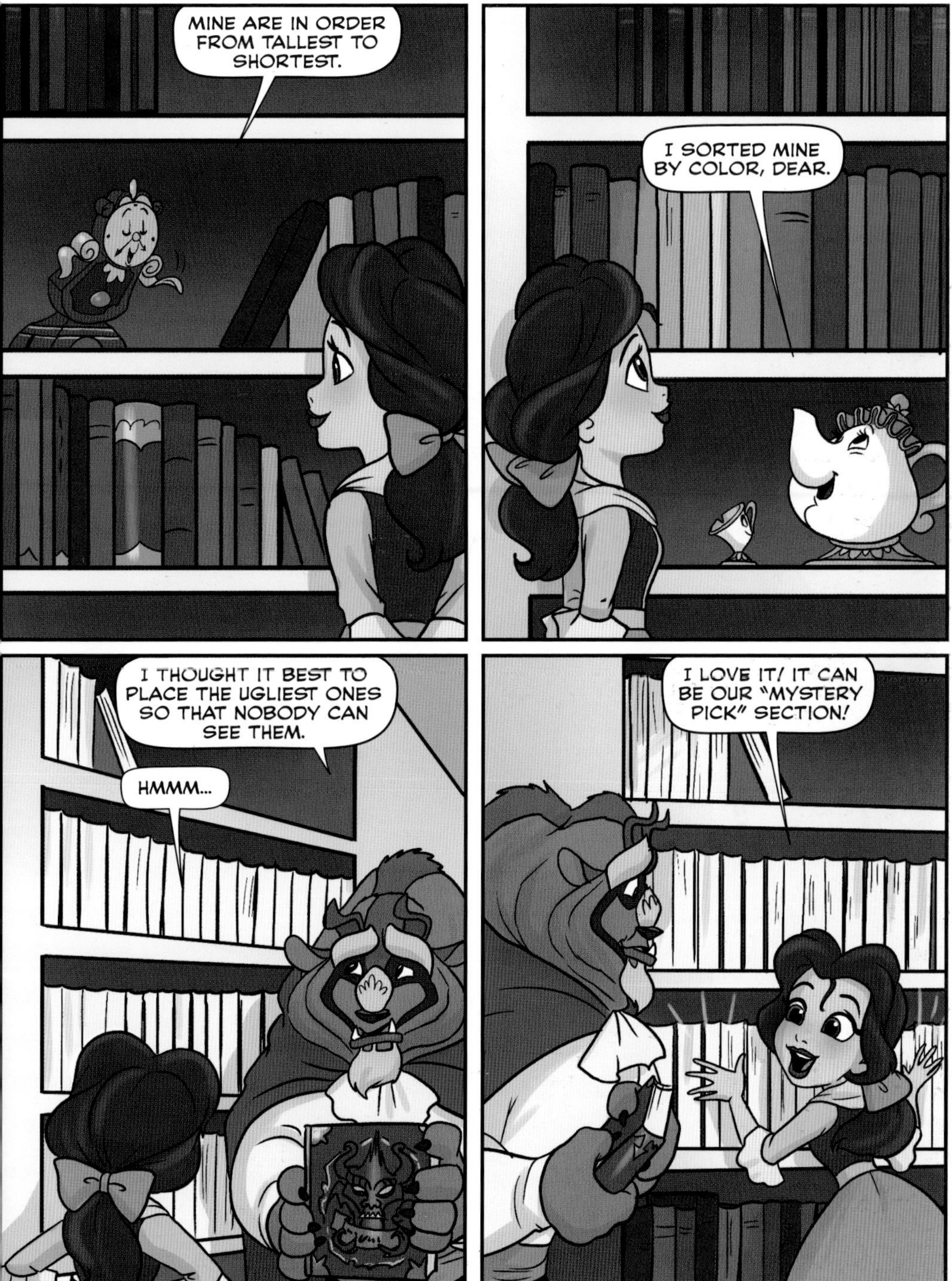
MINE ARE IN ORDER FROM TALLEST TO SHORTEST.
I SORTED MINE BY COLOR, DEAR.
I THOUGHT IT BEST TO PLACE THE UGLIEST ONES SO THAT NOBODY CAN SEE THEM.
HMMM...
I LOVE IT! IT CAN BE OUR "MYSTERY PICK" SECTION!

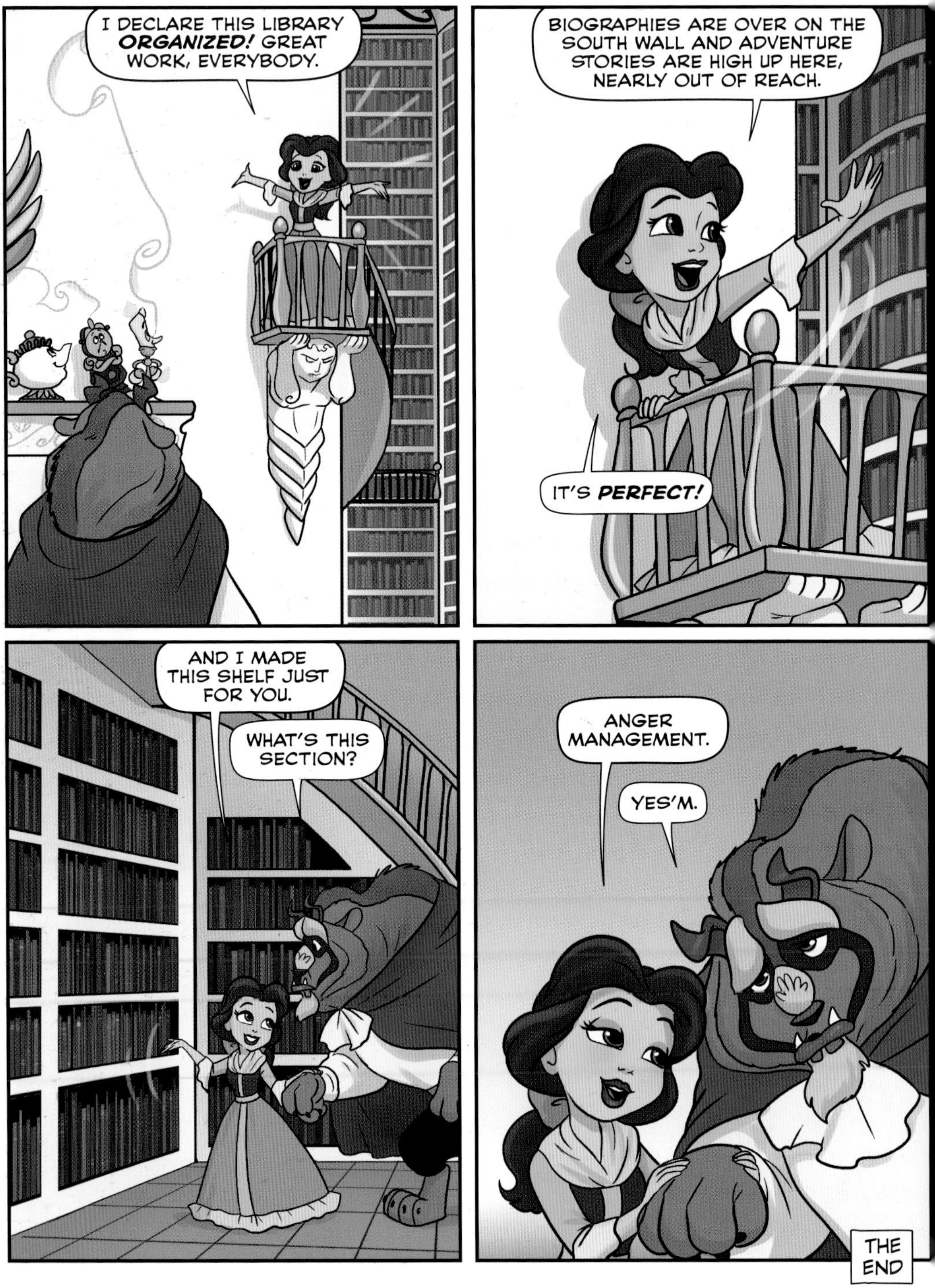
I DECLARE THIS LIBRARY ***ORGANIZED!*** GREAT WORK, EVERYBODY.
BIOGRAPHIES ARE OVER ON THE SOUTH WALL AND ADVENTURE STORIES ARE HIGH UP HERE, NEARLY OUT OF REACH.
IT'S ***PERFECT!***
AND I MADE THIS SHELF JUST FOR YOU.
WHAT'S THIS SECTION?
ANGER MANAGEMENT.
YES'M.
THE END

"EXPLORING THE CASTLE"

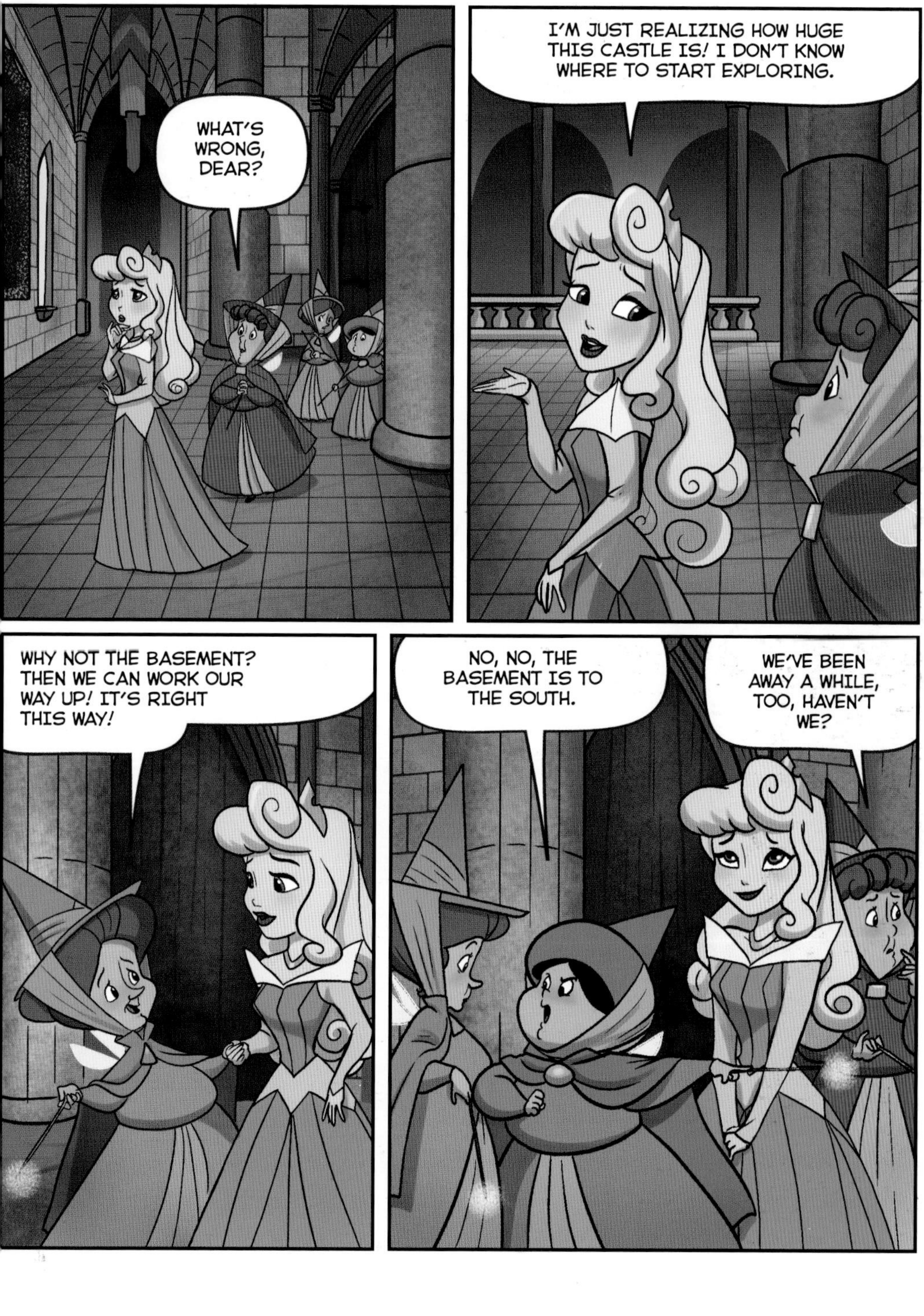
WHAT'S WRONG, DEAR?
I'M JUST REALIZING HOW HUGE THIS CASTLE IS! I DON'T KNOW WHERE TO START EXPLORING.
WHY NOT THE BASEMENT? THEN WE CAN WORK OUR WAY UP! IT'S RIGHT THIS WAY!
NO, NO, THE BASEMENT IS TO THE SOUTH.
WE'VE BEEN AWAY A WHILE, TOO, HAVEN'T WE?

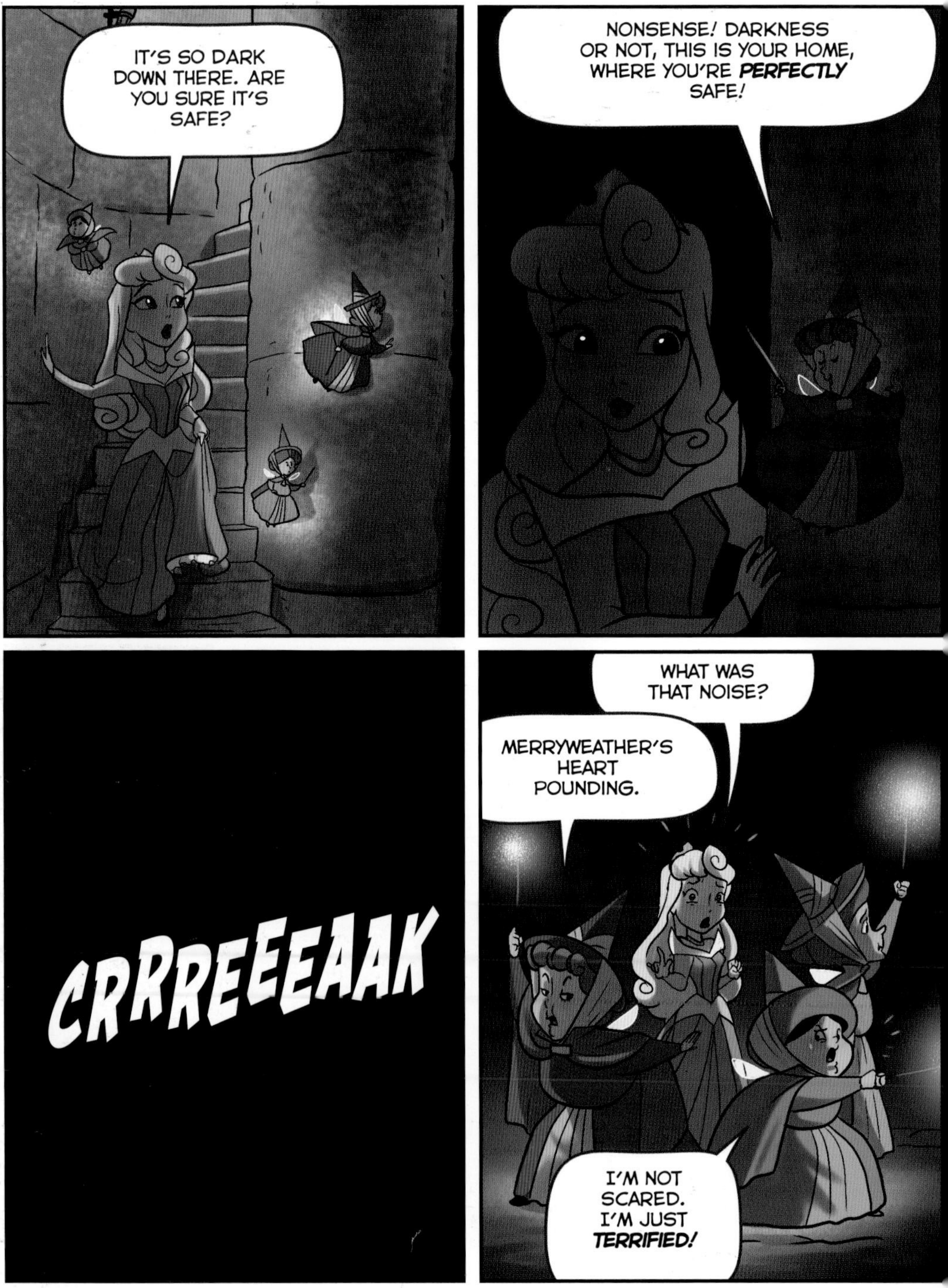
IT'S SO DARK DOWN THERE. ARE YOU SURE IT'S SAFE?
NONSENSE! DARKNESS OR NOT, THIS IS YOUR HOME, WHERE YOU'RE **PERFECTLY** SAFE!
CRRREEEAAK
WHAT WAS THAT NOISE?
MERRYWEATHER'S HEART POUNDING.
I'M NOT SCARED. I'M JUST **TERRIFIED!**

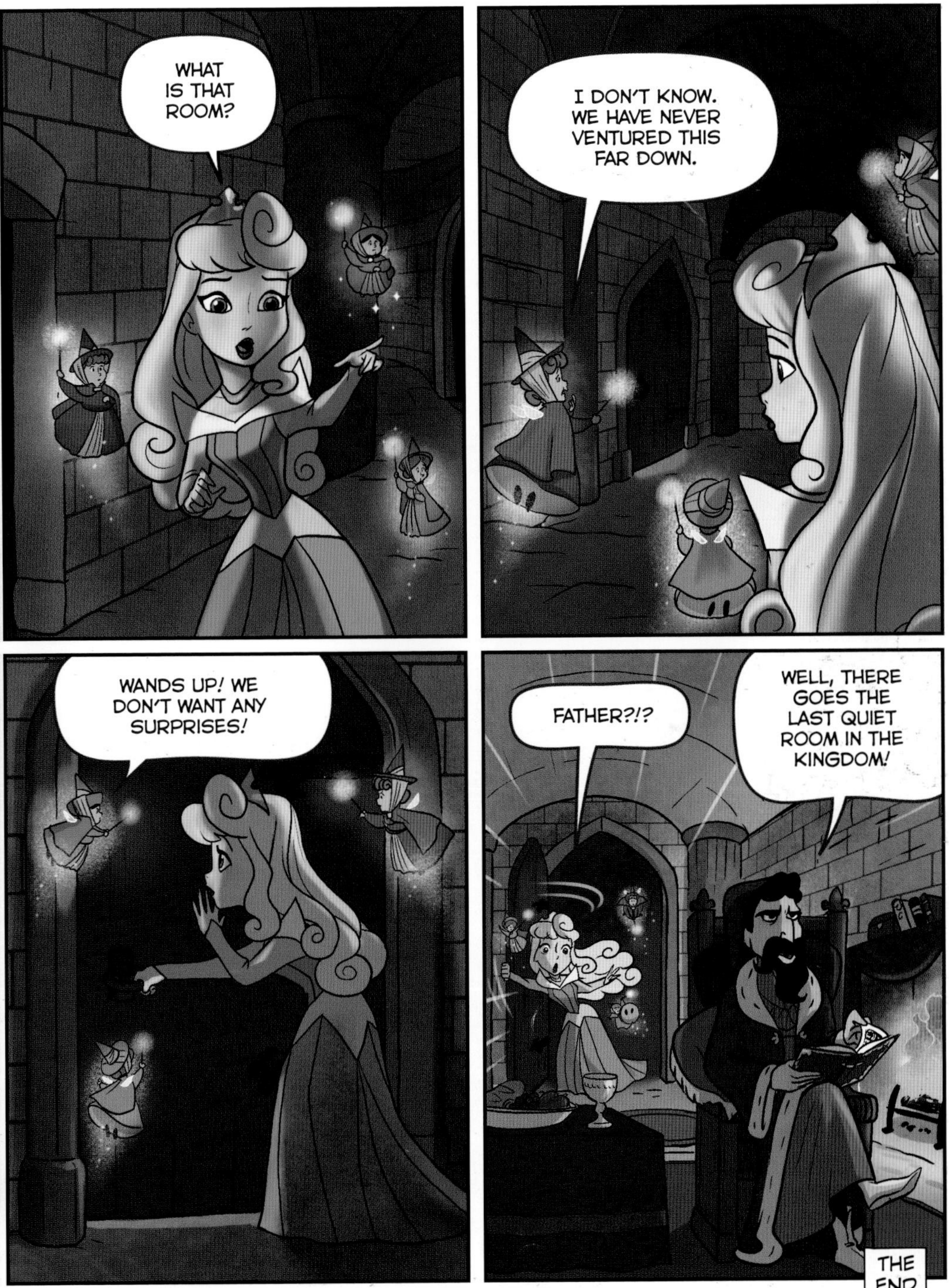
WHAT IS THAT ROOM?
I DON'T KNOW. WE HAVE NEVER VENTURED THIS FAR DOWN.
WANDS UP! WE DON'T WANT ANY SURPRISES!
FATHER?!?
WELL, THERE GOES THE LAST QUIET ROOM IN THE KINGDOM!
THE END

"BATHTIME"

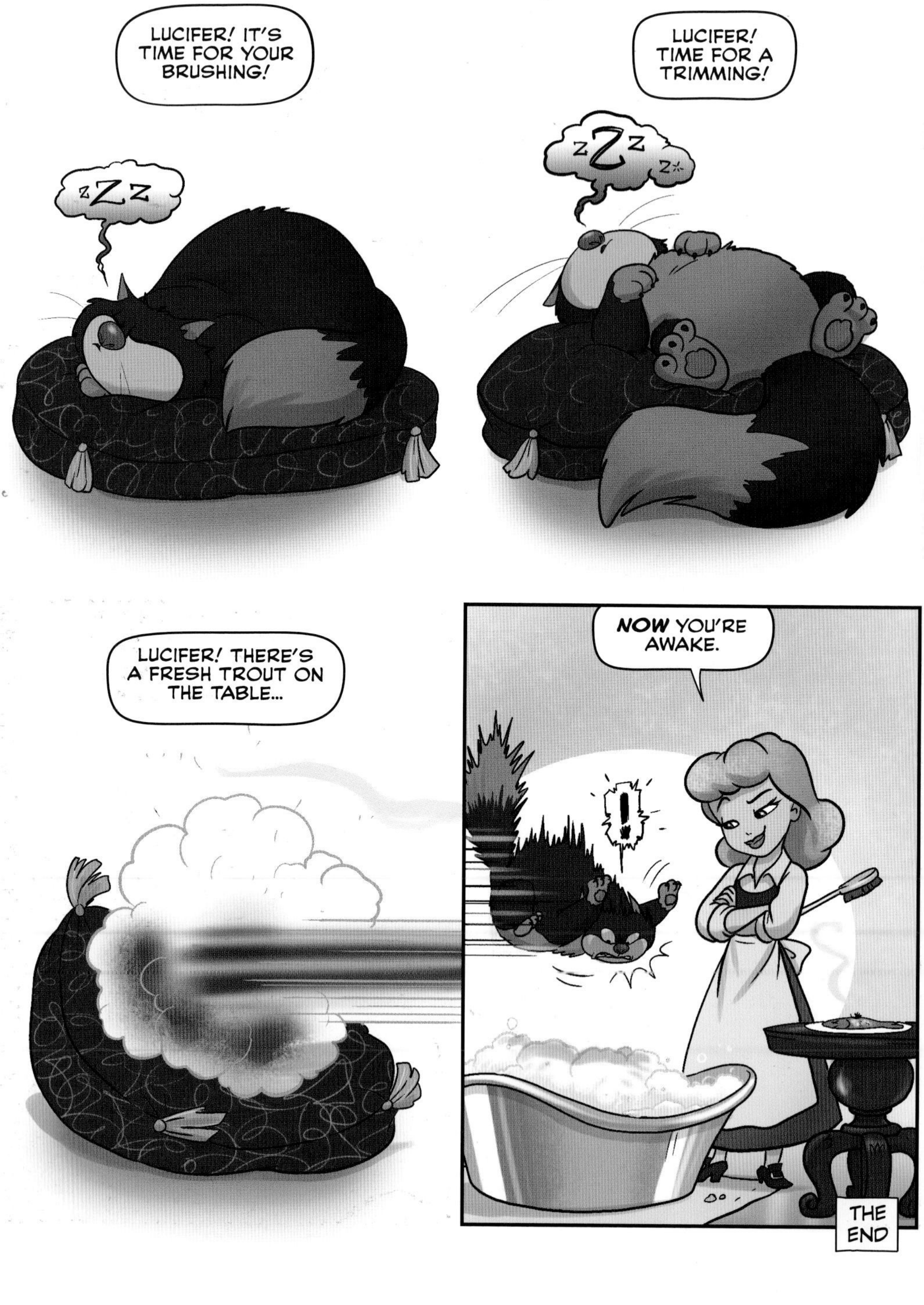

LUCIFER! IT'S TIME FOR YOUR BRUSHING!
zZz
LUCIFER! TIME FOR A TRIMMING!
zZz
LUCIFER! THERE'S A FRESH TROUT ON THE TABLE...
NOW YOU'RE AWAKE.
!
THE END

"MUSHU'S REVIEW"

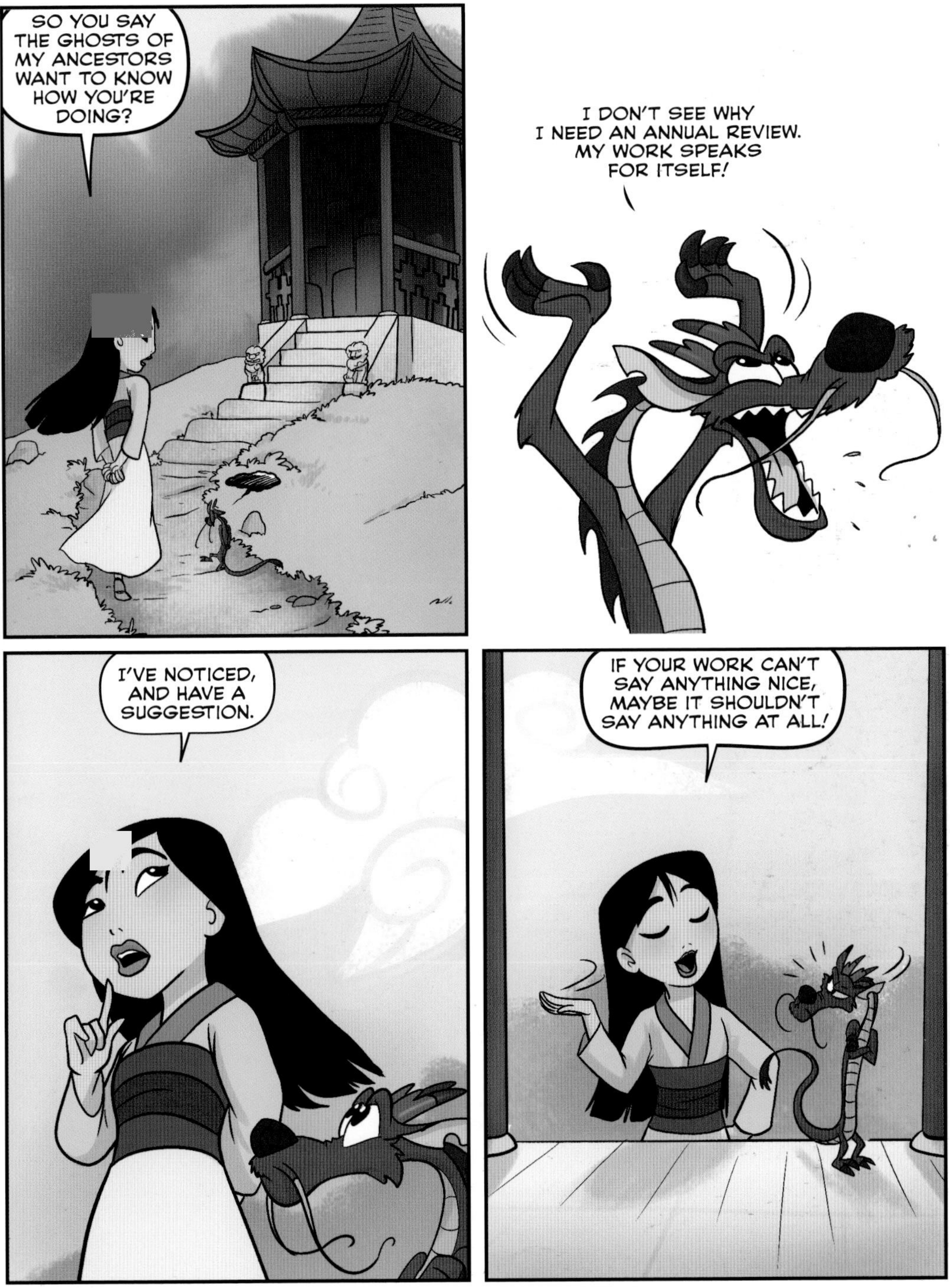
SO YOU SAY THE GHOSTS OF MY ANCESTORS WANT TO KNOW HOW YOU'RE DOING?
I DON'T SEE WHY I NEED AN ANNUAL REVIEW. MY WORK SPEAKS FOR ITSELF!
I'VE NOTICED, AND HAVE A SUGGESTION.
IF YOUR WORK CAN'T SAY ANYTHING NICE, MAYBE IT SHOULDN'T SAY ANYTHING AT ALL!

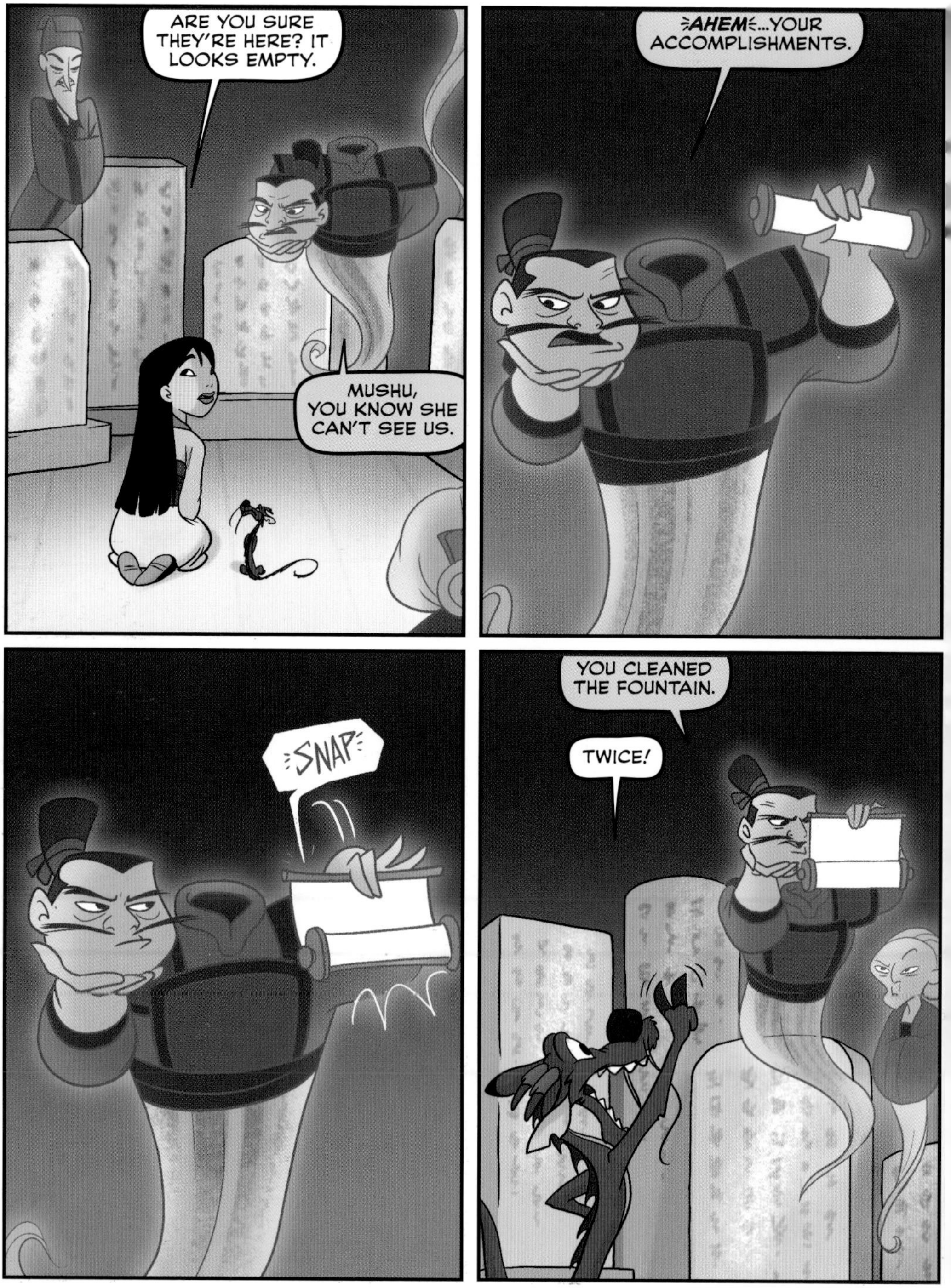
ARE YOU SURE THEY'RE HERE? IT LOOKS EMPTY.
MUSHU, YOU KNOW SHE CAN'T SEE US.
AHEM...YOUR ACCOMPLISHMENTS.
SNAP
YOU CLEANED THE FOUNTAIN.
TWICE!

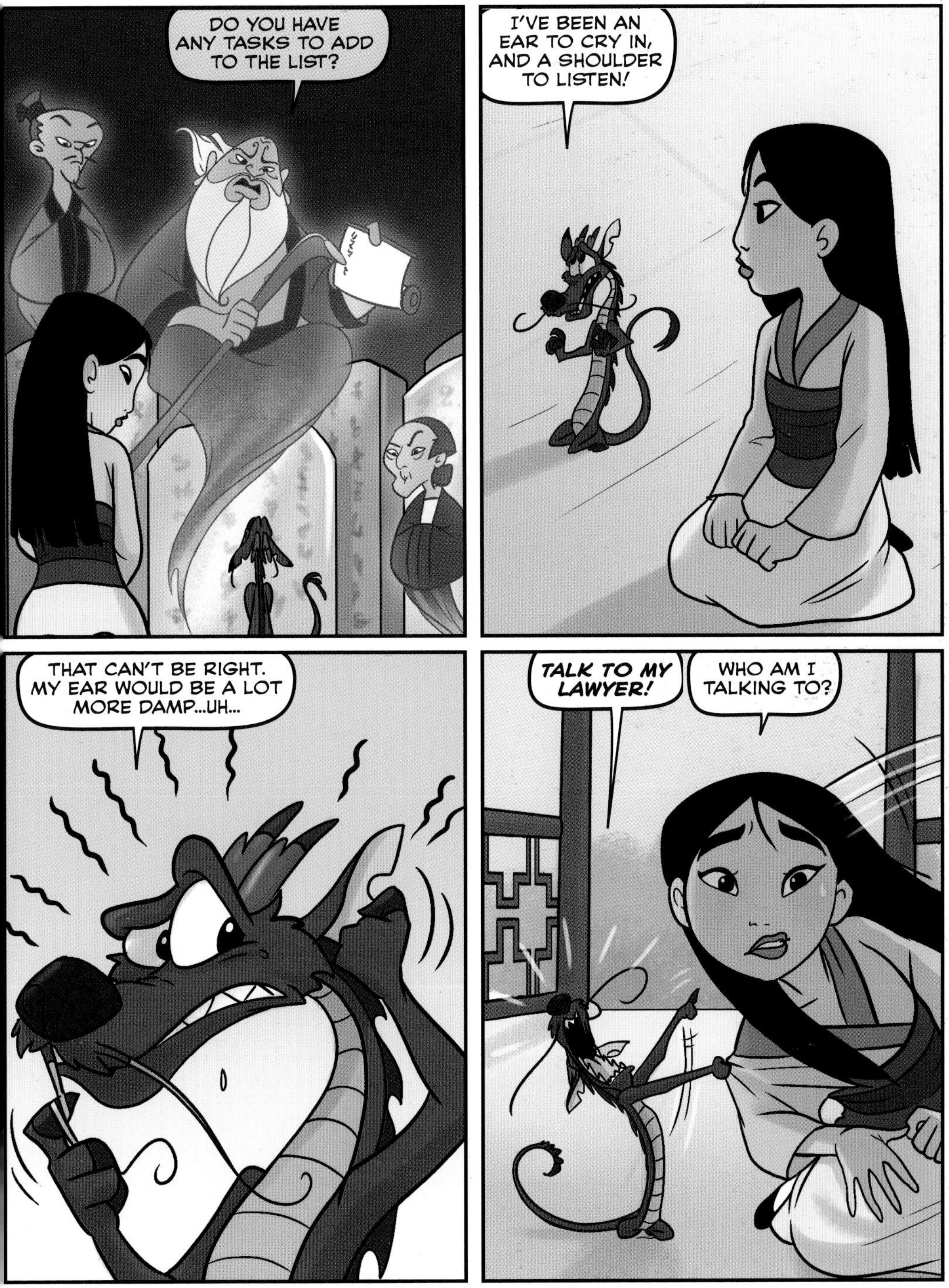
DO YOU HAVE ANY TASKS TO ADD TO THE LIST?
I'VE BEEN AN EAR TO CRY IN, AND A SHOULDER TO LISTEN!
THAT CAN'T BE RIGHT. MY EAR WOULD BE A LOT MORE DAMP...UH...
TALK TO MY LAWYER!
WHO AM I TALKING TO?

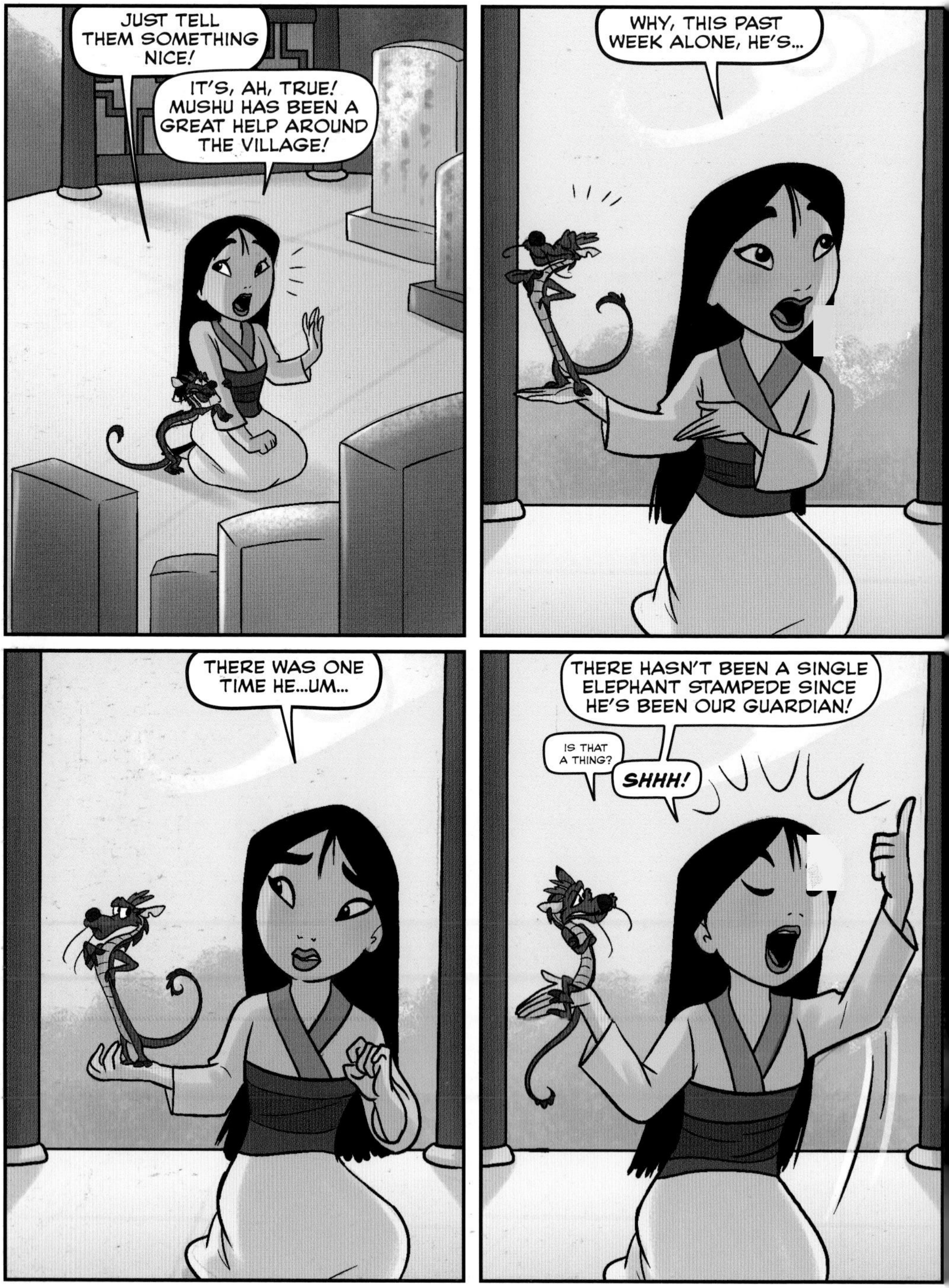
JUST TELL THEM SOMETHING NICE!
IT'S, AH, TRUE! MUSHU HAS BEEN A GREAT HELP AROUND THE VILLAGE!
WHY, THIS PAST WEEK ALONE, HE'S...
THERE WAS ONE TIME HE...UM...
THERE HASN'T BEEN A SINGLE ELEPHANT STAMPEDE SINCE HE'S BEEN OUR GUARDIAN!
IS THAT A THING?
SHHH!

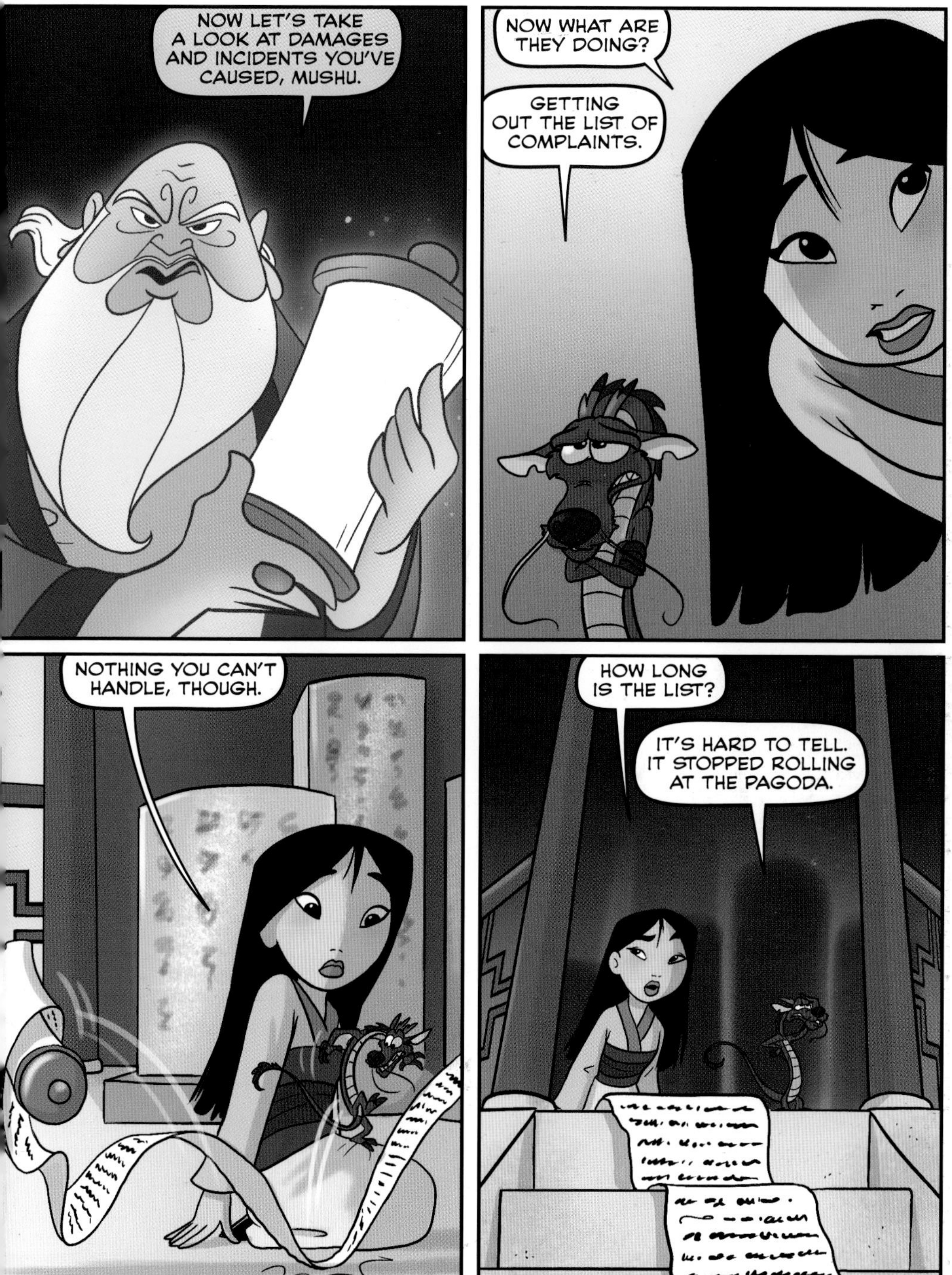
NOW LET'S TAKE A LOOK AT DAMAGES AND INCIDENTS YOU'VE CAUSED, MUSHU.
NOW WHAT ARE THEY DOING?
GETTING OUT THE LIST OF COMPLAINTS.
NOTHING YOU CAN'T HANDLE, THOUGH.
HOW LONG IS THE LIST?
IT'S HARD TO TELL. IT STOPPED ROLLING AT THE PAGODA.

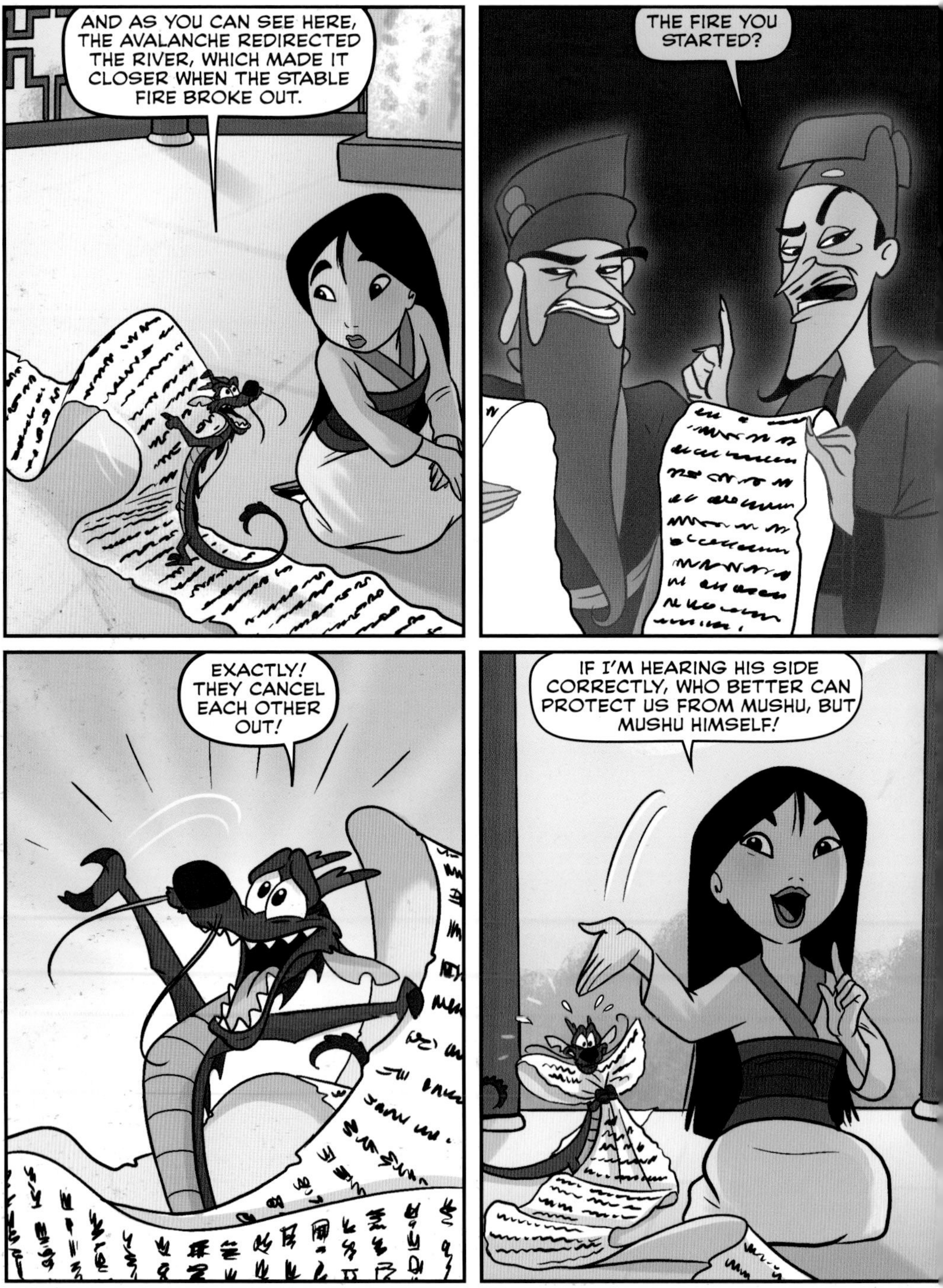
AND AS YOU CAN SEE HERE, THE AVALANCHE REDIRECTED THE RIVER, WHICH MADE IT CLOSER WHEN THE STABLE FIRE BROKE OUT.
THE FIRE YOU STARTED?
EXACTLY! THEY CANCEL EACH OTHER OUT!
IF I'M HEARING HIS SIDE CORRECTLY, WHO BETTER CAN PROTECT US FROM MUSHU, BUT MUSHU HIMSELF!

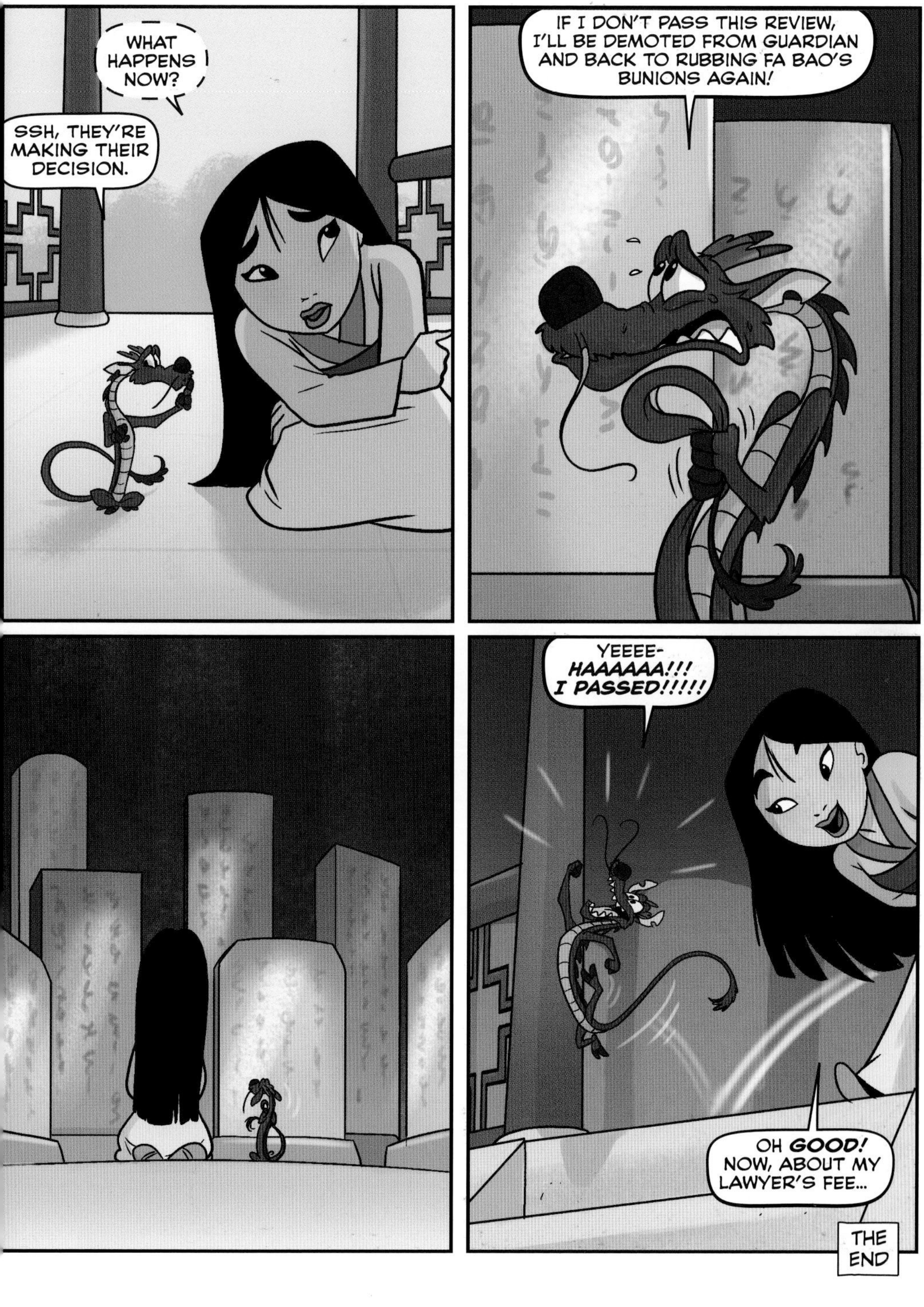

WHAT HAPPENS NOW?
SSH, THEY'RE MAKING THEIR DECISION.
IF I DON'T PASS THIS REVIEW, I'LL BE DEMOTED FROM GUARDIAN AND BACK TO RUBBING FA BAO'S BUNIONS AGAIN!
YEEEE-HAAAAAAA!!! I PASSED!!!!!
OH GOOD! NOW, ABOUT MY LAWYER'S FEE...
THE END

"ROMEO AND JULIET"

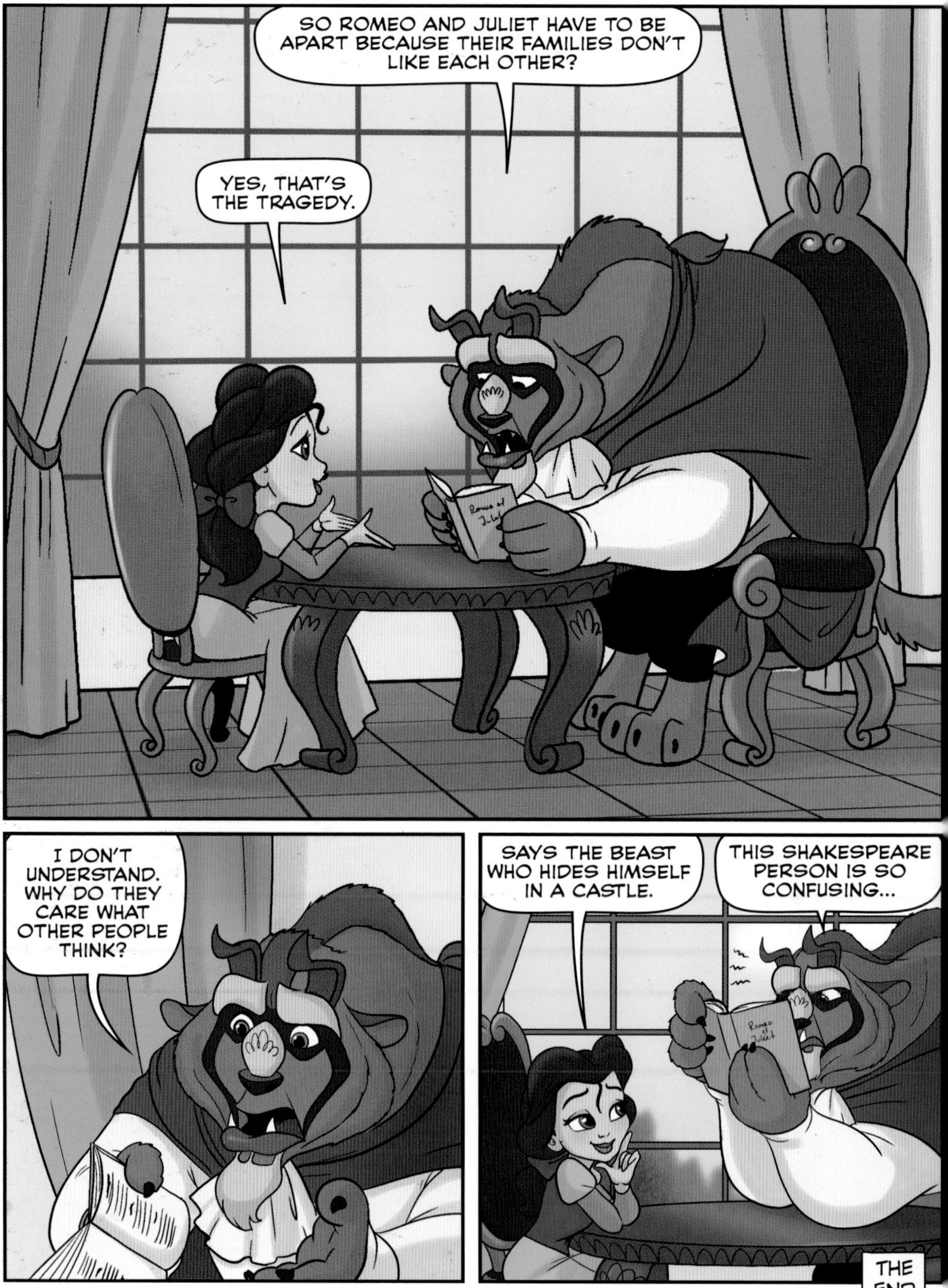

SO ROMEO AND JULIET HAVE TO BE APART BECAUSE THEIR FAMILIES DON'T LIKE EACH OTHER?
YES, THAT'S THE TRAGEDY.
I DON'T UNDERSTAND. WHY DO THEY CARE WHAT OTHER PEOPLE THINK?
SAYS THE BEAST WHO HIDES HIMSELF IN A CASTLE.
THIS SHAKESPEARE PERSON IS SO CONFUSING...
THE END

"SO YOU SAY IT'S YOUR BIRTHDAY"

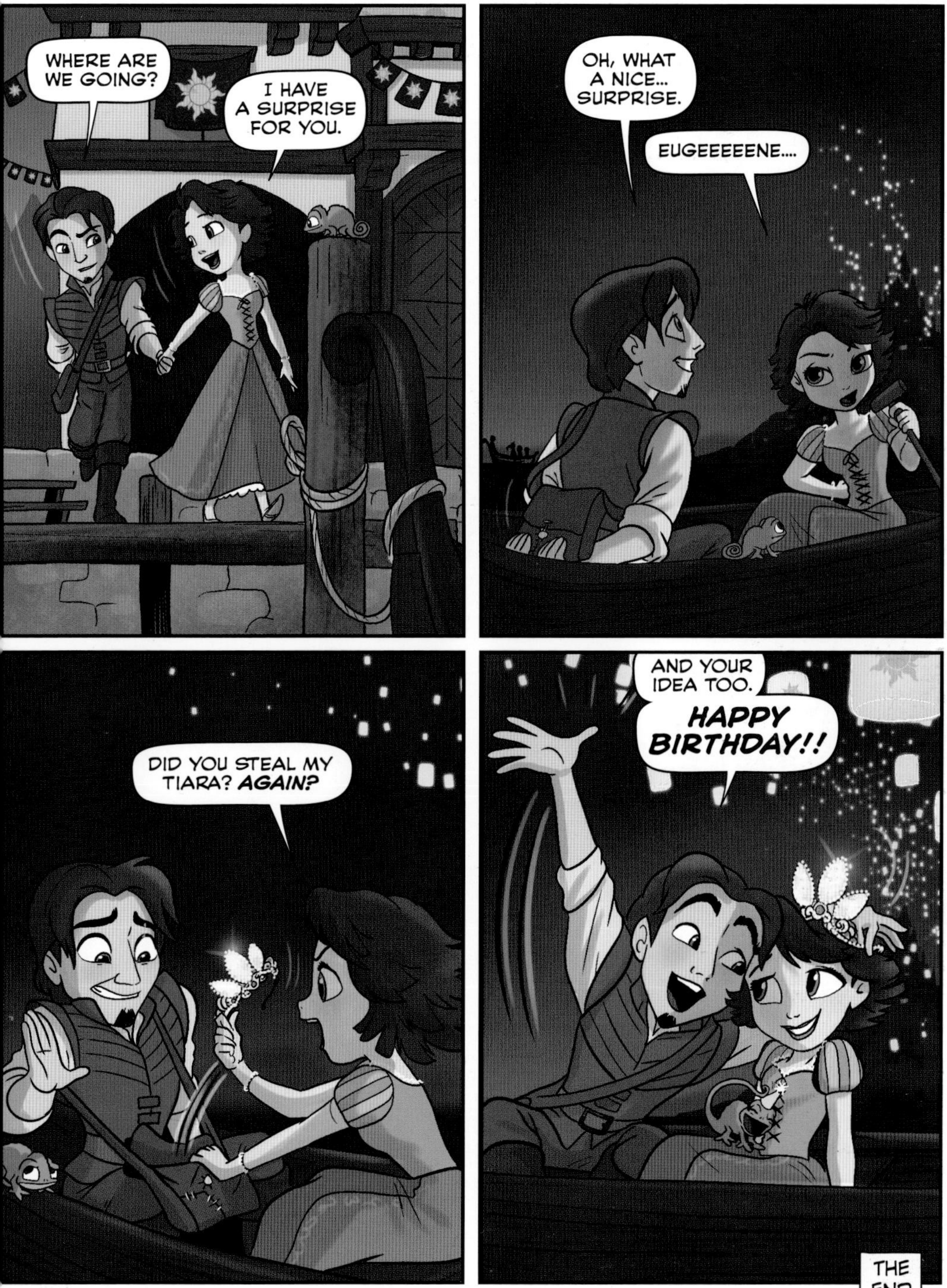

WHERE ARE WE GOING?
I HAVE A SURPRISE FOR YOU.
OH, WHAT A NICE... SURPRISE.
EUGEEEEENE....
DID YOU STEAL MY TIARA? *AGAIN?*
AND YOUR IDEA TOO.
HAPPY BIRTHDAY!!
THE END

"PUNS"

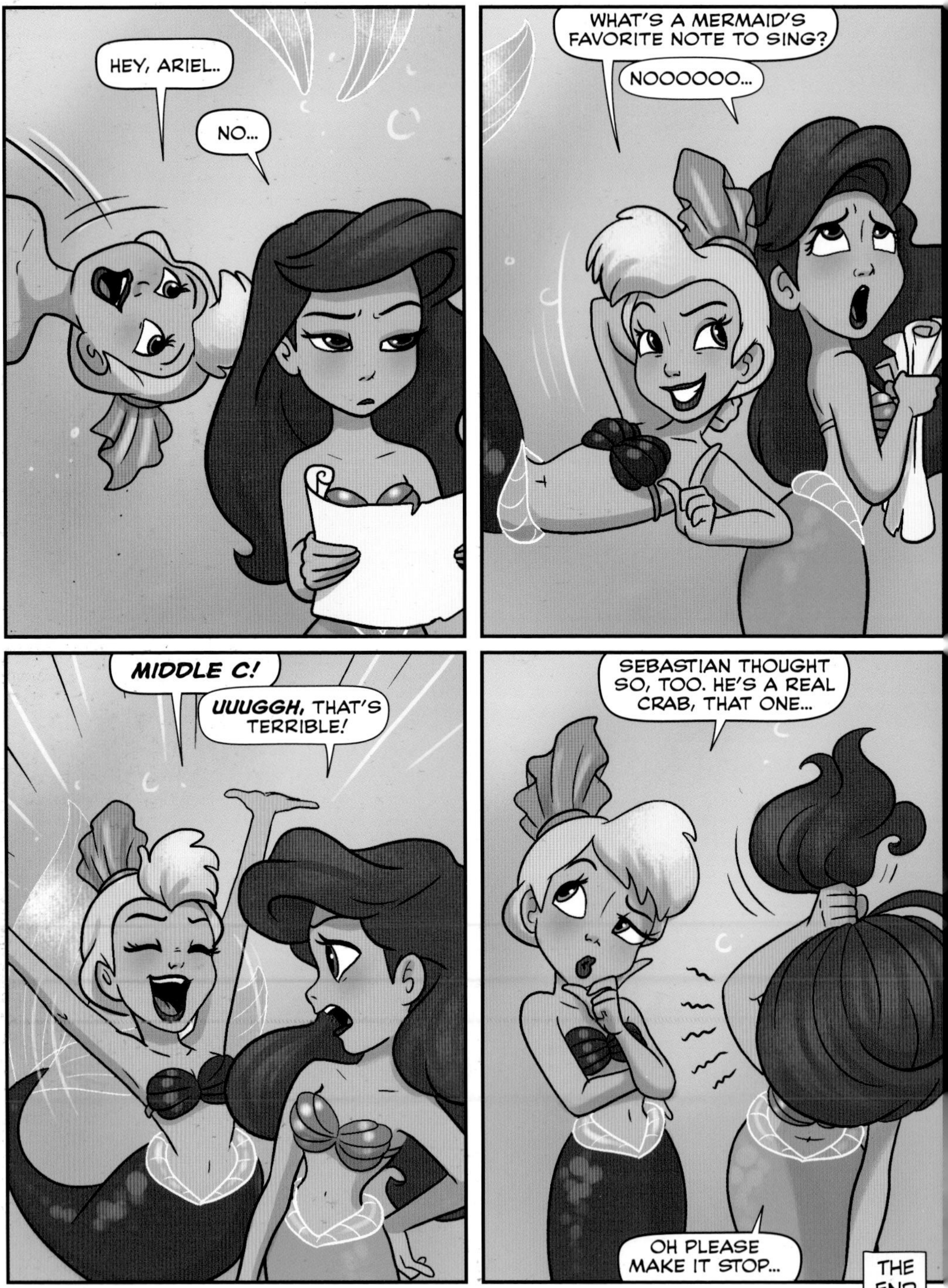
HEY, ARIEL..
NO...
WHAT'S A MERMAID'S FAVORITE NOTE TO SING?
NOOOOOO...
MIDDLE C!
UUUGGH, THAT'S TERRIBLE!
SEBASTIAN THOUGHT SO, TOO. HE'S A REAL CRAB, THAT ONE...
OH PLEASE MAKE IT STOP...
THE END

"STOLEN PIE"

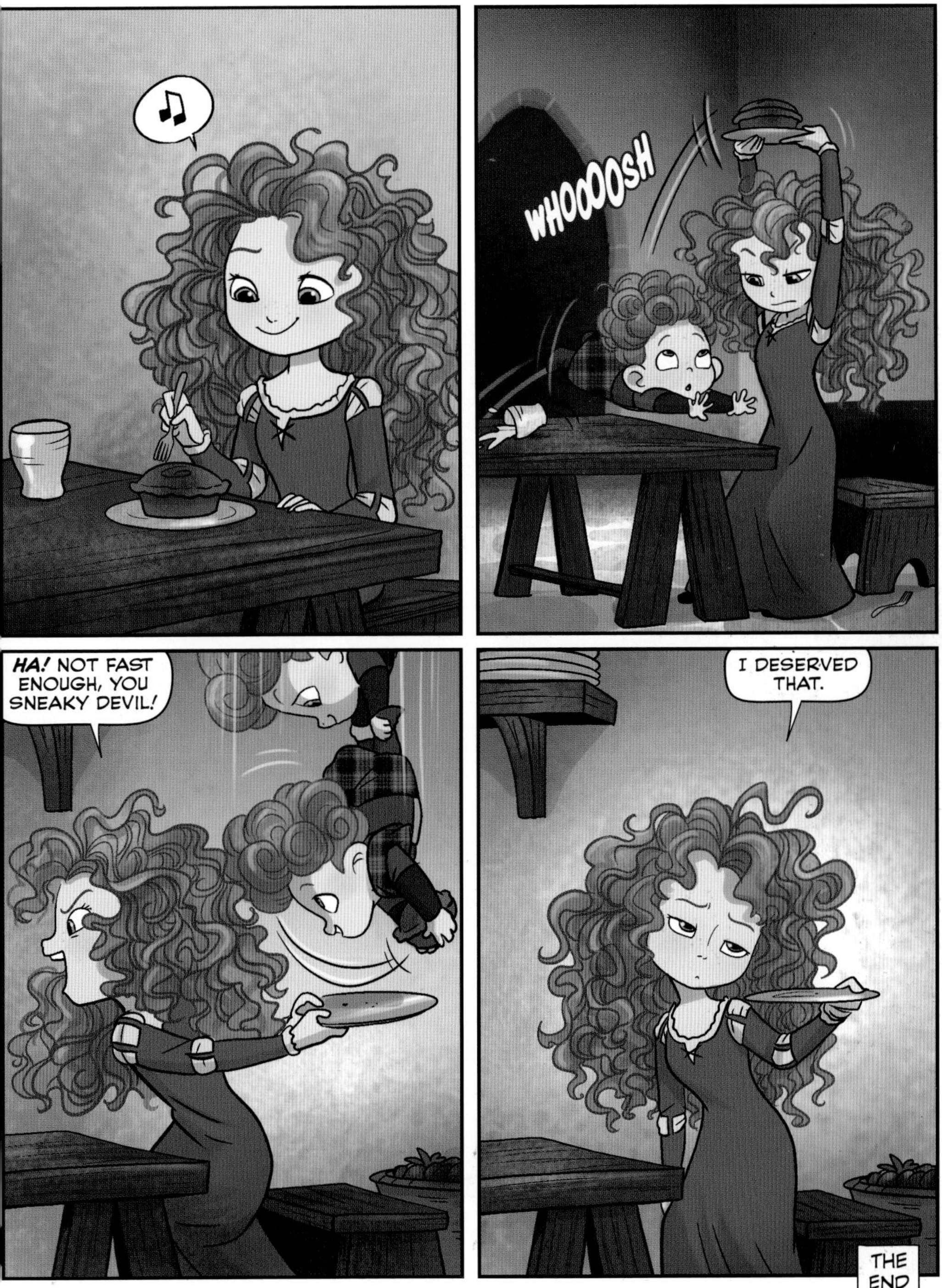
WHOOOOSH
HA! NOT FAST ENOUGH, YOU SNEAKY DEVIL!
I DESERVED THAT.

THE END

"SPICY ALLIGATOR"

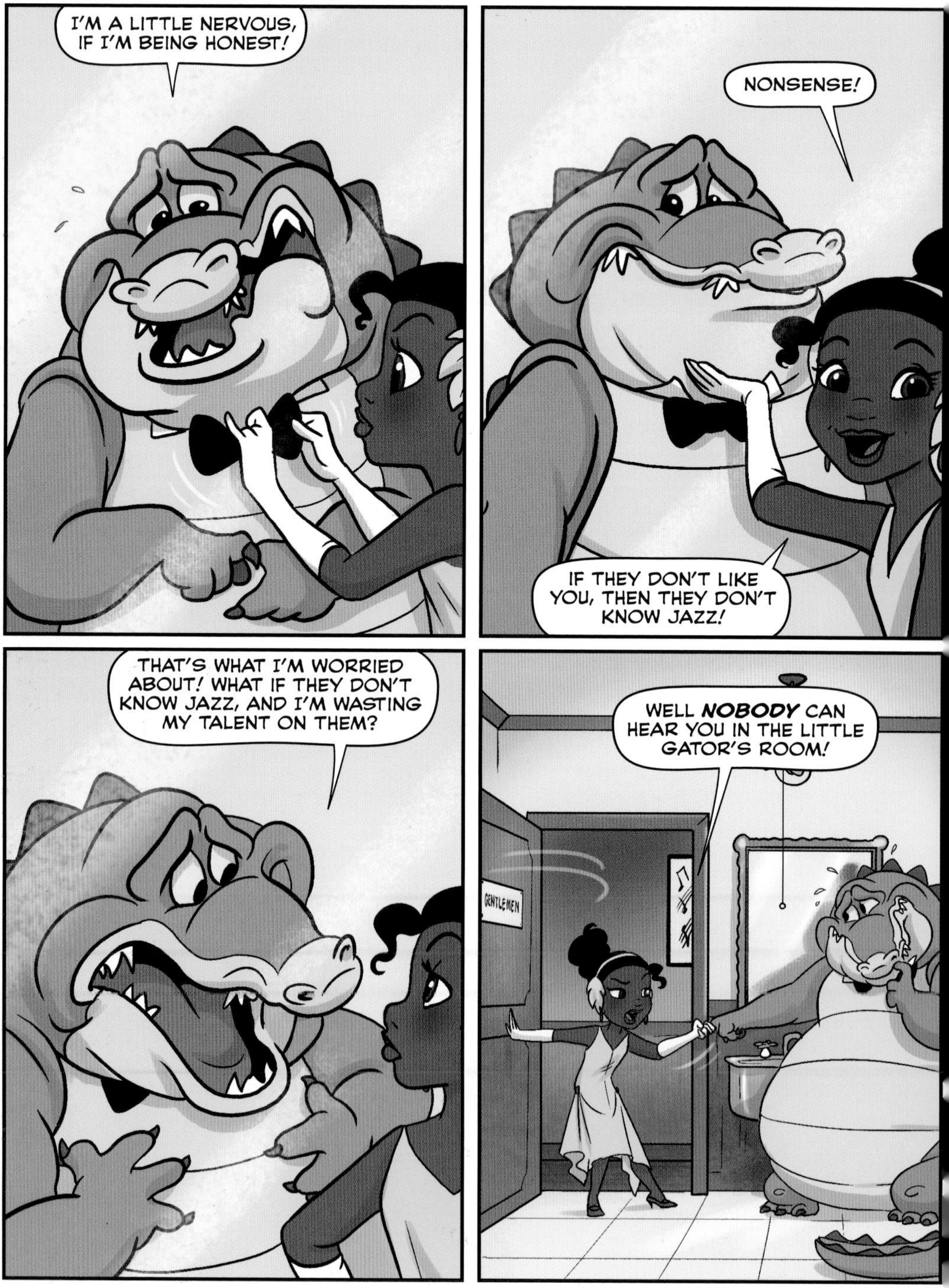
I'M A LITTLE NERVOUS, IF I'M BEING HONEST!
NONSENSE!
IF THEY DON'T LIKE YOU, THEN THEY DON'T KNOW JAZZ!
THAT'S WHAT I'M WORRIED ABOUT! WHAT IF THEY DON'T KNOW JAZZ, AND I'M WASTING MY TALENT ON THEM?
WELL *NOBODY* CAN HEAR YOU IN THE LITTLE GATOR'S ROOM!
GENTLEMEN

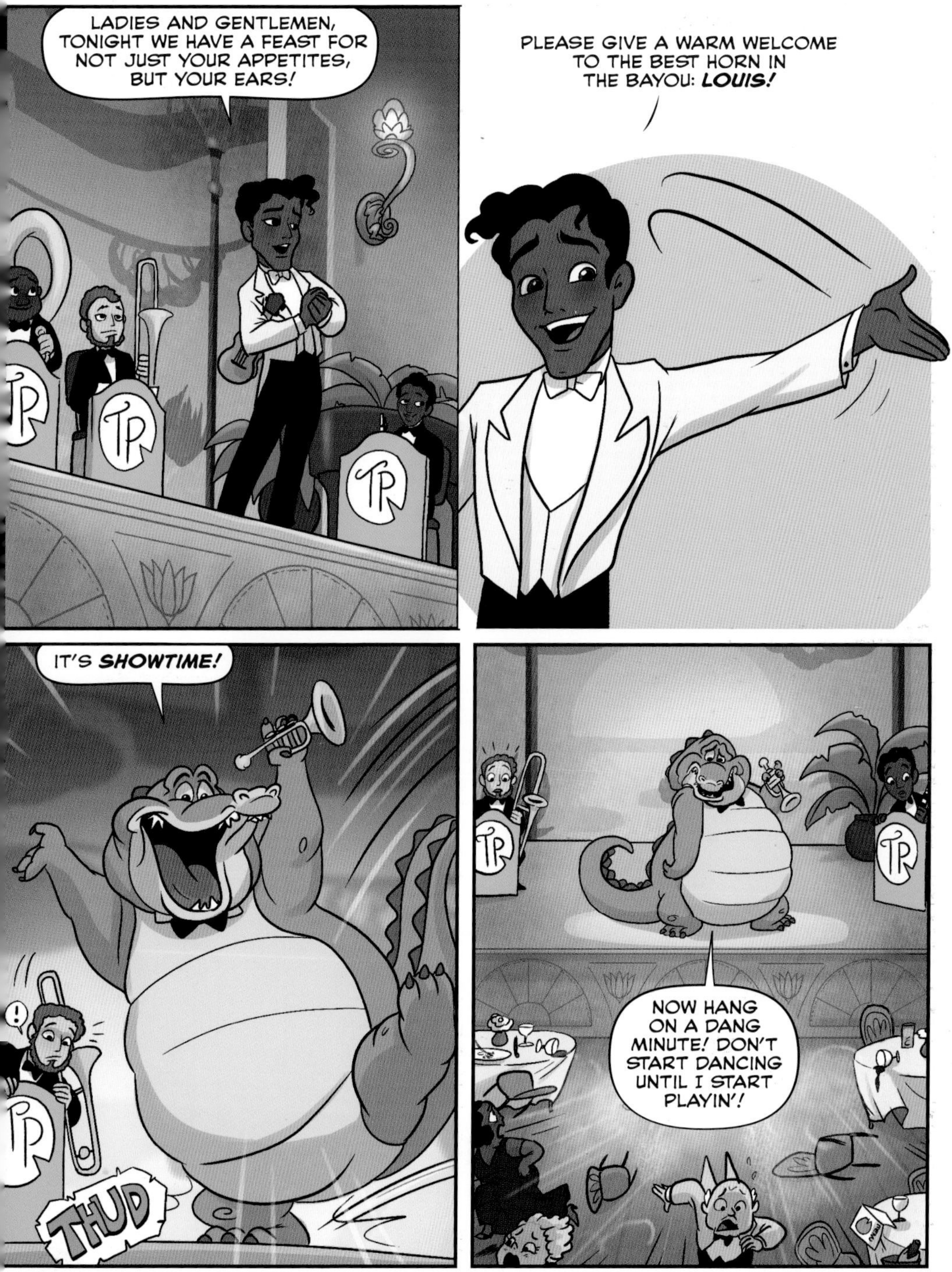
LADIES AND GENTLEMEN, TONIGHT WE HAVE A FEAST FOR NOT JUST YOUR APPETITES, BUT YOUR EARS!
PLEASE GIVE A WARM WELCOME TO THE BEST HORN IN THE BAYOU: LOUIS!
IT'S SHOWTIME!
!
THUD
NOW HANG ON A DANG MINUTE! DON'T START DANCING UNTIL I START PLAYIN'!

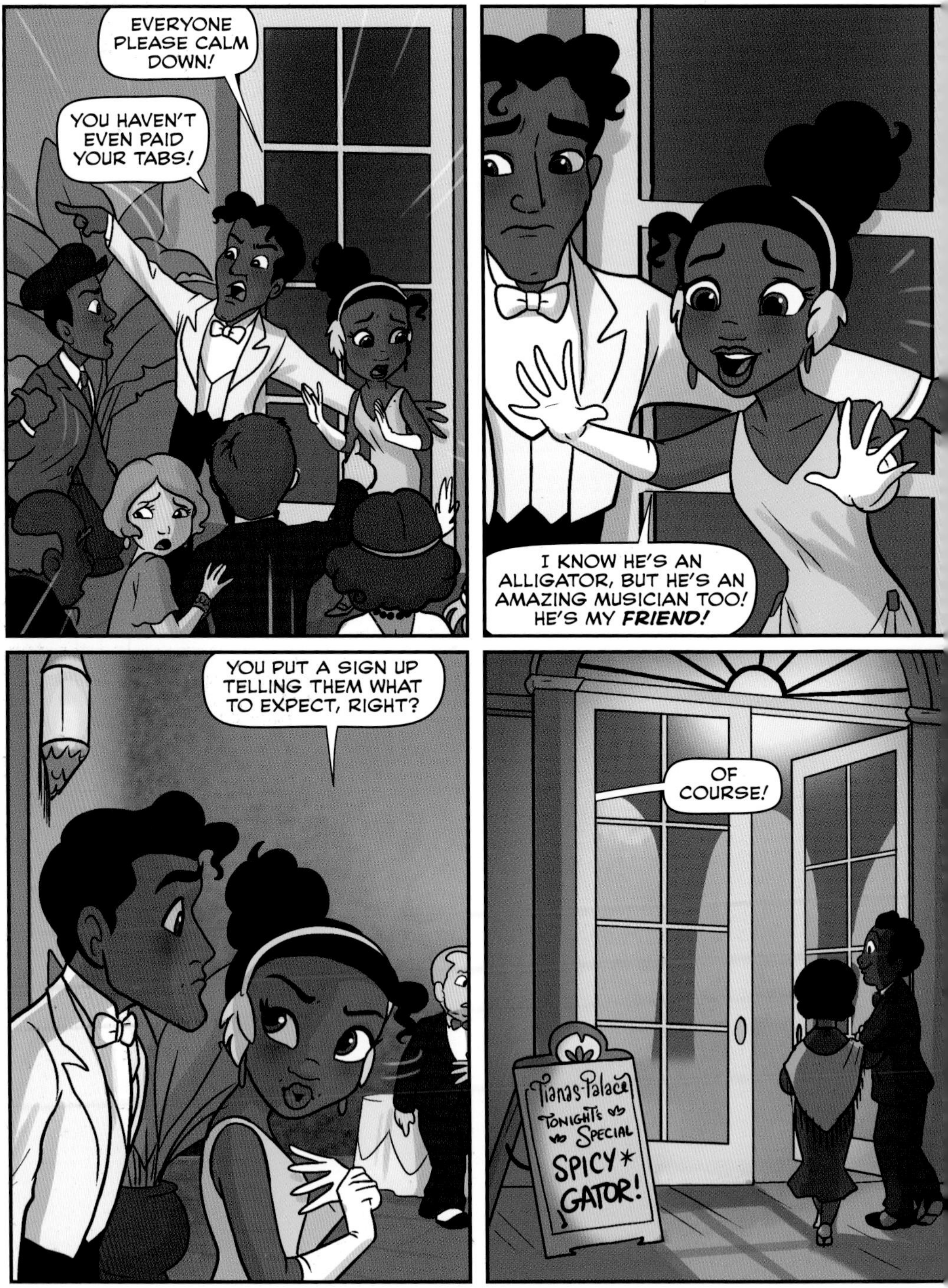
EVERYONE PLEASE CALM DOWN!
YOU HAVEN'T EVEN PAID YOUR TABS!
I KNOW HE'S AN ALLIGATOR, BUT HE'S AN AMAZING MUSICIAN TOO! HE'S MY **FRIEND!**
YOU PUT A SIGN UP TELLING THEM WHAT TO EXPECT, RIGHT?
OF COURSE!
Tianas-Palace
TONIGHT'S SPECIAL
SPICY GATOR!

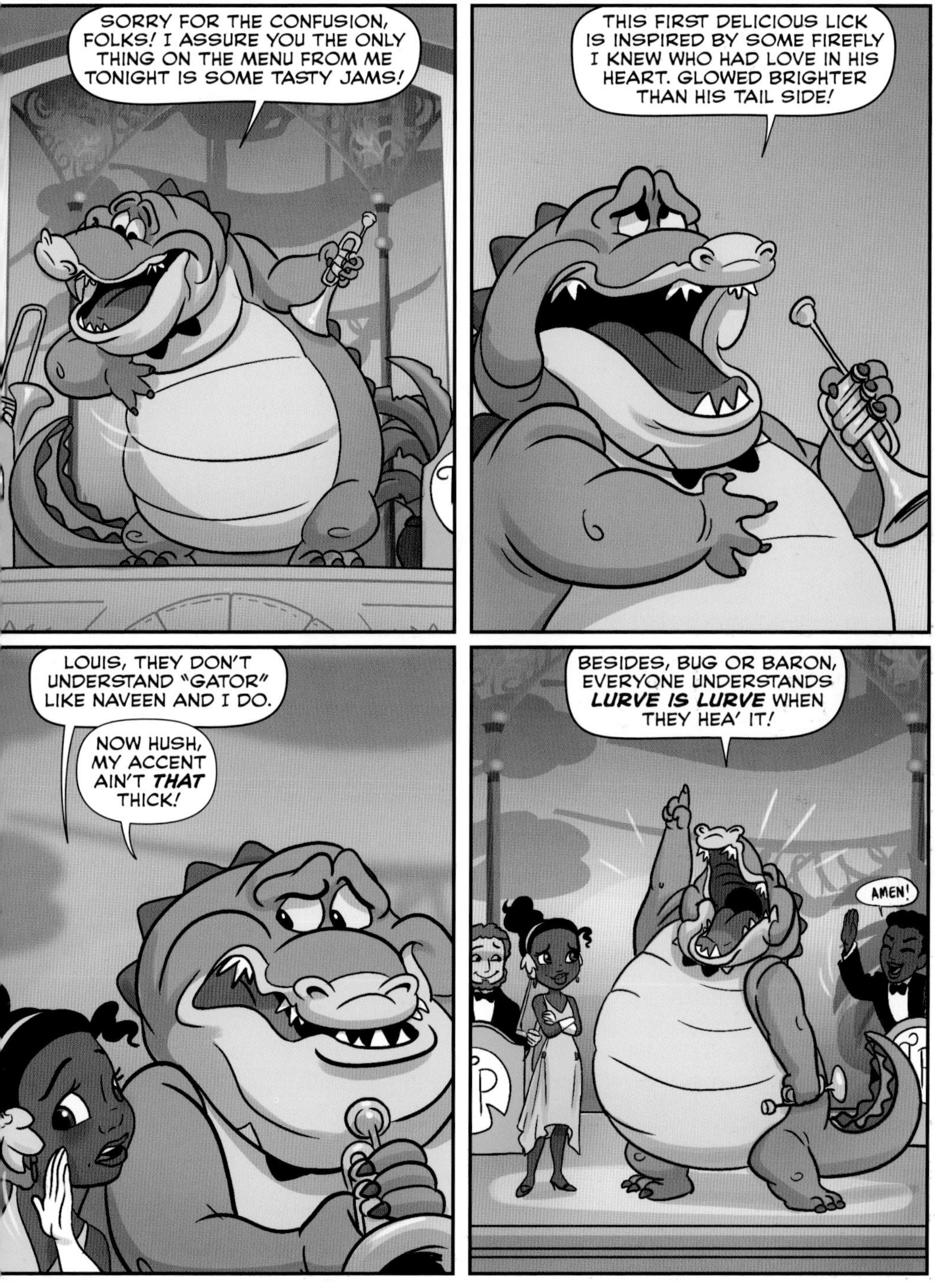
SORRY FOR THE CONFUSION, FOLKS! I ASSURE YOU THE ONLY THING ON THE MENU FROM ME TONIGHT IS SOME TASTY JAMS!
THIS FIRST DELICIOUS LICK IS INSPIRED BY SOME FIREFLY I KNEW WHO HAD LOVE IN HIS HEART. GLOWED BRIGHTER THAN HIS TAIL SIDE!
LOUIS, THEY DON'T UNDERSTAND "GATOR" LIKE NAVEEN AND I DO.
NOW HUSH, MY ACCENT AIN'T THAT THICK!
BESIDES, BUG OR BARON, EVERYONE UNDERSTANDS LURVE IS LURVE WHEN THEY HEA' IT!
AMEN!

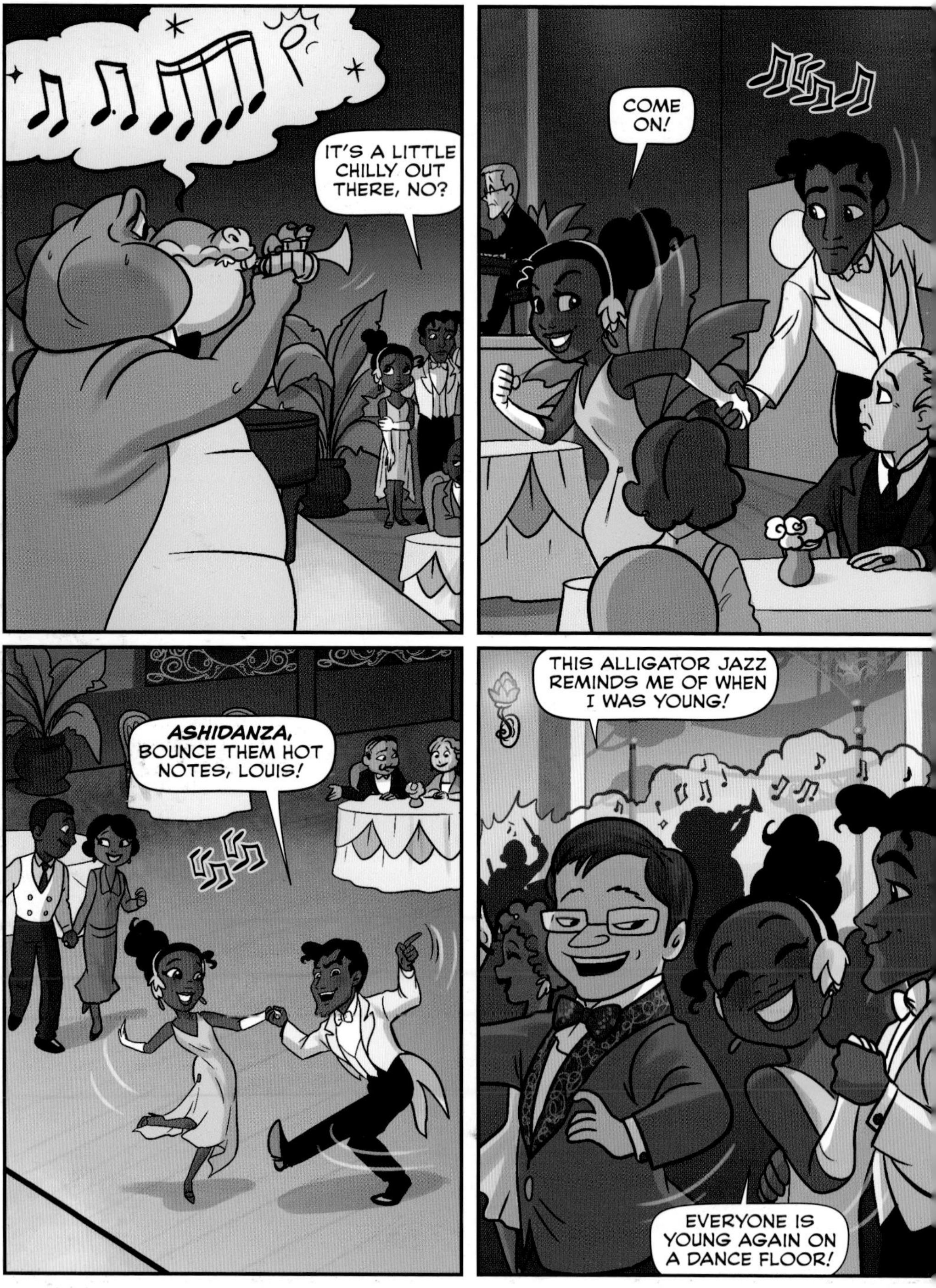
IT'S A LITTLE CHILLY OUT THERE, NO?
COME ON!
ASHIDANZA, BOUNCE THEM HOT NOTES, LOUIS!
THIS ALLIGATOR JAZZ REMINDS ME OF WHEN I WAS YOUNG!
EVERYONE IS YOUNG AGAIN ON A DANCE FLOOR!

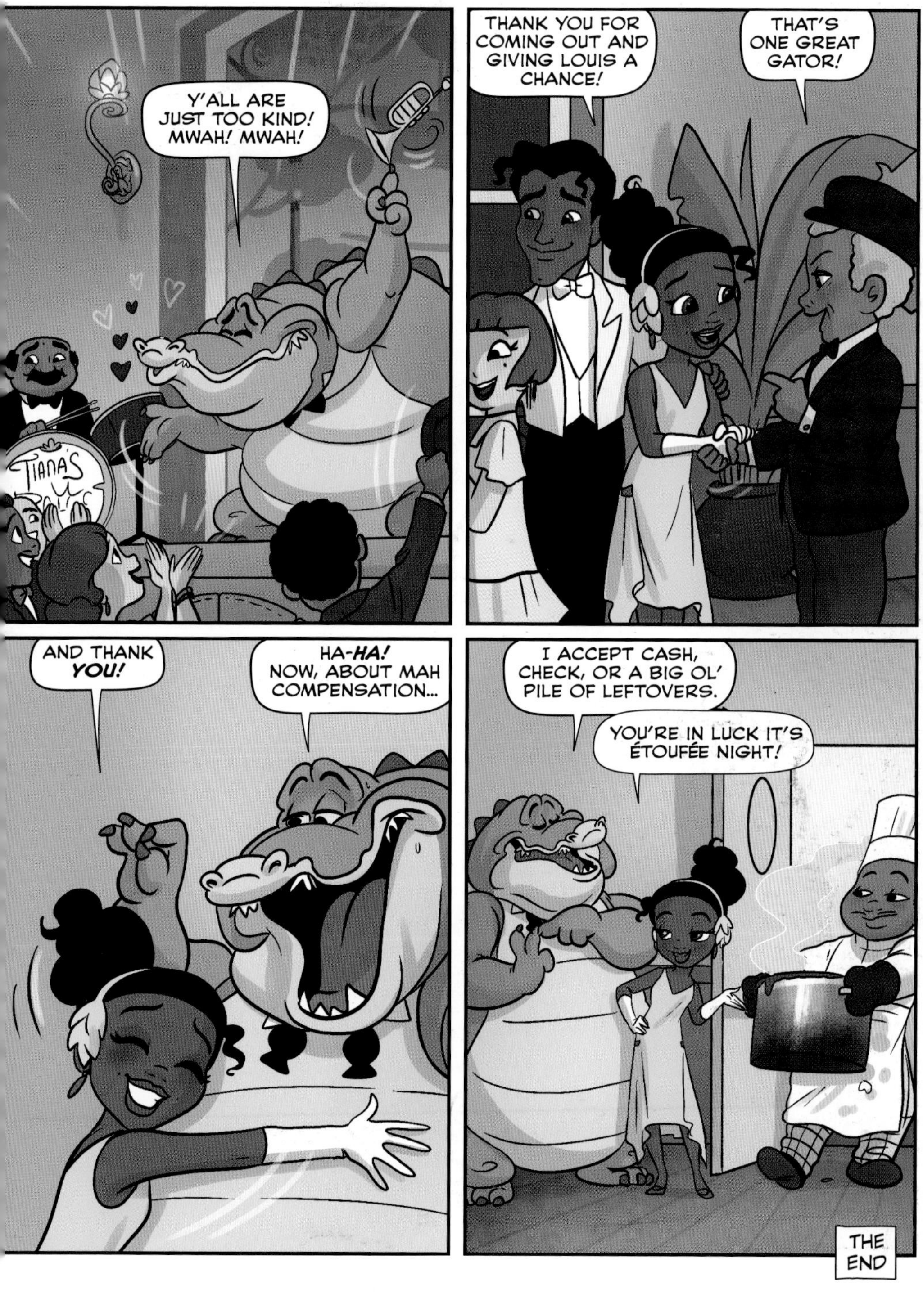
Y'ALL ARE JUST TOO KIND! MWAH! MWAH!
TIANA'S
THANK YOU FOR COMING OUT AND GIVING LOUIS A CHANCE!
THAT'S ONE GREAT GATOR!
AND THANK *YOU!*
HA-*HA!* NOW, ABOUT MAH COMPENSATION...
I ACCEPT CASH, CHECK, OR A BIG OL' PILE OF LEFTOVERS.
YOU'RE IN LUCK IT'S ÉTOUFÉE NIGHT!
THE END

"JOIN THE FLOCK"

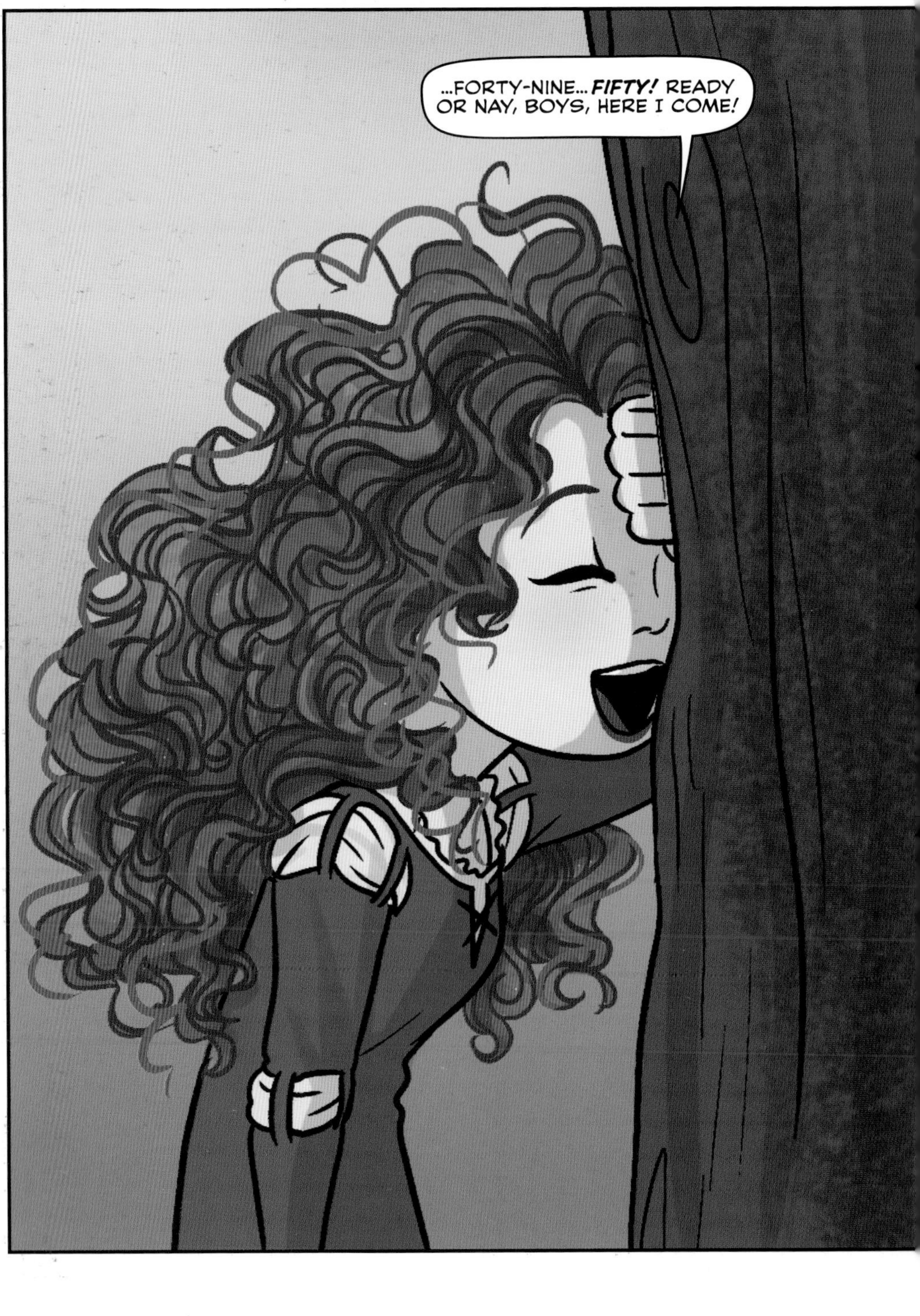
...FORTY-NINE... FIFTY! READY OR NAY, BOYS, HERE I COME!

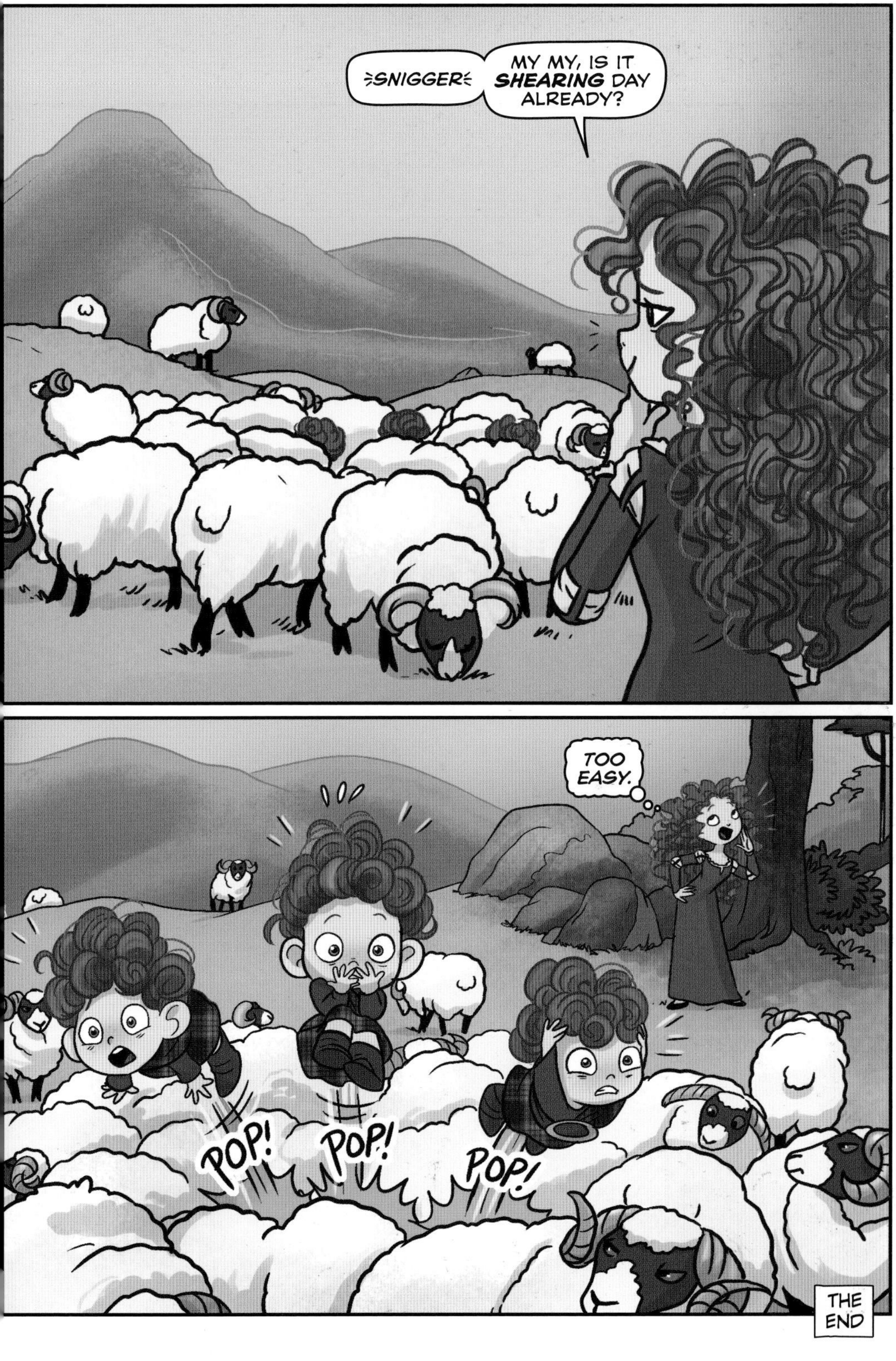

≋SNIGGER≋
MY MY, IS IT SHEARING DAY ALREADY?
TOO EASY.
POP!
POP!
POP!
THE END

"TWELFTH NIGHT"

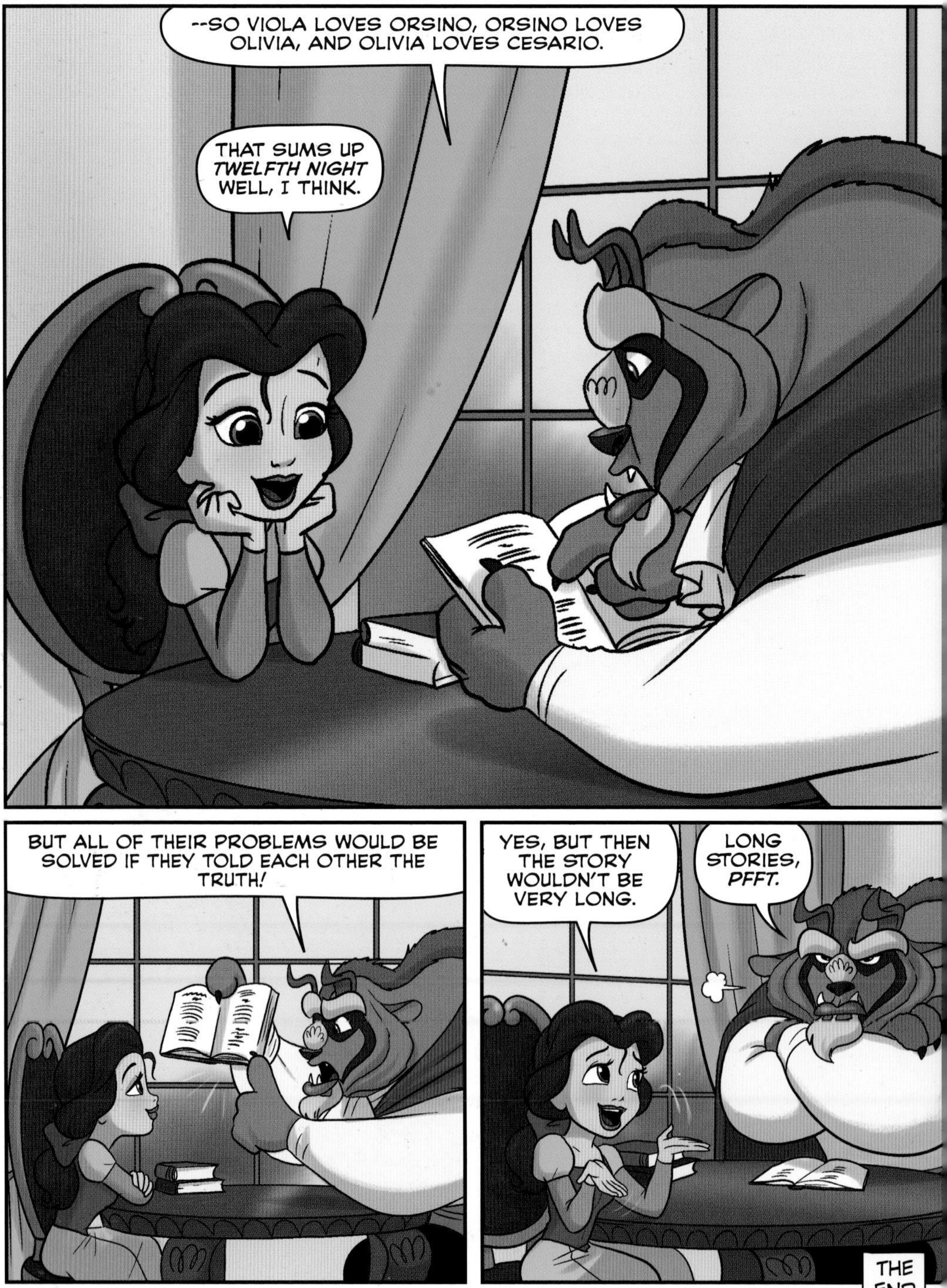
--SO VIOLA LOVES ORSINO, ORSINO LOVES OLIVIA, AND OLIVIA LOVES CESARIO.
THAT SUMS UP *TWELFTH NIGHT* WELL, I THINK.
BUT ALL OF THEIR PROBLEMS WOULD BE SOLVED IF THEY TOLD EACH OTHER THE TRUTH!
YES, BUT THEN THE STORY WOULDN'T BE VERY LONG.
LONG STORIES, *PFFT.*
THE END

"APPLE PIE"

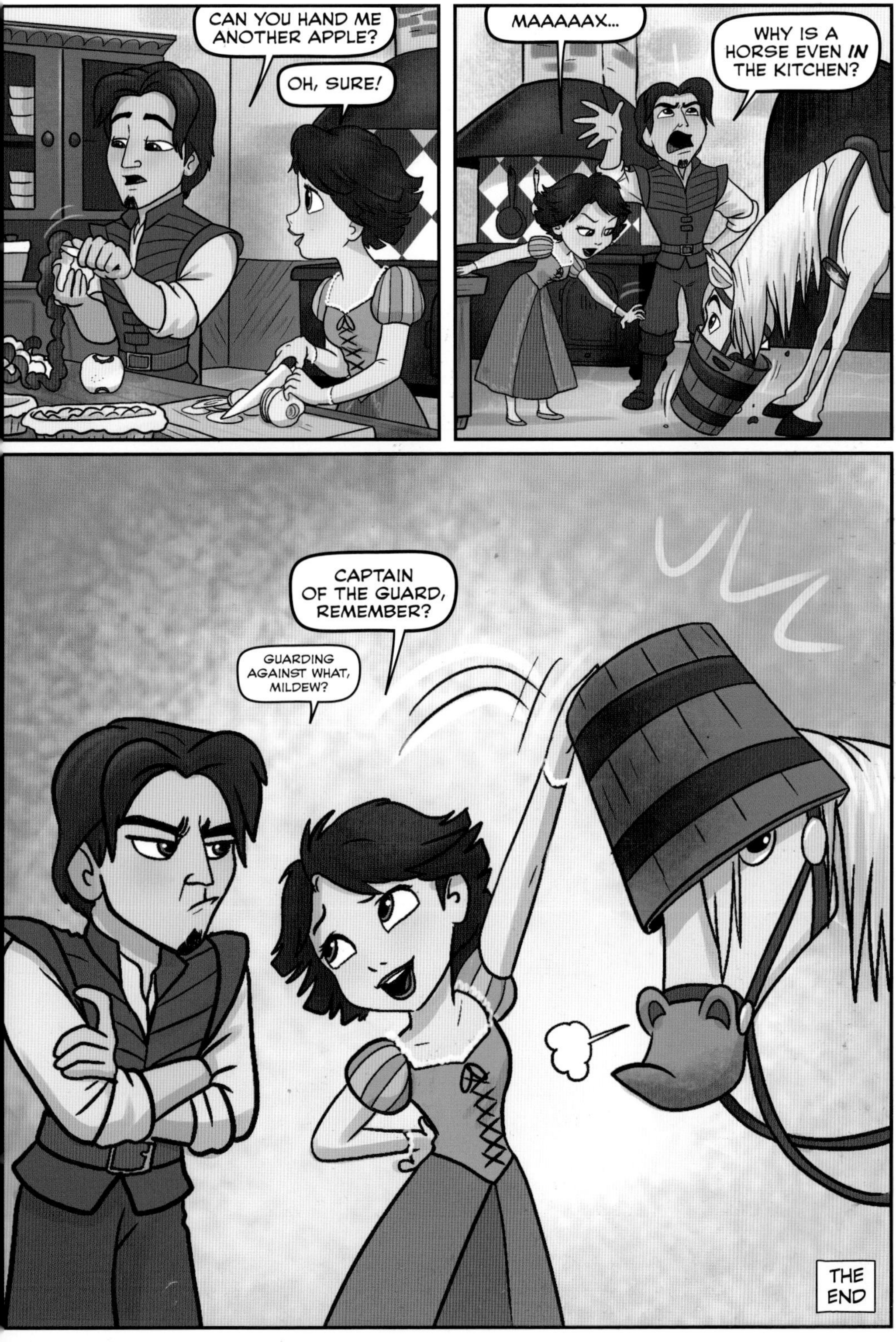
CAN YOU HAND ME ANOTHER APPLE?
OH, SURE!
MAAAAAX...
WHY IS A HORSE EVEN *IN* THE KITCHEN?
CAPTAIN OF THE GUARD, REMEMBER?
GUARDING AGAINST WHAT, MILDEW?
THE END

"BEDTIME STORY"

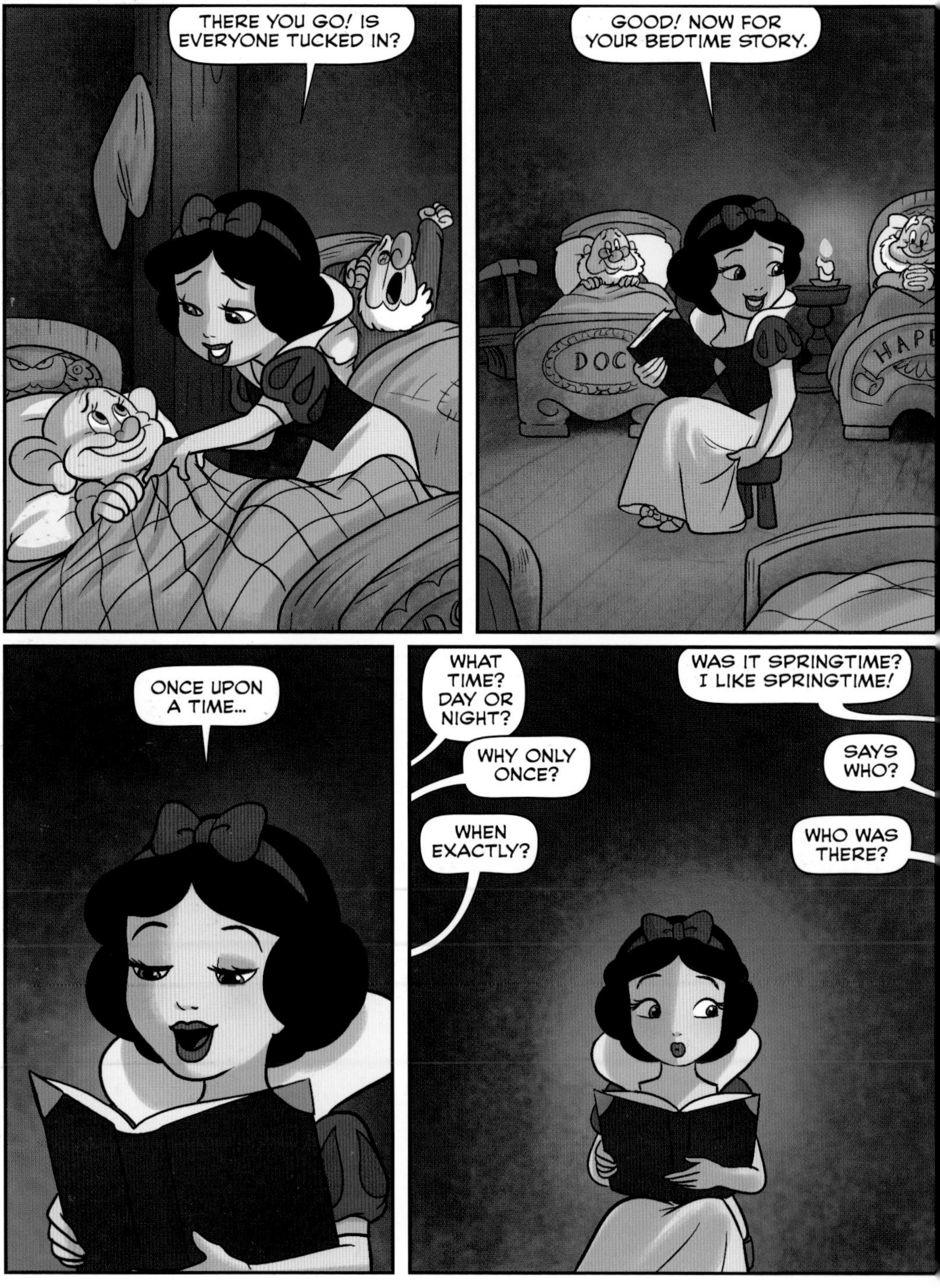

THERE YOU GO! IS EVERYONE TUCKED IN?
GOOD! NOW FOR YOUR BEDTIME STORY.
DOC
ONCE UPON A TIME...
WHAT TIME? DAY OR NIGHT?
WHY ONLY ONCE?
WHEN EXACTLY?
WAS IT SPRINGTIME? I LIKE SPRINGTIME!
SAYS WHO?
WHO WAS THERE?

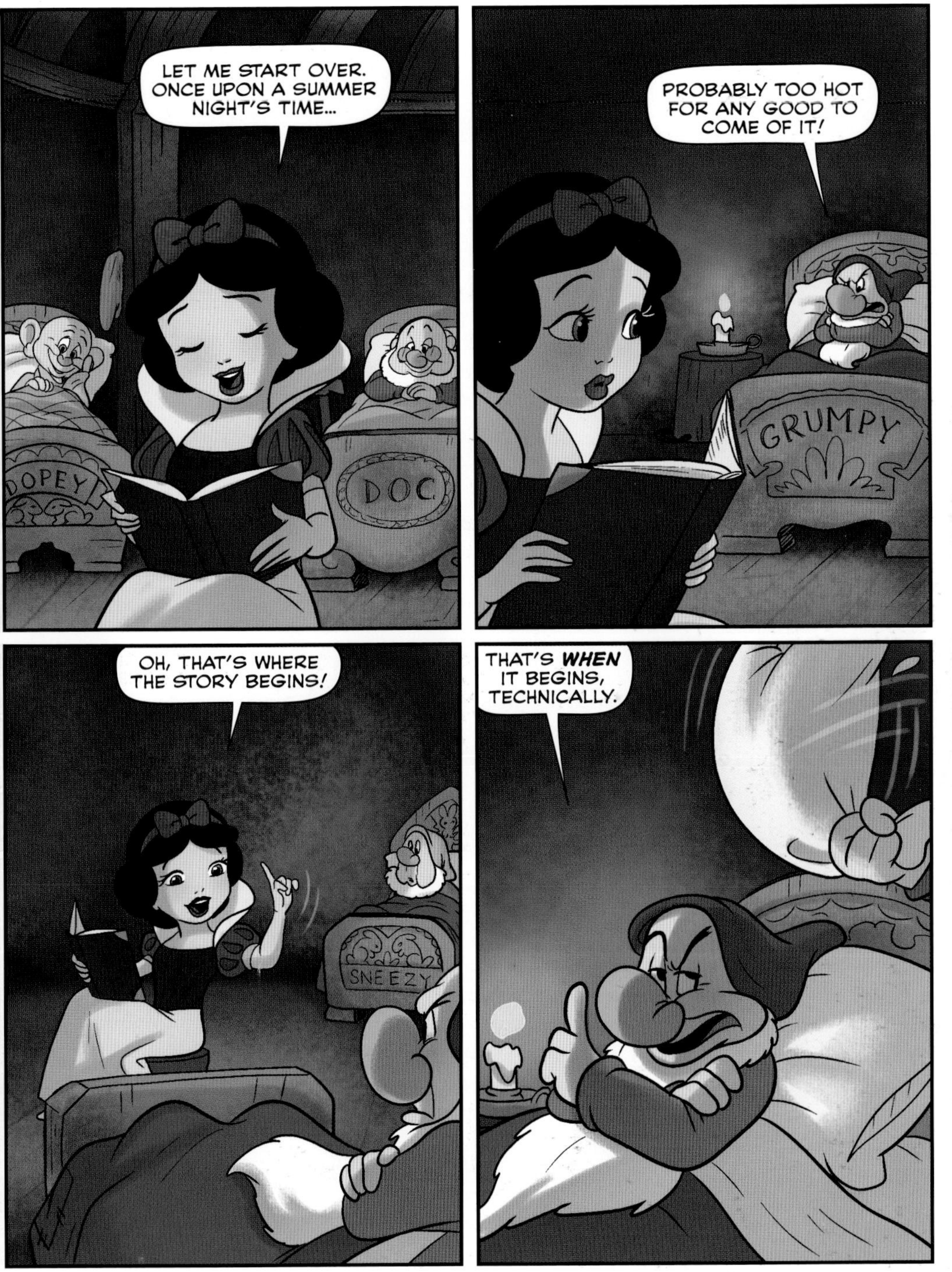
LET ME START OVER. ONCE UPON A SUMMER NIGHT'S TIME...
DOPEY
DOC
PROBABLY TOO HOT FOR ANY GOOD TO COME OF IT!
GRUMPY
OH, THAT'S WHERE THE STORY BEGINS!
SNEEZY
THAT'S ***WHEN*** IT BEGINS, TECHNICALLY.

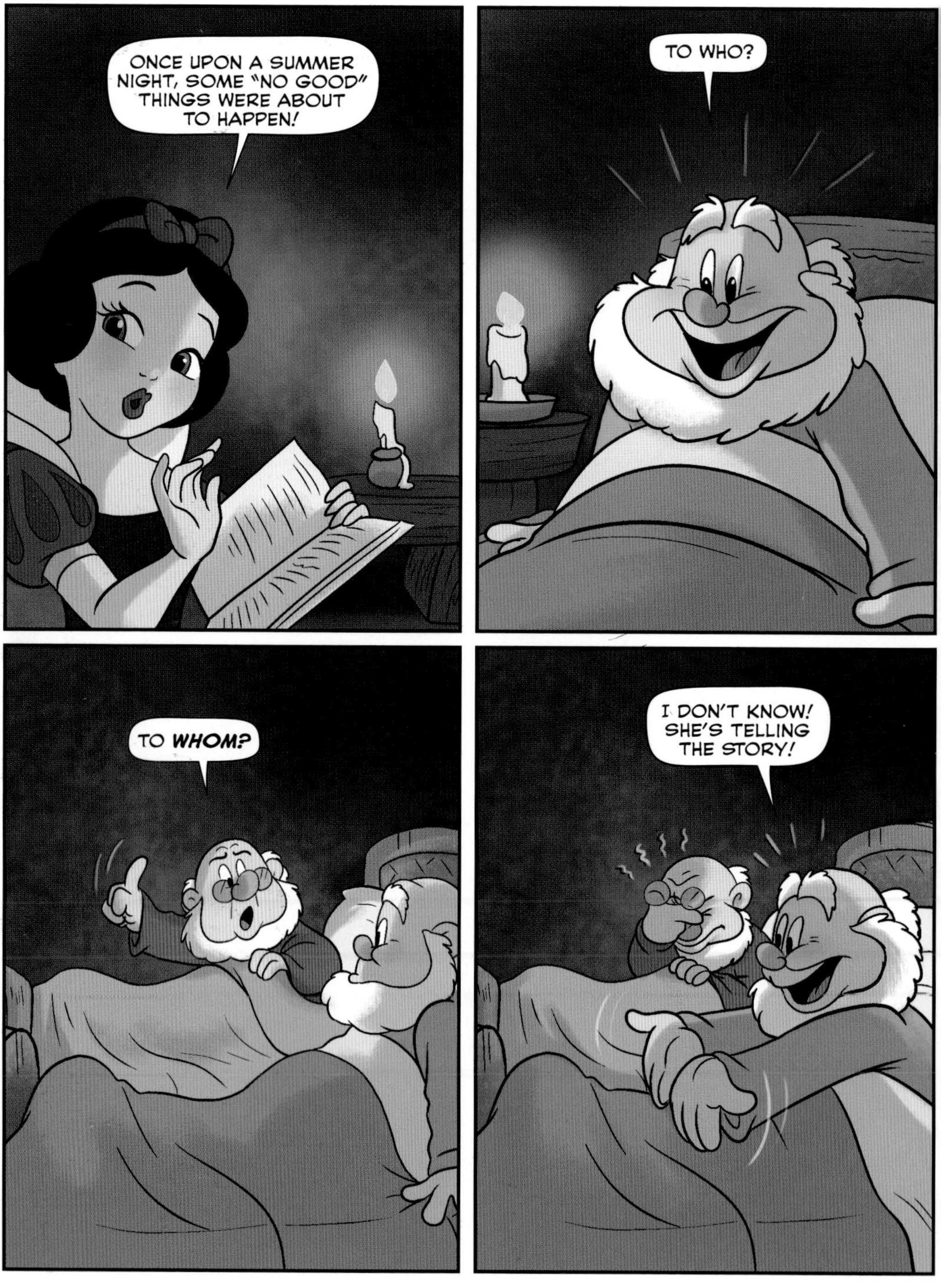
ONCE UPON A SUMMER NIGHT, SOME "NO GOOD" THINGS WERE ABOUT TO HAPPEN!
TO WHO?
TO *WHOM?*
I DON'T KNOW! SHE'S TELLING THE STORY!

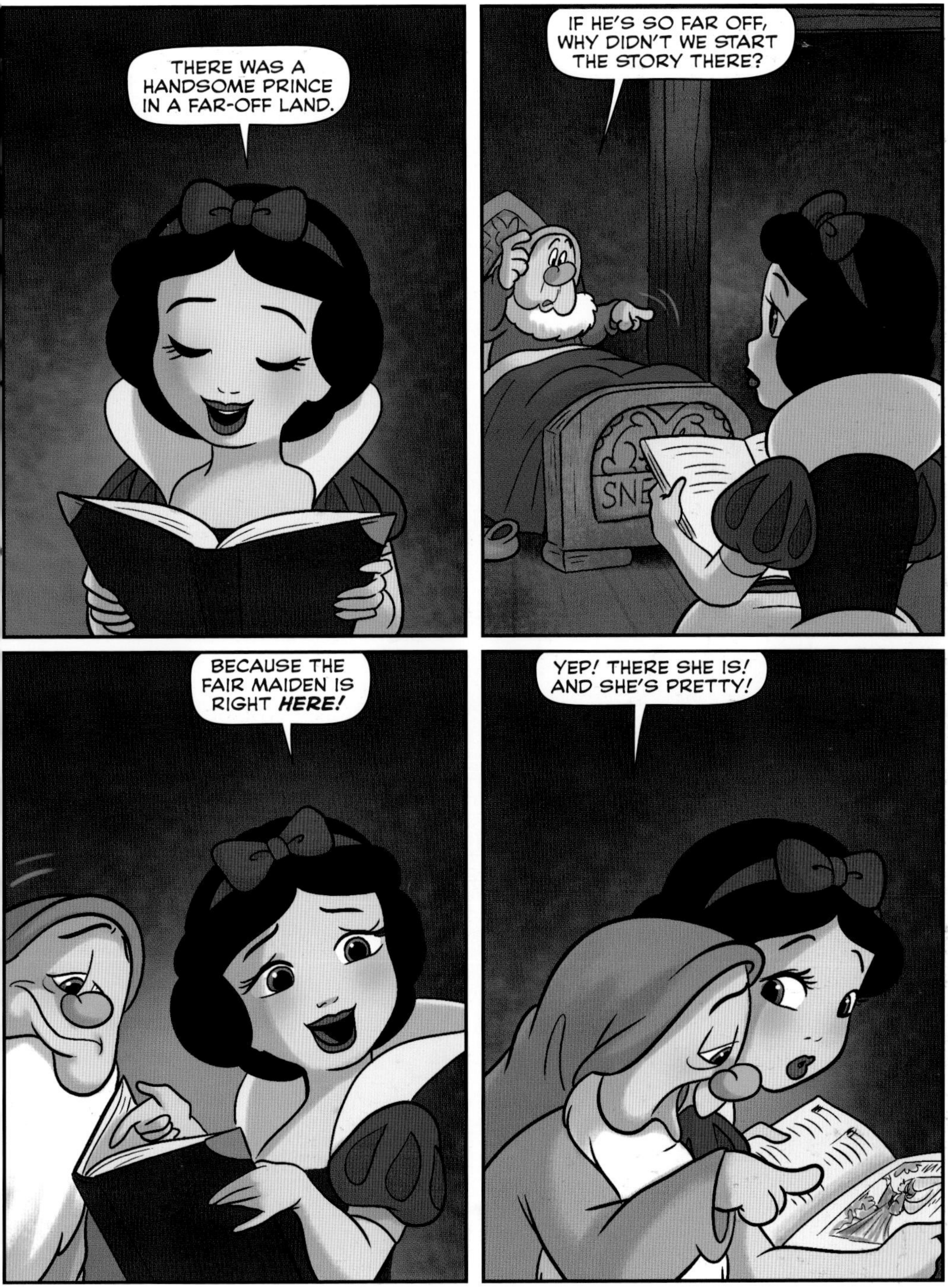
THERE WAS A HANDSOME PRINCE IN A FAR-OFF LAND.
IF HE'S SO FAR OFF, WHY DIDN'T WE START THE STORY THERE?
BECAUSE THE FAIR MAIDEN IS RIGHT *HERE!*
YEP! THERE SHE IS! AND SHE'S PRETTY!

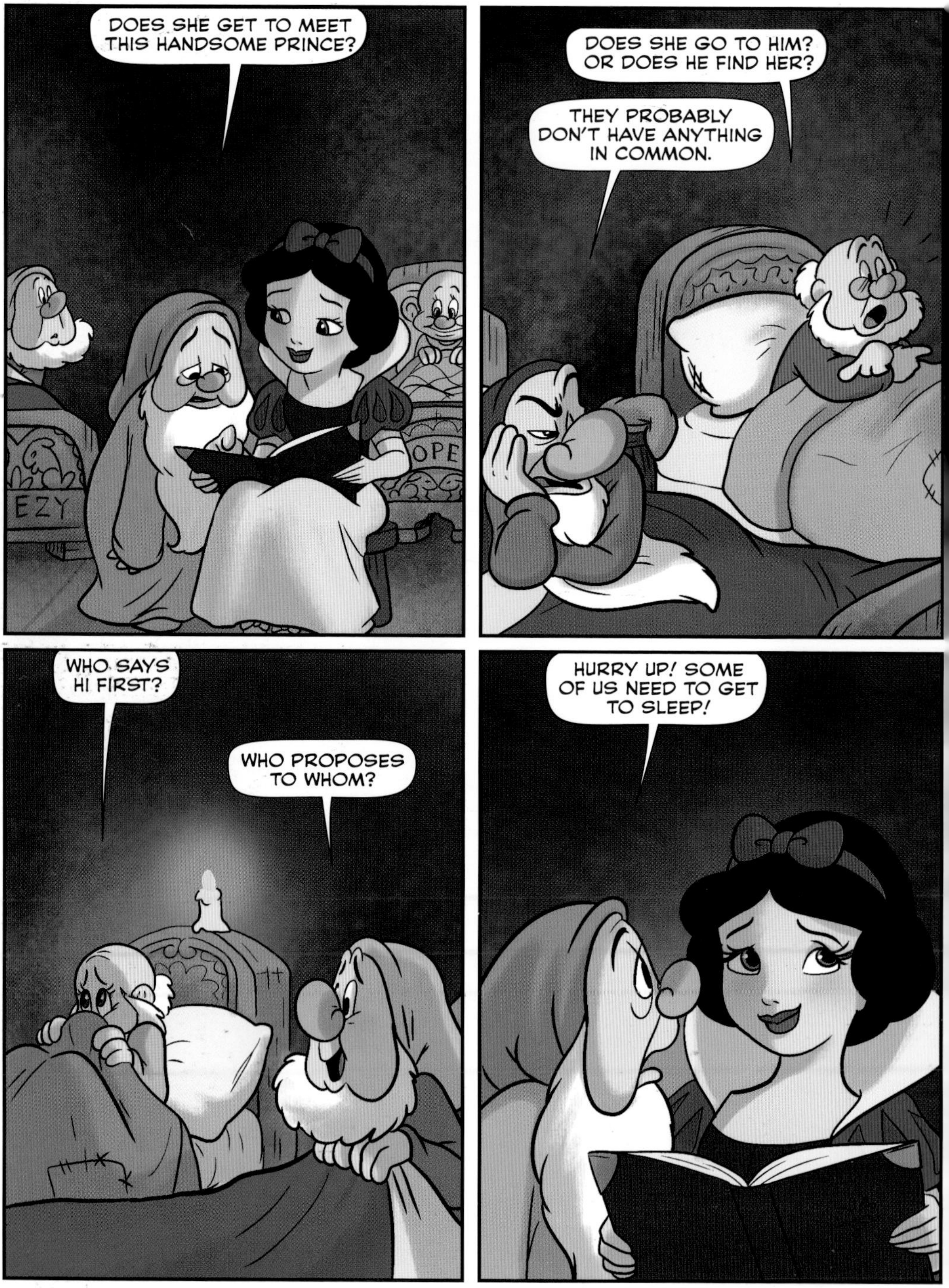
DOES SHE GET TO MEET THIS HANDSOME PRINCE?
EZY
OPE
DOES SHE GO TO HIM? OR DOES HE FIND HER?
THEY PROBABLY DON'T HAVE ANYTHING IN COMMON.
WHO SAYS HI FIRST?
WHO PROPOSES TO WHOM?
HURRY UP! SOME OF US NEED TO GET TO SLEEP!

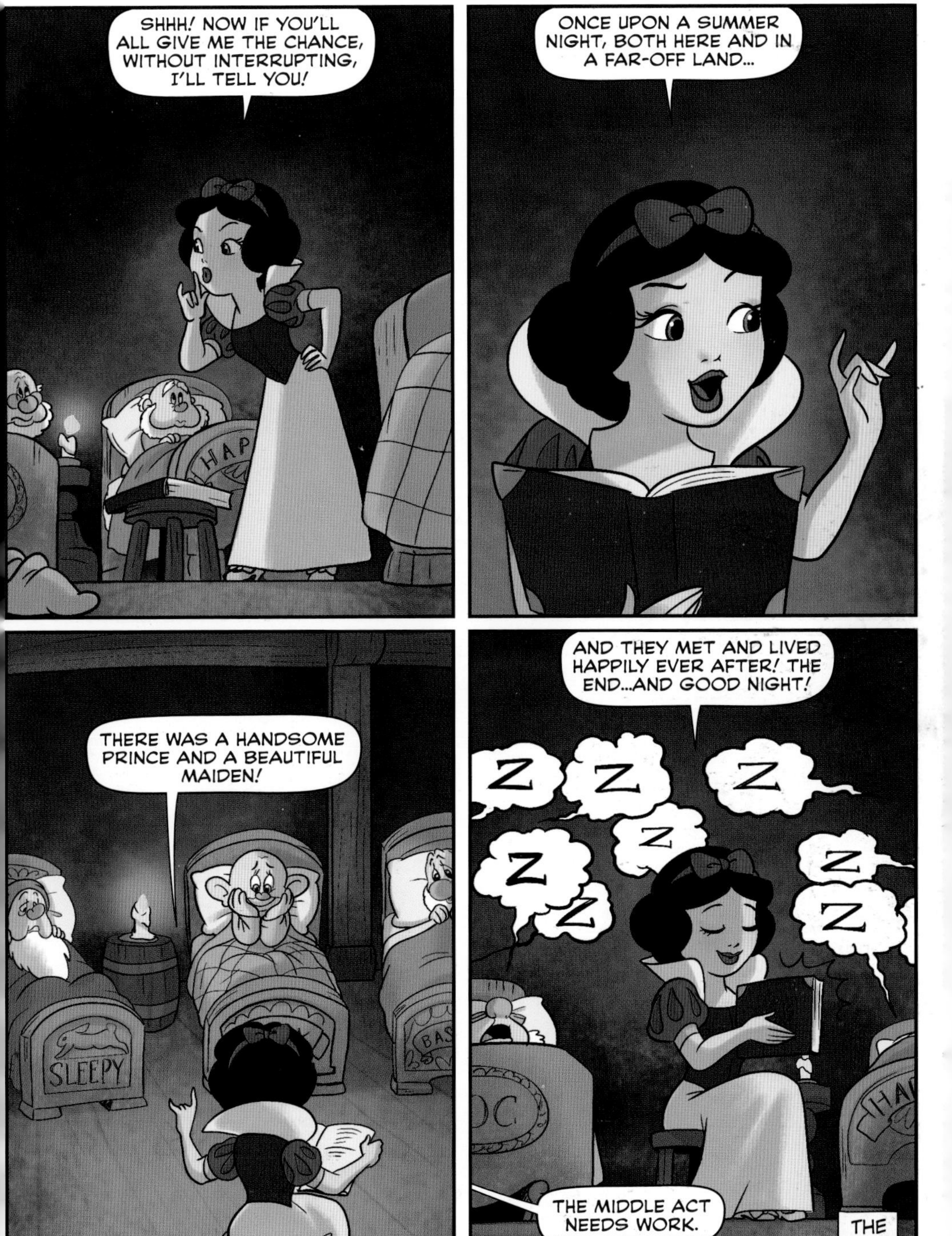
SHHH! NOW IF YOU'LL ALL GIVE ME THE CHANCE, WITHOUT INTERRUPTING, I'LL TELL YOU!
HAP
ONCE UPON A SUMMER NIGHT, BOTH HERE AND IN A FAR-OFF LAND...
THERE WAS A HANDSOME PRINCE AND A BEAUTIFUL MAIDEN!
SLEEPY
BAS
AND THEY MET AND LIVED HAPPILY EVER AFTER! THE END...AND GOOD NIGHT!
Z Z Z
Z
Z
Z
Z
Z
DOC
THE MIDDLE ACT NEEDS WORK.
THE END

"TREASURE HUNT"

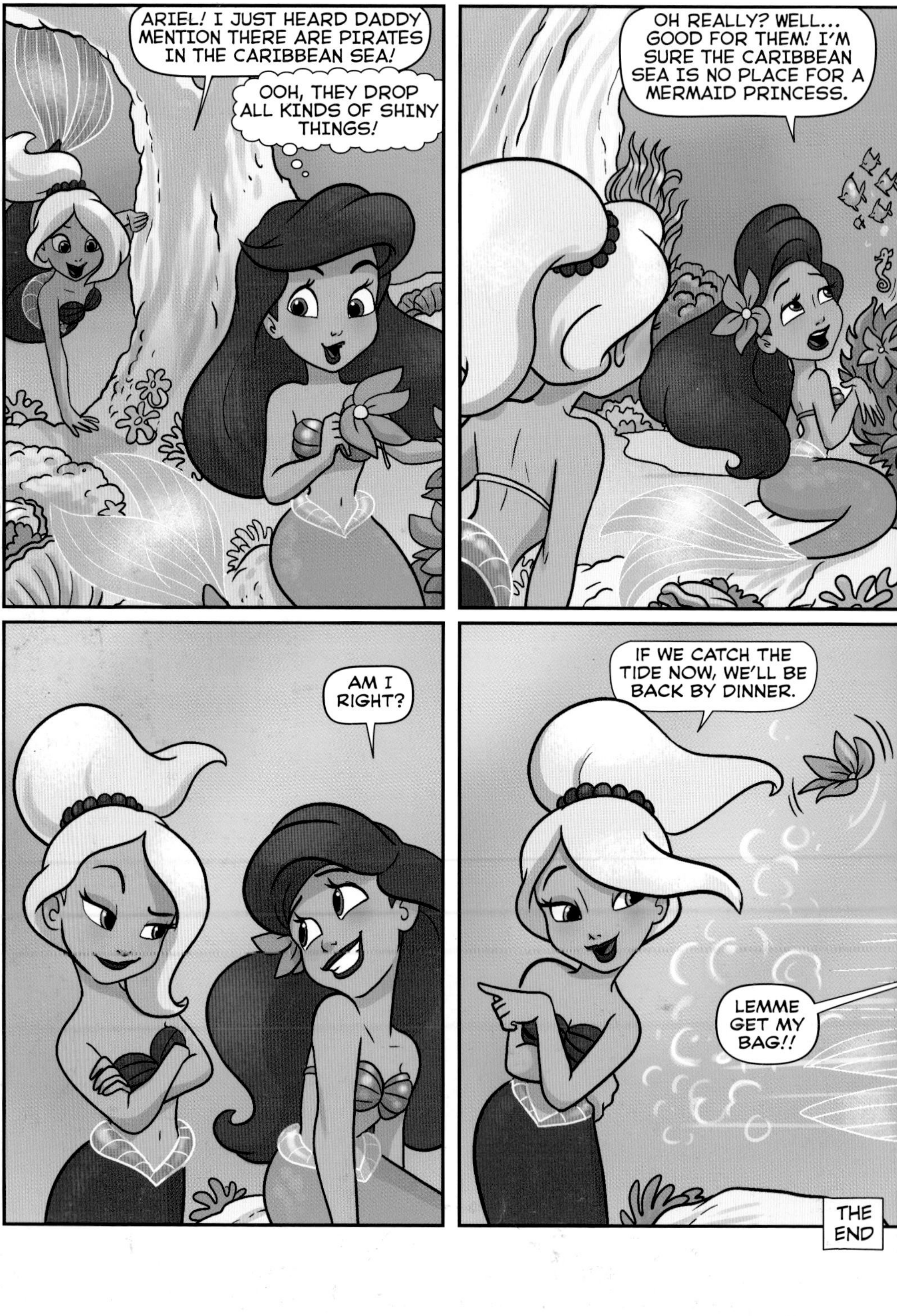
ARIEL! I JUST HEARD DADDY MENTION THERE ARE PIRATES IN THE CARIBBEAN SEA!
OOH, THEY DROP ALL KINDS OF SHINY THINGS!
OH REALLY? WELL... GOOD FOR THEM! I'M SURE THE CARIBBEAN SEA IS NO PLACE FOR A MERMAID PRINCESS.
AM I RIGHT?
IF WE CATCH THE TIDE NOW, WE'LL BE BACK BY DINNER.
LEMME GET MY BAG!!
THE END

DARK HORSE BOOKS

president and publisher
Mike Richardson

series editors
Steffie Davis, Judy Khuu, Deanna McFaden, Amy Mebberson, Freddye Miller

collection editor
Freddye Miller

collection assistant editor
Judy Khuu

designer
Anita Magaña

digital art technicians
Christianne Gillenardo-Goudreau, Samantha Hummer

Neil Hankerson *Executive Vice President* ✦ **Tom Weddle** *Chief Financial Officer* ✦ **Randy Stradley** *Vice President of Publishing* ✦ **Nick McWhorter** *Chief Business Development Officer* ✦ **Dale LaFountain** *Chief Information Officer* ✦ **Matt Parkinson** *Vice President of Marketing* ✦ **Vanessa Todd-Holmes** *Vice President of Production and Scheduling* ✦ **Mark Bernardi** *Vice President of Book Trade and Digital Sales* ✦ **Ken Lizzi** *General Counsel* ✦ **Dave Marshall** *Editor in Chief* ✦ **Davey Estrada** *Editorial Director* ✦ **Chris Warner** *Senior Books Editor* ✦ **Cary Grazzini** *Director of Specialty Projects* ✦ **Lia Ribacchi** *Art Director* ✦ **Matt Dryer** *Director of Digital Art and Prepress* ✦ **Michael Gombos** *Senior Director of Licensed Publications* ✦ **Kari Yadro** *Director of Custom Programs* ✦ **Kari Torson** *Director of International Licensing* ✦ **Sean Brice** *Director of Trade Sales*

DISNEY PUBLISHING WORLDWIDE GLOBAL MAGAZINES, COMICS AND PARTWORKS
PUBLISHER Lynn Waggoner ✦ **EDITORIAL TEAM Bianca Coletti** *(Director, Magazines)*, **Guido Frazzini** *(Director, Comics)*, **Carlotta Quattrocolo** *(Executive Editor)*, **Stefano Ambrosio** *(Executive Editor, New IP)*, **Camilla Vedove** *(Senior Manager, Editorial Development)*, **Behnoosh Khalili** *(Senior Editor)*, **Julie Dorris** *(Senior Editor)*, **Mina Riazi** *(Assistant Editor)*, **Gabriela Capasso** *(Assistant Editor)* ✦ **DESIGN Enrico Soave** *(Senior Designer)* ✦ **ART Ken Shue** *(VP, Global Art)*, **Manny Mederos** *(Senior Illustration Manager, Comics and Magazines)*, **Roberto Santillo** *(Creative Director)*, **Marco Ghiglione** *(Creative Manager)*, **Stefano Attardi** *(Illustration Manager)* ✦ **PORTFOLIO MANAGEMENT Olivia Ciancarelli** *(Director)* ✦ **BUSINESS & MARKETING Mariantonietta Galla** *(Senior Manager, Franchise)*, **Virpi Korhonen** *(Editorial Manager)*

DISNEY PRINCESS: GLEAM, GLOW, AND LAUGH

Published by Dark Horse Books
A division of Dark Horse Comics LLC
10956 SE Main Street
Milwaukie, OR 97222

DarkHorse.com
To find a comics shop in your area, visit comicshoplocator.com

First edition: October 2020
Ebook ISBN 978-1-50671-674-9 | Trade Paperback ISBN 978-1-50671-669-5

1 3 5 7 9 10 8 6 4 2
Printed in China

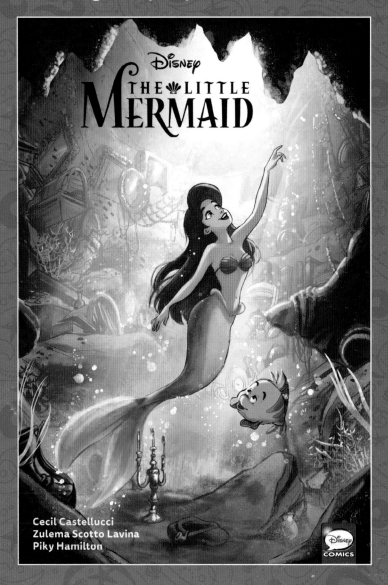